"…his aimlessness makes him an embodiment of uncertainty—no one knows when he'll show up, or how he'll break in, or what he'll do once he has arrived."

Lewis Hyde,
Trickster Makes This World: Mischief, Myth, and Art

I Bring the Fire Part I: Wolves

For permission requests, write to the author, subject "Attention: Permissions," at the email address below:

cgockel.publishing@gmail.com

ISBN-13: 978-1492394389

ISBN-10: 1492394386

I BRING THE FIRE
PART I ~ WOLVES

C. GOCKEL

Acknowledgements

First and foremost, I want to thank my editor, Kay McSpadden. Kay read and reread this story more times than I can count. I also would like to thank Gretchen Almoughraby. Her suggestions helped me clarify situations and make the action more believable. Also indispensable was Laura Stogdill. She consulted on legal aspects of this story. My brother, Thomas, was great as a myth reference, my dad James Merril Evans lent a hand in editing for content, and my mother and Christina Talbott-Clark helped with editing for grammar (I should note, if you see mistakes they are mine and mine alone). All of my readers weren't afraid to tell me when I screwed up; for that I am eternally grateful. For all their hard work, my editors may pop up in the story from time to time. I wish I could reward them more.

I also want to thank Lewis Hyde, author of *Trickster Makes This World: Mischief, Myth, and Art.* His book was tremendously inspiring and helped in shaping Loki's nature. He also gave me very generous permission to quote him.

Finally, thanks must go to my husband Eric. If he hadn't nagged at me to quit my job and work for him I still might be caught in a nine-to-five grind and the commute time would have eaten up my writing time. And if he hadn't nagged me to stop writing fan fiction and start writing something I can own, this story never would have happened.

Chapter 1

The gas station bathroom off route 44 is completely lined with white tiles. Overhead a fluorescent light buzzes and flickers. The bathroom smells like urine and Pinesol. A toilet with a cracked seat sits on one side of the little room. On the other is an ancient sink, hanging off the wall.

The toilet is unoccupied. The sink is not. In it is a writhing wet creature about the size of a dachshund but heavier set and tailless, with short, dark gray fur interspersed with tufts of light gray. Holding the creature under a cloud of foul smelling, antiseptic soap bubbles from the bathroom dispenser is Amy Lewis.

A splash of suds comes right at Amy's eyes. Blinking, she looks up at the mirror above the sink. Her long dishwater blonde hair is wet and plastered to her head where it isn't pulled back in a messy ponytail. Her wide blue eyes have dark circles from lack of sleep — she got up early to start the trip from Oklahoma to Chicago. She's not wearing any makeup.

She should not care; no one will see her out here. But she wishes she was wearing some under-eye concealer. Her nose has a large soap sud on it. Her wide lips are slightly chapped. She looks like she's been in her car for a week, not a few hours, and she looks far older than her twenty-four years.

Looking down with a sigh, Amy says, "Why, Fenrir? Why?"

Fenrir, the creature, makes a non-committal yip. Some of Amy's fellow vet school classmates insist that Fenrir is most likely a capybara, a large, tailless guinea pig-like rodent native to South America. But Fenrir's nose is far too narrow and rat-like for her to be a capybara. Other classmates have suggested that Fenrir is, in fact, a giant rat. However, her front teeth are not rodent teeth. Fenrir is a dog...and Amy and one of her professors did a DNA test just to prove it.

A few minutes ago Amy was walking Fenrir outside the gas station. Letting herself take a break from the long drive, Amy had idly watched the sparse traffic whiz by. When she felt the jerking of Fenrir's leash, it was too late. Fenrir was already joyfully rolling in something that would have been easier to identify before it had wandered onto the freeway, before whatever-it-was had cooked for a few days under a sweltering Great Plains sun.

"It's okay." Amy sighs. "I know why you did this." Animal psychology is somewhere between a hobby and an obsession for most vet wannabes. Lifting up the still soapy, still wiggling dog, she says, "You want to be a great big bad wolf. So you rolled on a dead thing to smell like your prey." It's a common behavior among dogs. And possibly rats.

Fenrir yips enthusiastically and licks Amy's nose.

"Ugh." Wincing away from the smell of roadkill, Amy sets

the dog on the floor. As Fenrir tears around the little room, Amy pulls off her fleece sweater. She's just trying to wrap it around the little animal when a knock comes at the door.

"Just a minute," she calls, scooping up the animal. The knock turns to a pound.

Hurriedly opening the door, she comes face to face with a middle-aged man with a puffy face and blond, almost white hair. Fenrir immediately starts growling and tries to lunge out of her arms.

Despite Amy's ferocious guardian, the man's eyes go directly to her chest. It's something Amy is used to. She is generously endowed, which is why she tends to wear large shapeless shirts. They make her look fat, but it is better than the stares. Now she is only wearing a slightly damp tee shirt. Pulling Fenrir's wet body protectively in front of her, Amy says, "I am so sorry she's growling. Really, she hardly ever does this."

Hunching slightly over her growling protector, Amy goes to the side and makes to slip by. The man does not move.

Amy can tell from Fenrir's growl and frantic wiggling that the dog is close to foaming at the mouth. "Shhhh..." Amy says. "I am so sorry," she says to the man. "She's normally not like this."

Well, normally Amy's dog isn't actively trying to lunge at people, but Fenrir isn't precisely friendly, especially not towards males.

Outside a horn honks. The man looks over his shoulder and then steps out of the way.

As Amy walks by him, he calls out, "Are you traveling by yourself?"

The hairs on the back of Amy's neck stand on end. She

turns to look at the man. He is smiling. It's a perfectly innocuous smile. She lies anyway. "No."

His smile widens as he closes the bathroom door. Fenrir makes a gurgling noise like she's choking on her own fury and nearly jumps out of Amy's arms.

Squeezing her tight, Amy says, "Really trying to live up to your namesake today?"

Amy's grandfather was a folklore buff. In Norse mythology, Fenrir was the wolf child of the Norse God of Mischief, Loki. The real Fenrir was so vicious that the gods bound him to a tree on a remote uninhabited island — but someday Fenrir is supposed to be the downfall of Odin, the head of the Norse gods himself.

Eyeing the door, Fenrir just growls.

A few minutes later Amy's in her Toyota Camry, releasing the clutch, tearing out of the gas station and on her way.

It's 768 miles from Stillwater to Chicago, mostly open road and farm land. It's about a twelve hour drive most times — and totally worth it.

The Oklahoma State University, Stillwater, is one of the best veterinary schools in the country and she's got a full ride. But she's spent every spring and summer since high school graduation with her grandparents in Chicago. There are lots of jobs in Chicago, and Amy's full-ride doesn't pay for things like rent, food, books, and the always mysterious 'miscellaneous fees' universities charge. Amy goes to Chicago to work during breaks. With occasional work as a tech for a veterinarian in Stillwater, she manages just to coast by.

Slipping a CD into the player, Amy cranks down the window. It's not so bad to have her fleece pullover off. Heat is beginning to rise off the freeway in waves. With the window down she's comfortable and the smell of wet Fenrir isn't as overpowering.

She glances over at her companion belted into a safety harness in the front seat. Fenrir's fur is starting to dry and she looks more like a rodent-like dog than dog-like rodent. As near as Amy and her vet-wannabe friends can determine, Fenrir is a mix of toy poodle and chihuahua, somehow minus a tail. Fenrir's fur couldn't decide to be chihuahua or poodle, so it's both, some places long and some places short. As it dries this oddity becomes more prominent. Her ex-boyfriend summed up Fenrir as, "Carlos meets princess, a love story gone terribly wrong."

You can't even say Fenrir is so ugly she's cute. She's just ugly. And with her less than charming personality, no one would have adopted Fenrir if Amy hadn't, which is why Amy had to.

Shifting into fifth gear, Amy says, "Well, despite the jackknifed semi in Tulsa that held us up 3 hours, and your little diversion, looks like we'll be home by midnight. Still on schedule."

Fenrir turns her panting muzzle in Amy's direction as though she's laughing at her.

After two more traffic jams, road construction, and some pit stops for Fenrir that might have been roadkill-induced, it's close to midnight and they're not even in Illinois. As Amy drives through Mark Twain National Forest, she is not the only one the road, but company is few and far between. Trees rise up on either side of her. The air coming in the open windows is humid and hot.

Beside her Fenrir whines.

Biting her lip, Amy says, "I told you...and I told Grandma,

we'll stop for the night outside of St. Louis." She should have stopped earlier — but she didn't want to deviate from her plan. Get home. Get a job. Work.

Granted, that careful planning could be undone by death. Despite the coffee she's been drinking all day, she's tired. She's getting to that stage of sleepiness when reminding her brain that if she falls asleep, she'll die, is no longer working. Her brain is rebelling, reminding her if she dies she'll be asleep. Blessed, wonderful sleep.

Amy grabs a CD from the armrest and holds it up near the steering wheel — Nine Inch Nails, Pretty Hate Machine. Totally retro, but with enough angst and anger to do the job.

Glancing down quickly, she hits the eject button and pulls out her current disc. As she lifts her head, an orange light in the trees catches her eye. Almost certain it's a forest fire, she briefly turns her head. It is a jet of flame, reaching high up into the sky...

And then it is gone.

She turns back to the road and sees two small lights ahead on the road. It takes a few moments for her brain to register it's a deer's eyes.

Braking and swerving quickly, Amy lets out a quick breath as her tires skid across the gravel on the shoulder. An old memory kicks in and she turns into the skid, but not fast enough. Her car slides into a shallow ditch on the side of the road. The next thing she knows the world is turning over, her neck jerking back and forth, her seatbelt cutting into her chest and hips. There is the sound of crumpling metal from the roof, and a loud crack from the windshield as it caves inward. The glass doesn't shatter completely, but it cracks into hard splinters that knock into Amy's hands. With a cry she pulls her hands away from the wheel. And then it's just the sound of her breathing as she and Fenrir hang upside down by their seat belts.

Amy swallows. It's hard to think, her heart is beating so fast and so loud. Don't cars sometimes catch fire in the movies when they tip over? That's probably overdramatized. Or not.

Get out, she has to get herself and Fenrir out of the car. Unbuckling her seatbelt, she manages to hold onto the strap and not bang her head against the ceiling. Turning, she tries to release Fenrir. It isn't easy. Just turning her neck is painful, and the little animal is whining and twisting furiously. When she finally frees Fenrir, she realizes she probably should have found the leash first. She's got a wiggling little dog under one arm, and it doesn't make crawling out of the window particularly easy.

Her headlights are still on, so she has just enough light to assess her situation. She's actually only a few yards from the road, even though it felt like she rolled for miles. There doesn't seem to be any smoke coming from the car. Nodding to herself, she tells herself all of this is good. Someone will see her from the road and call for help.

Just as she has that thought, she sees headlights approaching. Pulling Fenrir to her chest to better control the dog and her own body's shaking, Amy walks towards the highway. A burgundy minivan approaches, slows, and then stops. Its lights go off. Amy's stomach drops.

Maybe it would have been better not to be seen. She nervously scratches between Fenrir's ears. She's being foolish. The risk of being killed by a serial killer is less than the risk of being hit by lightning, and that risk is less than 1 in 750,000. Most people are good.

Still, she freezes in her tracks.

A door slams on the opposite side of the van.

"Having some trouble?" says a voice that sounds familiar. Why should it sound familiar?

Fenrir starts to growl and jumps from her arms just as the man from the gas station rounds the front of the van.

The next thing she hears is a dull thud and a loud yelp of pain. "Nice try," says the man.

Amy has pepper spray on her keychain. Patting her pockets, she feels nothing. Her eyes widen. It has to be in the ignition. Spinning quickly, Amy bolts towards her car.

She hears footsteps behind her, and a low chuckle.

Dropping and diving through the open window, she tries to roll over to grab her keys. Before she can, she feels pressure on her ankles and the next thing she knows, she's being dragged out of her car on her stomach.

As she tries to claw her way forward, weight settles on her back and pins her to the ground. Something cold and round settles against her temple and she stills.

"Now," says the man. "You make a single peep, you struggle at all, and I'll blow your brains out."

Amy closes her eyes. She doesn't make a sound, but her brain is screaming. *Someone, anyone, help me.*

Loki awakes with his cheek pressed to a cold stone slab, not sure where he is. This is not precisely unprecedented. What is strange is that he doesn't reek of alcohol and his mouth does not taste like vomit.

Blinking his eyes, he tries to focus. There is light, wan and diffuse as though from a northern window. There is a dull pain in his left temple, and the back of his neck is in agony. That is not so worrisome.

What is worrisome is what he doesn't see, feel, hear or taste. There is no magic in the room, no soft glow of light and shifting color, no slight tingle on his tongue and fingertips or murmur in his ear. He might as well be a dumb beast. No, it's worse than that. Beasts have some sense of magic in their whiskers, feathers, and flicks of their tongues. He might as well be a mortal human, blind to magic, and with no magic tricks save one.

His magical abilities cannot be taken from him. But magic can be removed from a place, folded back upon itself, held back for short periods of time in places of great power. Loki knows of only one such place in all of the nine realms. Which means...

Sitting up as quickly as he can with the pain in his neck, he looks around. The room he is in is lined with dull, flat, gray stones that stretch up to a high ceiling. The light is coming from a single skylight. He knows without looking there is a door made of iron bars to his left. There will be at least one sentry on guard beyond.

He's in his home, Asgard, realm of the Aesir, in the Tower. Again. But he can't remember doing anything wrong.

Loki hears the footsteps behind him again. He recognizes them. Loki smiles bitterly. "Thor, what is the charge?"

The footsteps circle around, and there is Thor, towering above him.

"You will be told in due time," Thor rumbles. Mjölnir, Thor's hammer, hangs at his side. But behind the shield of magic, it is just an ordinary piece of iron.

As are Loki's knives if...

Patting his body, Loki looks down. He is only in a shirt and breeches. His armor, boots and belt, and all his knives are gone.

"I don't know all the hiding places of your toys," Thor rumbles. "So I took away all the places they might hide."

Rubbing his neck, Loki winces and remembers Thor's fist connecting with his temple, and a blow to the back of his neck. "Surely I can know the charge?"

Bowing his head, Thor does not meet Loki's gaze.

Loki scowls up at him.

Thor and Loki look so alike they could be brothers. They are both red haired, though Thor's hair tends towards brown, and Loki's towards a brighter strawberry blond. Both are blue eyed, but Thor's eyes are as dark as a storm cloud, and Loki's are a pale gray. Thor has more generous features. He's slightly taller with wider shoulders, an expressive open face, prominent nose, full mouth and raging eyebrows. Loki is a bit more delicate, his chin a little narrower, and his frame leaner. Loki keeps his face clean shaven and his hair shorter — though it tends to be uneven. Thor sports a red beard, and his hair is long, though neatly groomed.

The biggest difference between them is their skin. Thor's father, Odin, leader of the Aesir, is half Jotunn, the race of the Frost Giants. Thor's mother, Jord, is full Jotunn. Despite his dominant Jotunn blood, Thor's skin is a lovely shade of gold.

Loki's skin by contrast is so pale it is nearly translucent. He does not tan. Without ointments and spells he burns. By most accounts Loki is full Jotunn. Rumors in court say his mother was Laufey and his father Fárbauti, and he was abandoned to die as a baby after they were murdered by their own kind. There are some who whisper that while Laufey was his mother, Odin is his father, and that is why he was brought to the court when Odin found him. Whatever his origins, Loki has the ability to cast illusions like a fisherman casts line — when he has access to magical energy.

While Loki was raised by the servants of Odin and Frigga, Thor was sent away to be raised by the winged Vingnir and Hlora, and only came to court when he reached the end of his twenties. Thor and Loki were almost friends once.

That was a long time ago.

"I was told only to see you here. Not to discuss the reason for your confinement," Thor says with vehemence that sounds forced.

"You've been following the rules since your brother Baldur died," Loki says, gingerly getting to his feet. Smirking, Loki says, "Don't you think if there was any real hope of Odin granting you the crown he would have announced it by now?" Poor Thor.

"Watch your mouth, Silvertongue," says Thor.

Silvertongue is one of Loki's favorite nicknames. It's better than Trickster, Fool, or simply Liar. Thor isn't terribly mad at him. Still, Loki can feel a chill of worry creeping into his bones. Last time he was in the Tower, things did not go well. Smiling despite his fear, Loki says, "I can't watch my mouth, it's attached to my face. As are my eyes, which..."

It's a gentle jibe, but Thor's hands go to the front of Loki's shirt and he's shoved against the wall so hard his teeth rattle. Too winded to speak, Loki just stares at Thor's face, inches from his own. Thor's lips are turned down and his eyes are narrowed in anger...or in despair.

Feeling dread uncoil in his stomach, Loki whispers, "Oh,

Thor. Has your daddy made you do something terrible?"

Loki knows something of the terrible things Odin would compel someone to do.

Releasing him, Thor drops Loki to the floor and backs away. For a moment Loki feels sorry for him.

From the door comes a sentry's call. "Visitor to see the prisoner."

Loki blinks. There are few people who would wish to see him.

Thor says quietly, "I was told there were to be no visitors..." but makes no protest as a slender form emerges with the sentry on the other side of the door.

"Sigyn," Loki and Thor say almost at once.

The sentry's key clicks in the lock and Sigyn, Loki's ex-wife, enters.

Asgard is experiencing a 13th century European revival. Sigyn's golden hair is held back by a circlet of braided gold at her crown. She wears a draping seafoam green dress. A cloak of moss green hangs back from her shoulders. But what catches Loki's eye is a large golden pendant on a chain around her neck. He wonders what man has given it to her, and his heart sinks a bit.

Sigyn says nothing until the lock clicks behind her. "Has Thor told you the charges?" Sigyn says.

"No," says Loki, turning to the other man. Thor actually looks a little afraid. Pain and death are not things Thor fears. Loss of honor, on the other hand...

Odin has convinced him to do something very bad indeed.

"They're not against you, Loki," Sigyn says, and Loki turns sharply to her.

Lips trembling she says, "Valli and Nari have been accused of treason by Heimdall and are to be thrown into the Void."

Valli and Nari are their sons.

Loki bites the inside of his cheek. He must stay in control; he must fight with his mind...that is how Loki always wins, the only way he wins.

But his hands are already going to Thor's cloak. As he pulls Thor so their faces are just inches apart, the words he means to say in a low whisper come out a scream. "You swore an oath to protect my sons as though they were your own!"

In the hallway he hears a sentry running and shouting for help.

Thor's hands go to Loki's shirt, as though he might push him away, but he doesn't. Instead he stammers, "Loki, I..." Thor stops, looks sideways, his hands fumbling at his belt.

Loki screams again. "Look at me when you lie to me, oath breaker!"

Thor's eyes go to him. There is so much shame there — it verifies every horrible suspicion Loki has. His sons will perish, Loki will die unable to help them, and the mighty, valiant, honest Thor is to blame.

He isn't thinking clearly when he tries to twist and throw Thor. Thor's magic is partially responsible for his strength, but even without it he is bigger and stronger than Loki, more practiced at these things, and he isn't completely blind with rage. All Loki can see is red, and the only thing he can feel is his blood pounding beneath his skin too hot and too fast. Too quickly Loki is pinned on the floor, snarling at Thor and reaching for magic that isn't there.

And then Thor's body goes limp and slumps forward. Wrestling the large frame off him, Loki looks up to see Sigyn,

Thor's hammer hanging heavy in her hands.

Loki's eyes go wide and his lips curl. A mortal might have died from even a non-magical blow from Mjölnir, but Loki knows Thor isn't dead. Scrambling up from the floor, he moves to take the hammer from Sigyn and finish the job.

Drawing back, she scowls. "No."

Loki wants to scream, wants to argue. His blood is pounding in his ears, his skin feels too hot and too tight and their sons are going to die. Killing another one of Odin's sons seems fitting retribution.

"He let us win," Sigyn says. "Let him live."

Clenching his teeth, Loki stifles his protest.

Sigyn presses firmly at the sides of the pendant around her neck, and the casing in front springs open. Inside is a human-style wind-up stopwatch. "Is it working?" she says. "Hoenir gave it to me; Mimir said he's been devising it since the last time you were here."

Loki is about to speak, something angry and unkind, but his eyes widen instead. The stopwatch is beginning to pulse with magic.

"Yes," Loki says, coming forward.

Staring down at it, Sigyn says, "He said that it..."

"Pulls magic from out of time," Loki says in wonderment. "I see it...how?"

"We don't have time," Sigyn says. "Your armor is at the guard station. I have a hairpin; maybe you can pick the lock?"

Loki can pick just about any lock with a hairpin, but there are faster ways. Clutching the stopwatch, he pulls the magic around him. Closing his eyes he lifts his other hand towards the door. The lock clicks and the door swings open with a creak.

Without hesitation Sigyn runs out, lugging Thor's hammer. Loki follows her into a hallway lined with empty cells. At the end of the hall is the empty guard room, a large ovoid booth set partially into a wall with glass windows on all sides.

Going forward, Sigyn says, "They found out about Valli and Nari's dream of a constitutional monarchy."

Loki's heart falls. Odin is an absolute monarch not interested in sharing his power...and most Asgardians are happy with things that way.

"You knew about that?" Loki says. He'd expressly told his sons to leave their mother out of that folly.

Glaring at him, she says, "I approve of that," and Loki looks quickly away.

As they step through the guard room door, Sigyn says, "Mimir talked the guards downstairs into letting me visit. And then he and Hoenir went back to their hut."

Loki swallows. Hoenir and Mimir have always been kind to Loki and his family, but this...

"Hoenir and Mimir will be confined to the hut until Ragnarok," he says, using the Viking word for the end times.

Glancing at him, Sigyn gives him a tight smile. This escape will spell death warrants for them all; he is not sure even Hoenir's hut can protect them. From down the corridor Loki hears the sound of footsteps on the stairs.

Up ahead is a small guard room with a large window looking out at the cell block. Loki's armor and his sword, Lævatein, hang against the far wall. Entering the room, Loki and Sigyn move towards the armor as one. Without speaking, Sigyn sets down the hammer and helps Loki slip on the breastplate as he fastens his simple unadorned helmet. The helmet's most notable feature is a visor of dwarven crystal.

With magic it is shatterproof, but without magic he can't trust it to protect his eyes. He flips it up.

Loki's hands never collide with Sigyn's as they finish the fastenings. They've done this many times before. As the last buckle is finished and Lævatein is on his hip, their eyes meet.

Since Sigyn opened the stopwatch, magic has been creeping into the tower. But his armor is still not fully enchanted, nor will his knives be. It's doubtful they'll make it out alive.

Loki can't speak, and Sigyn looks quickly away.

Down the hall, a guard shouts, "Come out of there! Hands above your heads."

Darting to the far corner, Sigyn says, "Hoenir said these magic eggs were yours, and they might help us...although the guards didn't detect any magic in them..."

"Eggs?" says Loki. He has no magic eggs. Going to the door, he peers quickly out and catches sight of four guards. A crossbow arrow whistles and he pulls back in.

Crouching on the floor, Sigyn holds up a drab olive green knapsack with the words U.S. Army stenciled on top. "They wouldn't let me take them to your cell — insisted on keeping them here," she says.

Mementos from his last trip to Midgard — Earth. Loki smirks. "Throw it here."

Sigyn tosses the bag. Catching it, Loki deftly pulls out one of six 'eggs'. They are thankfully not magical, and therefore fully operational in the dampened magic of the tower. Pulling on the pin at the top with his teeth, he tosses the Mk 2 World War II era grenade down the hall.

For a moment nothing happens.

The guards chuckle. One shouts. "Your magic tricks won't work here, you fool!"

Sigyn looks at him, eyes wide. Almost too late, Loki hurls himself towards her and covers her body with his. An earsplitting boom ricochets through the tower, and the glass in the guardroom window implodes and showers down on Loki's armor.

Getting quickly to his feet, Loki helps Sigyn up. Together they step out of the guardroom and towards the stairs, avoiding the bodies of the guards, Sigyn clutching Thor's hammer in both hands. Neither speaks.

At the top of the circular staircase, Loki takes out another grenade, swings the knapsack over his shoulder, and gestures for Sigyn to stand back.

The staircase has an echo. He hears more guards but can't tell how far away they are. The sound of his and Sigyn's breathing seems unnaturally loud.

"Loki, they were already taking Valli and Nari to the Center. There isn't much time," Sigyn whispers.

"Shhhhhh…" Loki says, trying to determine just how far away the footsteps are.

Close enough. Pulling the pin he throws the grenade at the far wall. He watches it bounce down the stairwell and out of sight. He hears footsteps, and breathing, and the grenade…. plink, plink, plink down the stairs. Loki pushes Sigyn back behind him so his armor will catch any shrapnel.

"An egg?" someone says. Someone else out of Loki's line of vision shouts.

There is another explosion accompanied by the sound of falling rock, groans, and screams. And then Loki hears a telltale whistling in the air. Before he can move, or even think, Sigyn's body slumps against his, and Thor's heavy hammer falls to the ground.

Lifting his head, Loki sees a guard at the top of the stairs. His face is bloodied, and he has an upraised crossbow.

A knife is in Loki's hand and whipping through the air before he even thinks about it. There is just enough magic now that when the knife hits the guard, it explodes, and the guard crumples to the floor.

Throwing Sigyn over his shoulder, Loki looks at the hammer on the stone step. It is a powerful toy — but as soon as Thor wakes up it will rebound to his hands. Cursing silently, he turns and goes as quickly as he can down the stairs.

"Put me down," Sigyn mutters into his back. "You have to save them, Loki. My boys...my beautiful boys."

He's too busy pulling out another grenade to even tell her to shut up. He hears guards mustering in the open chamber at the base of the tower. Pulling the pin just before the bottom of the stairs, he waits for the explosion and then rushes forward. Magic is thick enough in the air now for him to pull it to them and wrap them in a blanket of invisibility.

Outside the tower he sees men gathering near Sigyn's steeds. Less well protected is Thor's chariot. Thor favors attaching it to goats so he always has something tasty to eat, but the chariot is perfectly capable of flying on its own, and there are no goats today.

Loki slides Sigyn from his back and lays her on her side in the chariot. She is invisible to those around him, but in Loki's eyes she shimmers and glows, as does the arrow protruding from her back. He breaks it as close to her body as he can.

"Leave me," she whispers as he sits her up.

Glaring at her, Loki climbs into the chariot and seats himself next to her, facing the back. "To the Center," he shouts.

The chariot rises in the air with the crackle of magic.

Shouts rise up, and Loki hears the thunk of magical arrows in the floor beneath them. Flames dance near his feet as the arrows catch fire, but Thor's chariot was designed to withstand lightning — a little fire from magical arrows won't hurt it.

Moments later, Loki and Sigyn are whisking forward, over and through the illusions of flying buttresses and steeples that are part of this decade's 13th century revival. There are faster ways for Loki to travel, secret ways that he alone knows. But they would leave him too drained to fight — and he can't use them to transport others.

He'll need all his power to fight soon. He lets the invisibility spell drop.

Narrowing her eyes in his direction, Sigyn says, "Must you always make things difficult? I'm as good as dead. You should have left me!"

Her lips are horribly pale, and the color has left her cheeks. She is full Asgardian, but looks nearly Jotunn. Leave it to Sigyn to waste her last breaths berating him. Smiling with brightness he doesn't feel, Loki says, "My dear, have you forgotten that among some humans I am regarded as the patron god of lost causes?" Not that he believes he or any of the Aesir are gods.

Sigyn's head lolls to the side, and she makes a sound like, "Pfffttt." She heaves a ragged breath and Loki does his best not to look concerned. "What are you planning?" she whispers, her eyelids slipping closed. "To swoop down, pick them up, and carry us all away in this bucket?"

That actually was close to Loki's plan, but he says nothing, just glares at her one more time before standing to look out of the chariot. They are close to their destination. Nearly below them is a wide plain. In it are eight circles of white stone, each about 50 yards in diameter, with wide gates and toll booths around and between them. The white circles are where the "branches" of the World Tree connect with Asgard. Not "branches" at all, they are places where the fabric of space and time tears easily, and the largest, most efficient, gateways to the eight other realms.

The white circles themselves form a larger circle around a small raised dais, its surface unnaturally dark. It is the entrance to the Void, where the Asgardians dump their trash, their spent potions, hopelessly broken magic tools, and the condemned.

Normally most of the circular gateways would be buzzing with merchants and delegates to visit and barter with the Aesir and each other. However, all the white circles and the toll booths at their peripheries are empty; instead, a crowd is gathered in the great dark circle at the center, their attention focused on the black dais.

From aloft, Loki can see Valli and Nari at the base of the dais, their blond heads bent, their hands bound at their backs. Behind them stands Odin, the staff Gungnir in his hands. A great armed host stands in a circle around Odin, Loki's sons, and the dais. A crowd of civilians from the friendly worlds mill about in a dense crowd just beyond the warriors.

"Have you forgotten the Valkyries?" Sigyn asks.

There is a stirring below among the armed host. In the distance Loki sees Heimdall, the guardian of the gates, pointing in their direction. Around Heimdall, the Valkyries, winged warrior women, rise. Bolts of fire hurtle toward the chariot from the staffs in their hands. Loki slumps down next to Sigyn.

"Actually," he says, "I did forget about them."

Sigyn takes a deep, ragged breath. Clutching the edge of the chariot, Loki tries to clear his head as they rock under the Valkyrie onslaught.

"Chariot, down!" he says. He nearly loses his seat as the chariot falls. "Gently," he cries and the descent slows. "Move to hover just above the crowd!"

As Loki suspected, the barrage of fire stops as they get close to the civilians.

"What are you doing?" Sigyn whispers.

"I can't help you," Loki says, pulling a grenade from the olive green bag. "I'm no good at healing...and this bucket will never get close enough to Valli and Nari."

He looks down. They're close enough to the ground. Smiling at Sigyn, he says, "Chariot, to Hoenir's hut!"

"What!" says Sigyn, the anger in her voice nearly blood curdling.

Loki jumps out just before the chariot takes off, and Sigyn's scream fades away. The crowd parts only enough for him to land. Straightening quickly, he holds the grenade above his head and smiles across the crowds in Odin and Heimdall's direction.

"What do you have there, fool?" someone says.

"A rotten egg," he responds with a grin.

The crowd closes in around him. From where they stand, now on top of the dais, Loki hears Valli or Nari shout, "Father!" The crowd starts to roar, but then Odin's voice rings out, "Let him pass!"

Odin knows Loki is no fool.

The crowd parts and murmurs. Loki walks forward, still smiling, still clutching the pin of the grenade. He is within a few paces of the dais when Odin thumps the black stone beneath his feet with Gungnir and shouts, "Stop." The rich velvet blackness that is Odin's magic whips out across the plain.

Loki's legs suddenly feel like lead. He feels like the gravity in Asgard has increased by ten, as though he's consumed vast quantities of magical energy, enough to set a world on fire. He blinks, takes a breath, and moves onward. It takes him a moment but then he realizes that the crowd is dead silent, and except for Odin and him, no one seems to be moving.

"Nice trick," he says. An incredibly powerful trick. Odin must be using nearly all of Gungnir's power for this. Not for the first time Loki wishes he'd never given Odin the damn thing. Loki's eyes flit nervously to the side. Just beyond the plain he can see Odin's raven messengers, Huginn and Munnin, soaring through the air, and he almost sighs with relief. Not everything has stopped.

He looks up to Odin. Unlike the other Aesir who all chose to appear closer to the age of 25, Odin appears to be near the human age of 50. He wears a patch over a missing eye; he purportedly exchanged that eye for wisdom. As Loki draws closer, he sees Odin's one eye widen, as though in alarm.

Loki blinks, and Odin's gaze is its normal steely calm. "You have something you wish to discuss?" Odin says.

Walking up and around until he stands just a pace from Odin, his back to Valli and Nari, Loki says, "Let my sons go."

"I don't think you understand how dangerous Valli and Nari have become," Odin says, his one eye unblinking.

Scowling, Loki says, "You're wrong." They aren't strong in magic, not like Helen.

"No," says Odin. "I am not." Sighing, Odin says, "You know I will do anything to preserve the safety of the nine realms."

Loki waves a hand. "Yes, yes, I know. Even allowing the death of your own beautiful son." Tilting his head he sneers. "I'm not that selfless."

"Loki," Odin says. "There are things happening now, new passages opening between the realms that should remain closed, branches from other realms approaching ours. Asgard cannot afford to be divided by this idea they have...this democracy..."

Rolling his eyes, Loki says, "It's more of a proto-democracy, hardly a threat."

"Heimdall and the Diar demand this," Odin says, thumping his spear again. "For the stability of the realms, for order, I must do what must be done."

Loki's eyes flick to the immobilized figure of Heimdall, the "all seeing god" of order. He and Loki do not get along well.

Loki looks back at Odin. How long has he carried the weight of Odin's desire to preserve the nine realms? How long has he carried Odin's secrets? How often has he, as the Christians say, turned the other cheek...after Helen?

For Helen alone Odin owes him. "Let them go," Loki whispers. "Or you make me your enemy."

Odin blinks, and for a moment Loki imagines he sees hesitation. The other man's face softens, perhaps in compassion or understanding. Odin certainly can't be afraid of Loki. For a moment everything is worth it: obeying Odin, playing the fool, letting himself be cast as the coward, the shirker. But then Odin bangs his spear down three times and Loki feels the air pressure behind him drop.

"Hurry and you might catch them," Odin says, his face flat.

With a cry of rage, Loki pulls the pin from the grenade, hurls it into the air, and rushes up the stairs of the dais. The sky is already opening up to the Void, a long tear in space time, like the funnel of a tornado twisting downwards.

Loki sees Valli spin so his back is to Nari's side, and then they are gone, sucked up into the blackness. With a cry Loki follows, dimly aware of the ring of the grenade behind him.

In the glow of starlight, and nearly spent and broken magical objects, Loki sees his sons hovering before him, their mouths and eyes open wide, Vali's hands desperately clasped around Nari's scabbard. They've never been in this place before, but Loki has. Fifteen seconds. They can survive 15 seconds in the vacuum of space. Loki tries to use the threads of magic to move towards them, for what purpose he doesn't even know. So they can all die together?

It is the only plan he has, but as he tries to implement it, something sucks him backwards.

Loki looks down in panic. A renegade branch of the World Tree, another tear in space and time has caught him... but there shouldn't be one here. He looks back up for an instant and sees his sons vanish. Were they pulled backwards by another renegade branch? Suddenly there is a flash of color, and then he is blinded by sunlight, gasping in hot, humid air and falling backwards to the ground.

He failed. His world is gone. Blackness overtakes him.

Loki hears a voice, like a child's, say, "Zd`rastvuyte," and then, "'Kak `Vas za`vut?"

He opens his eyes. Loki has the gift for tongues, but it

takes him a moment to recognize the language. A very power-ful magical something is saying, "Hello. What's your name?" far too cheerfully in Russian. He looks around — he's in a forest on Earth. Instead of Russia, the stars overhead suggest the continent of North America. There is magic in a thick red glow around him like a mist. Whatever it is, the magic is very powerful. But there are no magical creatures on Midgard anymore, just beasts and humans, with their one, very weak, though intriguing, magical trick.

"Loki," he says. Whatever the Russian speaking mist is, he doesn't want to annoy it.

"You hear me, Comrade!" says the thing, still in Russian. Its voice fades; the mist dissipates.

Loki is alone on the ground. He is too filled with despair to worry about the magical Russian-speaking creature. Sitting up, he pulls up his knees, leans forward and buries his face in his hands. He sees Sigyn slumped in the chariot, he sees his sons' terror-stricken faces in the Void flash before his eyes. He remembers the way they clung together, Valli clasping his hands to Nari's scabbard.

...The scabbard! Nari's scabbard. Long ago Loki gave it to him as a gift. Nari is an anglophile and the scabbard comes from that isle. It is enchanted to protect the bearer from harm. Is it powerful enough to save its bearer in the Void? Perhaps it could suspend them in time, just as Odin did to the crowd with Gungnir?

It is such a slim hope that Loki drops his hands and laughs. But he has to believe it. Not because it's likely, but because he must believe it or he might stay here, in this spot, in this forest for a millennium.

He swallows and assesses his situation. Physically he is

unharmed, but he's very hungry. Using magic always makes him famished, and resisting whatever Odin did with his staff drained Loki tremendously.

He opens the knapsack quickly and pulls out the grenades. When he stole the grenades he also stole C-rations for their novelty. He scowls. The C-rations aren't there. Belatedly he remembers discarding them decades ago. But there is something else, something wonderful. A small book, bound in white leather, the size of his palm. It is the Journal of Lothur. Hoenir must have packed it. Loki presses the book to his forehead and squeezes his eyes shut. More than a journal, it is a book of magic with maps of many of the secret back road branches of the World Tree. Having it is a small miracle.

Not that he can open space-time to travel any of those branches now. He is famished, and exhausted.

He sees a far off glow in the distance. Perhaps it is a human habitation where he can steal food. Climbing to his feet, he starts trudging towards the glow. There is the cry of a raven above his head, and for a moment he panics. But when he looks up at the shadows of the trees he sees only common ravens, not Odin's messengers.

He hears a roar not far away. He hasn't been here since the 1940's, but he recognizes it as the sound of a roadway. It will be far easier to travel if he walks along it. That thought is just through his mind when he trips over something. Nearly falling to the ground, he curses, and a spurt of flame rises from his hand to the treetops. In the flame's orange glow he sees an outcropping of stone rising at his feet.

His flame dissipates, and he does his best to walk around the rocks in the dark.

His brain, as it is wont to do, starts to scheme. After he

gets to the human village and eats his fill, then what? How will he find Valli and Nari in the Void? No, not the Void, they disappeared before he did. To what realm? He'll have to search them all.

Swallowing, he tries not to let the enormity of the task overwhelm him. He is rather good at achieving impossible things. Even Odin will give him that. Scowling at the thought of the would-be executioner of his sons, he feels his body go hot.

From up ahead he hears the sound of tires screeching and some loud noises he can't identify. He's too hungry to be curious. He just steps onto the gravel on the side of the road. Concentrating, he creates an illusion of the attire that was popular the last time he was on this planet. His armor is still on. If anyone touches him they will feel it, but he will look like he belongs. With a deep breath he starts walking towards the lights of human habitation.

An automobile approaches him. It has a shape he's never seen before, trapezoidish, large and boxy. Thinking perhaps that the driver will give him a lift, he raises his hand. It slows for a moment, and Loki sees a flash of white hair, but then it speeds away. Loki scowls and keeps going, every step dragging more than the last.

Far up ahead the boxy, trapezoidish automobile slows and stops. Loki hears a voice in the distance and something that sounds like a growl and maybe a yelp.

A few minutes later he feels something. Something that makes every hair on the back of his neck stand on end. It's something he has not felt in centuries, the one, small, intriguing human magical trick: A prayer.

Someone, anyone, help me.

CHAPTER 2

Amy lies on the ground, one side of her face pressed in the dirt, the other side with the cold end of a gun to her cheek. She can hear her breath in her ears, or is that his breath? The guy's knee is on her back. He's silent. The hand is trembling. In fear...or...she swallows...or excitement.

Closing her eyes, she tries to remember her self defense courses she took with Grandma. The first rule was to verify that your attacker's weapon is genuine.

Licking her lips, she says, "Is that a...a...real gun?"

He laughs. "You want me to take it away from your cheek, don't you? Don't you?"

He pushes the muzzle more tightly against her, and Amy screws her eyes shut.

From the grass towards the road there is the sound of a high-pitched growl punctuated by occasional whimpering.

Fenrir! Screwing her eyes tighter, Amy desperately thinks, Fenrir, please, just distract him...

From the direction of the man's van comes another voice. "Fenrir?" Amy's heart stops. There are two guys? Oh, no.

"Who's there?" shouts the man that's holding her down. The trembling of the gun's muzzle stops and steadies.

Amy hears the snap of a twig close to her and Fenrir's pathetic growl and tiny yips a little further off.

"I'm not moving this gun from her face!" the man says.

The whimpering disappears. The high-pitched growl changes and deepens.

"What the..." her captor stutters and pulls the gun away. Amy darts into the car, rolls over and tries to yank her keychain out of the ignition, but it's jammed. Fumbling, she manages to detach the pepper spray.

She hears the sound of gunshots and the man cursing. Looking out the window, she sees an enormous wolf the size of a small pony, muzzle white with foam, crouching as though about to spring. The bullets seem to have no effect on it, and Amy draws back further into her overturned car.

And then there is a shadow over the window, a dull thudding noise over and over again, and then the sound of a crack. The deep growling is gone. There is just Fenrir's pathetic whimpering.

The shadow moves away and Amy blinks in confusion. And there, just visible in the indirect light of her headlights, is the man who was attacking her. He's face down on the ground. The white hair on his head appears slick, black and shiny. Just beyond him is Fenrir, licking her tiny jaws, and wiggling forward on her belly.

A new face pops too suddenly into the window, younger, clean shaven, with sharp features. He's wearing a fedora. "It's going to be all right — ."

It's the fedora that freaks her out. Amy fires the pepper spray. In slow motion it arcs towards him in a long stream.

The stranger throws up a hand just before it reaches his face. He blinks and then screams. "Aaauuuggghhhhhh!!!!"

Jumping back from the window, he shouts, "That stings!"

Unable to bear the sound of Fenrir's whimpering, Amy scoots forward and out of the car. The man is shaking his hand. He seems to be shimmering. It looks like he's wearing a fedora, a white shirt and dark, well-tailored pants that are sort of retro looking. And it also looks like he's wearing a suit of weird armor, a sword waving at his hip.

Shaking his hand, he turns to her, "That's how you reward someone, anyone, who saves your life? Firing snake venom at them?"

He slumps to the ground, still shaking his hand. The fedora, white shirt, and black pants seem to solidify around him. "I don't know why I bothered."

A shape wriggles towards him on the ground, whimpering and wagging its body.

"Fenrir!" Amy says.

Looking in the little dog's direction, the man says, "Fenrir," his voice sounding a little far off. Still shaking his one hand, he holds his other out to Amy's dog. Fenrir tries to lick it.

Running forward, Amy holds up the pepper spray. "Don't you dare hurt her!"

The look he gives her. It is such a look of what-are-you-some-kind-of-idiot that it actually makes Amy think he really won't hurt Fenrir — or her. Also, Fenrir is licking his hand. Fenrir doesn't lick men's hands.

Fenrir is limping, actually almost crawling. Forgetting all

about the stranger, Amy goes into full diagnostic mode. The angle of her leg, the way her hip is jutting..."Fenrir," she says, "You've dislocated your hip. Oh, poor Baby."

Fenrir turns to Amy and pants. She was trying to save Amy a few minutes ago...with a dislocated hip. Sitting down next to her, Amy says, "You are the best doggie in the world, thank you, thank you, thank you." Fenrir wags her body and whimpers again.

"I am so sorry about this," Amy says to Fenrir. She looks at Strange Man. "She likes you. Would you hold her front steady?"

He raises an eyebrow. "Aren't you going to thank me?"

"Hold her," says Amy, her brain going into fix-the-injured-little-creature mode.

Sighing, the man wraps his hands around Fenrir's torso.

"I'm so sorry about this, Fenrir," Amy says. "She may bite you," she says to the stranger.

Before he can withdraw his hand, Amy's already got her hands on the dislocated joint. It takes only seconds to relocate Fenrir's hip. The dog yelps pitifully, but amazingly doesn't bite. As soon as Amy's done, she wiggles and jumps into Amy's arms.

"That was well done," says the stranger.

"Thank you," says Amy. Her eyes fall on the man lying prone in front of her overturned car. The enormity of what has happened suddenly catches up to her. Looking down, she says, "And thank you."

"Do you have any food?" the man asks. "That would be thanks enough."

Clutching Fenrir to her chest and rubbing her sore neck, Amy looks towards her car. She has a cooler in the back seat if she can get it out, but... Her eyes fall to the man on the ground.

"I don't think you have to worry about him," the stranger says.

Amy's eyes widen and she squeezes Fenrir a little tighter.

The stranger is silent. Somewhere an owl hoots.

"Your first time to see a corpse," says the stranger softly. Amy looks quickly at him. "No," she says, "I've seen plenty in the anatomy lab."

He stares at her for a moment. His face is young, he can't be much older than she is, but his expression is weary. "Do you have food in your automobile?" he says.

Amy blinks at the non-sequitur. "Yes, in the back seat. In the cooler."

"Cooler?" he says.

Nodding her head towards the car, she says, "Just the cheap Styrofoam white box you get at the convenience mart..."

The stranger stands up quickly and goes to her car. Amy's not really paying attention to what he's doing. She thinks she hears a car on the road. Running up out of the ditch she just catches sight of a car's retreating rear lights. She almost swears. They didn't even stop!

Putting Fenrir down, she goes back to her car and crawls through the window. The stranger is already pulling the cooler out of the backseat. It takes a while, but Amy finds her iPhone.

She tries to dial 911 but gets the no-service message.

Scowling in frustration, she stares at the man on the ground. She doesn't want to stay here, not with the dead or dying man — oh, God, should she check if he's dead? Will she be charged with manslaughter if she doesn't? Will Strange

Guy be charged with murder?

Crawling out of her car, she feels for a pulse. She can't find anything and is both relieved and disgusted by the fact that she is relieved.

She has to get out of here. She begins frantically patting down the dead man's body.

"What are you looking for?" Strange Guy says.

Amy glances up to see him sitting on the bank of the ditch, a box of Life cereal between his knees, Fenrir sitting in front of him. He throws a handful into his mouth and tosses a piece to her dog.

He looks so much calmer than she feels, and it's not fair. She begins patting down the man again.

Not finding what she's looking for, she murmurs, "They're not here."

"What?" Strange Guy says.

Amy looks up at the minivan. Getting up from the ground she runs around the corpse and out of the ditch. She lifts the latch on the passenger side door. It's open. Maybe his keys are in here. She can drive the minivan to find help.

Stranger's voice comes from close behind her. "I don't think you should go into that man's automobile."

Ignoring him, Amy opens the glove box. There's a narrow folio in there, long and leather bound.

"Don't," says Stranger, and his hand is suddenly coming from behind to grab it from her. But it's too late. Amy's already opening it, and pictures are spilling out. There are pictures of women in there, but mostly of children. For an instant the pictures shake in Amy's bloody knuckles, and then she screams.

The man behind her says something, a curse or a swear or

an exclamation. Whatever, he sounds shocked and horrified and the photo album bursts into flame.

Amy drops it, and the man says, "I'm sorry...I didn't..."

Some sense finally coming back to her, Amy begins to stamp out the fire with her foot. The people in the pictures... their families will need to know.

When the last of the flames are out she backs up — right into Stranger Guy's chest. He feels weird, too hard. She's in shock. Obviously. He brings a hand to her shoulder; it is warm and comforting and normal.

In the distance she hears sirens — maybe the car that drove off didn't belong to an ass after all. Stranger starts to pull his hand away. "Don't," she says, turning to him and looking up. He is really tall, maybe 6' 3" or 6' 4". She's not afraid of him anymore. She presses his hand more tightly and wills him not to go.

His jaw goes tight. And then he says, "All right, I won't."

When the man had a gun on her, she was terrified. But now, after seeing the pictures and what she almost did not escape... Her whole body trembles. The sirens in the distance get louder. Clutching Stranger's hand to her face, she begins to cry. She's safe now, she knows it. The words, "I am so afraid," are on the tip of her tongue, but she doesn't say them.

"I know. I know," the Stranger says. And in the pit of Amy's stomach she can feel it. He does understand. He does know.

Loki is about eleven years old. He is in Asgard. Odin is off on a campaign in the realm of the dwarfs and Loki's snuck off to play with Hoenir — Odin discourages Loki's visits to Hoenir's hut when he is home. Odin claims he doesn't want Loki disturbing Hoenir while he works. Hoenir never seems to be disturbed by Loki. In fact, Hoenir always seems happy to drop whatever he is doing when Loki comes about.

At the moment Loki and Hoenir are squatting in the grass outside Hoenir's hut. The hut is in a meadow between a copse of trees so high they completely shield the rest of Asgard from view. The trees are a gift from Frigga, Odin's wife and Loki's adoptive mother. She calls Hoenir's hut an eyesore.

Unlike all the other dwellings, buildings, and monuments in Asgard, Hoenir's hut isn't touched by any illusions that would make it conform to the current fashion for Egyptian architecture from the Old Kingdom. It looks as it always has. Made of rough wood, it leans slightly to one side. The chimney is made of natural stone and is crumbling slightly. The roof is thatch, and there are always little creatures peering out from the straw. Sometimes the creatures are recognizable, sometimes they are Hoenir's own invention — squirrels with bird beaks and peacock tails, snakes with butterfly wings, and birds with cat faces. These creatures are real, unlike the illusions created by Loki and Odin.

The hut normally has a glow about it, golden white, the color of Hoenir's magic. All magical beings have a color to their magic, but one can never see one's own color. Loki's been told, though, that his own magic is white, blue, orange and red — like a flame Mimir says. Or, as Odin says, because Loki is too fickle to pick a shade.

Loki isn't thinking about magical color, or paying attention to the denizens of the thatch. He is peering over Hoenir's shoulder and through a magnifying glass, a magical device Hoenir is holding over a small twig.

Hoenir, like Odin, doesn't look particularly youthful. He is balding and is a little round around the waist. Next to Hoenir is the severed head of Mimir the giant, propped up on top of an overturned crate. Like Loki, Mimir is wearing a wide brimmed hat to shield him from the sun.

Since Hoenir is mute, Mimir speaks for him. "Now you see, Loki, the magnifying glass captures and concentrates sunlight and turns it into heat."

Loki bends closer to the ground. He can see the concentrated beam of light Mimir speaks of. He waves his hand through the beam but only feels a disappointingly faint amount of warmth. The normal yellow golden glow of Hoenir's magic isn't present though, which means the glass needs none of Hoenir's magic to work. That is something, Loki supposes.

"The way a magnifying glass captures, concentrates and transforms sunlight is very much like how magical creatures capture, concentrate and transform magic," Mimir intones.

Loki nods at Mimir's head. Loki knows about magic. Most men of Asgard don't deign to toy with it, believing it makes them unmanly. But Odin and Hoenir are both powerful magicians, and Odin is king, and Hoenir is — Hoenir is Hoenir. Loki respects him as much as Odin. And he wants to be like them. At eleven he sees and feels magic everywhere, and is nearly as good at creating illusions as Odin. Loki gets the feeling that most people are uncomfortable with that, but Hoenir and Odin encourage his ability.

Looking back down to Hoenir and the magnifying glass, Loki asks, "May I try?"

"Ummmm…" says Mimir. "That might not…"

Hoenir hands Loki the magnifying glass.

Just as Loki takes the worn wooden handle in his grasp, he hears a loud shout, "Loki! Loki! Loki!!!"

Standing up in shock, Loki sends the concentrated beam of light dancing across the grass and the overturned crate Mimir sits on. In its wake, flames flare to life.

"Helllllppppppppp!" shouts Mimir.

Dropping the glass, Loki jumps over and pulls Mimir from the rising flames.

"Wow," Loki says, momentarily forgetting the shouting that distracted him. "That magnifying glass has powerful magic!"

"Ummm...no..." says Mimir. "Thank you, Loki. Turn me so that I face Hoenir."

Loki does as he is bidden and instantly regrets it.

"Hoenir, you had to expect that would happen if Loki touched the glass!" Mimir says, his voice so accusatory Loki feels pain on Hoenir's behalf.

Stamping out the flames, Hoenir just raises an eyebrow in Mimir's direction.

"What? He should know!" says Mimir.

Hoenir shrugs. Mimir says, "Pfffttt to what Odin says."

"Loki! Loki! Loki!!!" come the shouts again. Dropping Mimir on the ground, Loki spins around. "What was that?"

"What was what?" says Mimir, eyes staring at the sky.

"The voices calling my name!" says Loki. He doesn't recognize them. They sound almost like a chorus.

From Mimir there is silence. Loki looks to Hoenir. A quiet look is passing between the man and the severed head on the ground.

Blinking, Mimir says, "I suppose we might expect you to hear them early..."

"Hear what?" says Loki.

"Close your eyes, Loki," Mimir says. "What do you see?"

Loki tilts his head. Magic. He smiles. Closing his eyes, he finds he does see something. "I see the village by the lake from our camping trip this spring."

"Are you sure?" says Mimir.

How could he forget the place? Odin, Hoenir and Loki had gone camping on Earth. Their trip had been interrupted by some humans. It was the first time Loki had seen the creatures. In person they were smaller and more pathetic than he could have imagined. It seemed horribly cruel that Hoenir and Odin hadn't gifted them with magic.

The humans had spoken to Hoenir and Odin at length, and then Loki had been sent home under the watchful eyes of Huginn and Munnin, Odin's ravens. Nothing more had been said of the incident.

The scene behind Loki's eyelids changes, and he gasps. He sees something more. "I see a man with skulls around his belt!" Loki swallows. The skulls are too small to belong to adults.

"Do the voices in your head...do they say anything else?"

Loki's eyes open. "Yes, they say the giant's body has knit itself together, and he has sent a messenger from his fortress. In the morrow he will come to claim his sacrifice."

Hoenir's jaw drops. Mimir's eyes go wide. Swallowing, Mimir says, "Loki, the giant calls himself Cronus. I don't think he is the Cronus; he was Greek, and Odin, well, Zeus, well... Odin sort of..."

Loki's brow knits together.

Licking his lips, Mimir says, "Anyway, Cronus is not Aesir or Jotunn, but something other. He has been terrorizing humans for generations. Last fall, Hoenir hid the boy that Cronus chose to be *a sacrifice as wheat in a field — and Cronus found him. Odin disguised the boy as a swan, and Cronus found him yet again. Fortunately, Odin was able to kill Cronus."*

Loki nods. Of course, Hoenir wouldn't have been able to kill Cronus. Loki's never heard of Hoenir killing, or even hurting, anything.

Swallowing, Mimir says, "Or so we thought. If what your peasants say is true, Cronus was able to reassemble himself and seeks to claim his sacrifice again."

"Odin must come back!" Loki says, looking to the skies. He was sure he saw Huginn and Munnin, Odin's raven messengers earlier. If he gets their attention they can alert Odin.

Mimir sighs. "Loki, Odin is busy saving multitudes of children. He cannot come back for just one."

Loki swallows. In his head the voices rise again. "Loki! Loki! Save our son! Save our children!"

Loki starts walking to the Center and the World Gates. "I have to go." He feels as though the voices are pulling him by a thread.

"You won't be able to use your tricks of illusion against him!" Mimir says.

"I'll think of something," Loki says. He has to. The voices in his head...

He hears footsteps, and then Hoenir is at his side, Mimir in his hands. "You always do," Mimir says.

Loki blinks and Mimir winks at him.

Loki, along with Hoenir and Mimir, arrives at the village well after nightfall.

Even though Loki is only eleven, he is nearly as tall as the tallest man in the village — though that man is broader in shoulder, and probably stronger. The humans smell less than pleasant. Their *clothes look like rags. Many are missing teeth, and some have hor-rible scars. He is horrified by them, and at the same time, when they look at him their hope is palpable. It makes Loki feel older, wiser, and more powerful than he has ever felt before.*

And the boy that is to be sacrificed, Jonah...he is so small, he hardly comes up past Loki's waist. His eyes are so wide, fright-ened, innocent and trusting; Loki simply has to succeed.

Loki scans the horizon. As he does, the old man, who had talked to Odin and Hoenir last year, says, "We have tried to fight him, but our weapons bounce off, and he is terribly strong."

Loki blinks. Loki can't make weapons bounce off of him, but he knows it takes immense concentration. A surprise to break Cronus' concentration is needed.

A boathouse on the bank of the lake catches Loki's attention. He looks at the small stature of the humans and, to his own wonderment, he does think of something.

"Jonah," Loki asks, "can you swim?"

The boy nods.

Standing taller and trying to look important, Loki begins to tell Jonah, Hoenir, Mimir, and the assembled villagers his plan. When he is done, Jonah is quaking with fear.

Loki bites his own lip. He is very nearly a child himself, and he can relate. Kneeling down, he puts a hand on Jonah's shoulder. "Don't worry. All the time you are with Cronus, I'll be there with you."

Next to him, in Hoenir's arms, Mimir says, "Wait, now — " but Hoenir slaps a hand over his mouth.

In the morning before Cronus arrives, Loki casts an illusion over Jonah so he looks like a fish and commands him to go swim in the lake. Loki knows that Cronus will eventually see through the illusion, but he needs to buy the village men some time to enact their part of the plan.

As soon as Jonah is in the water, Loki goes off to meet Cronus. Cronus isn't tall for an Aesir, Vanir, or Jotunn, but he can see why the villagers think him a giant. Compared to the humans, he is immense. He has white hair and a face that is disturbingly pleasant, almost baby like in its roundness. It is in stark contrast to the belt of children's skulls that hangs at his waist. The belt is terrifying, but what is more frightening is the blanket of magic that hovers over him.

Cronus doesn't get angry when the villagers don't bring Jonah forward. He just smiles. And then he says, "I think I will go fishing." With that he turns around and walks to one of the boats on the shore. That was faster than Loki anticipated. Racing after Cronus he shouts, "Wait, I'll come with you."

"Of course, Little Giant," Cronus says with a laugh.

When they get in the boat, Loki says, "Let me row for you, Sir."

Narrowing his eyes, Cronus says, "Very well, Little Giant."

Loki takes the oars and proceeds to row in the wrong direction...as slowly as he can.

Smiling again, Cronus says, "You'll have to row faster than that, Little Giant, if you want your death to be an easy one."

Loki sits bolt upright and nearly drops the oars.

Laughing, Cronus says, "Oh, come now, you're a little bigger than I like, but you are very pretty. You don't think I'd let you get away?"

Fear unravels in the pit of Loki's stomach; it's all he can do not to quake in his seat.

With a wave of his hand, the oars fly from Loki's grasp and fall at the bottom of the boat. With another wave, Cronus sets the boat in motion again — this time in the right direction.

Loki swallows. The sun is bright, and its cheerfulness feels like a mockery of Loki and Jonah's plight.

Loki tries to confuse Cronus by illusioning schools of fish beneath the boat, and it does work somewhat. Cronus sees the fish, slows the boat, and drops the net that sat at the boat's stern. But after a few empty hauls, he sees through Loki's scheme. He weights the net down and dredges along the bottom.

By late morning he has Jonah in the net, and as soon as he lifts him into the boat, the illusion drops. With a gasp, Jonah runs to sit by Loki. Taking the smaller boy's hand, Loki squeezes — not sure who he's trying to reassure.

Cronus just smiles at them, waves a hand and the boat heads toward shore. As soon as the boat hits ground, Loki waves his hands and an illusionary wall of flame rises up in the middle of the small craft, a few hands lengths away from Cronus' nose. Pulling Jonah from the boat, Loki yells, "Run!"

They tear as fast as they can through the shallow water, out of the bright sunlight, into the boat house. Cronus, in a frenzy, follows right behind. He is nearly on them when his head runs straight into the trap Loki had the men set for him, a spear at just the right height to hit a full-grown Aesir, Jotunn or Vanir squarely in the head.

Dazed, Cronus takes a step back. "Now!" screams Loki. From the shadows village men come forward with axes. One presses an axe in Loki's own hand.

Loki has received a warrior's training. And he has killed animals in the hunt. But now, when he needs it most, he seems unable to fight. He just stands frozen. The human men do not hesitate. They begin furiously hacking at Cronus' limbs with their axes, and the boathouse fills with the thick smell of blood. Loki sees a leg separate at the knee. Almost instantly it reattaches.

Loki's eyes go wide and Cronus laughs.

"Think you're clever, Little Giant? I disguised how quickly I can heal from your brother, Odin! But I don't want you to get away."

With a roar he heaves one of the villagers through a wall.

Loki's mind uncoils. He doesn't know if it is fear or bravery which sets him in motion. "Keep going!" Loki shouts to the remaining villagers, running to the wall and grabbing several iron nails.

A villager separates the other leg with an axe, and this time, Loki stabs a nail into the severed knee, preventing a clean bond of the severed flesh. Cronus gives a cry of rage and tries to bend down to remove the nail, but the humans sense his weakness and redouble their efforts. An arm falls away, and again Loki is there, stabbing another iron nail into the wound.

They can't get to the head before all the limbs are severed and the joints secured from reattachment. Cronus is unaffected by loss of blood, and he manages to throw a few more villagers off of him with the power of his mind alone. But at last, when he can barely move, when he's just a torso and a head, he looks at Loki and his eyes open wide. "You," he says. And then he sneers, "Plan to flush me down the river like you did your brother?"

Loki feels like he's been struck. He wants to demand to know what Cronus is talking about but then a villager's axe falls down on Cronus' neck and his eyes go blank.

Loki falls back gasping. He starts to shake; he's not sure why. He's safe now...safe...

CHAPTER 3

Sheriff Ken McSpadden sits in his office, the driver's license of Thor Odinson in his hand. It's an Oklahoma driver's license, just like Amy Lewis' license. The picture on this license is definitely the man who saved Amy Lewis by killing Ed Malson — a name that was soon to go down in serial killer history.

On his computer monitor Thor's license information is displayed again. It took a while to pull the record up. They had some computer problems first.

Thor's social security number checks out...but that's a little weird, too. Like the license details, before Thor's social security number cleared they had computer trouble, a flicker, an error...and then...everything was okay.

Thor's got a clean record as far as the criminal databases are concerned. McSpadden tried Googling him, too — but all he got was a comic book character.

Leaning back in his chair, McSpadden taps the armrest in agitation. It's not the comic book name, the computer glitches, or the girl's story about a wolf distracting Malson that's really putting him on edge. It's Deputy Patches, the station cat.

Patches is a very fat cat. Sometimes the officers affectionately refer to her as a bowling ball. She's famously lazy, but right now she is rubbing her head vigorously against the edge of his computer monitor. McSpadden puts the license down. Patches begins batting it with her paw, and then chewing its edge. Abruptly she hops down from the desk and begins chasing an imaginary mouse around the room.

McSpadden sighs. Patches hasn't been this excited since they found that crazy carpet at the edge of the road. Darn thing kept rolling and unrolling, and then it would levitate a few inches off the ground before collapsing. Patches had scratched and rolled over every part of it until the thing was covered with fur.

Nix that. She had been more excited by the monkey paw. McSpadden's dogs had found it while he'd been out coon hunting with the boys. The dogs had formed a circle around it and growled up a storm. McSpadden picked it up and put it in his pocket. It had been a long evening, he was hungry, and he found himself wishing for a pastrami sandwich. Not five minutes later he and the boys discovered the hiker — dead for days, a rotting pastrami sandwich miraculously not eaten by scavengers in his hands. That's when McSpadden remembered reading a horror story back when he was a kid about a monkey's paw that granted its bearer's wishes — but at a price.

McSpadden feels a chill run up his spine at the memory. He wouldn't have put two and two together, but after the carpet incident and all the damn unicorn sightings in Mark Twain National Forest, he had the sense to bring the paw back to the station and call it in. Patches had thrown a hissing fit. She has a sense for these...weird things. Some of the boys call it magic.

"Yo, Colbert!" McSpadden calls through the open door.

Deputy Colbert tears himself away from CNN and comes into McSpadden's office. "Give this back to Thor," says McSpadden.

Colbert opens his mouth to speak, but McSpadden points to Patches. She hops up onto McSpadden's desk again and starts rubbing her head against the computer.

Colbert's eyebrows go up at Patches' unusual display of activity. Nodding, he takes the license and leaves the office, wisely not saying a word.

McSpadden picks up Patches and carries her outside. It's 4 a.m. and still dark. He walks over to one of the cars in the parking lot and sets Patches down on the hood. She sprawls out and does what she normally does best. She sleeps.

Feeling a little more confident and a little less watched than he did inside, McSpadden pulls out his cell phone. He clicks on a contact he's never actually met, but he's all too familiar with.

After three rings the call's picked up on the other end. "Laura Stodgill here, U.S. Department of Anomalous Devices of Unknown Origin. McSpadden, what do you have for me in your vortex of weirdness?" Her voice sounds sleepy and a bit disoriented.

"You mean this shit isn't happening all over?" McSpadden says.

Suddenly sounding very alert and awake, Laura says, "I

can neither confirm nor deny that. What do you have?"

"The question is who do I have," McSpadden says.

Laura sounds distressingly nonplussed by that response. "Does he or she have pointy ears or green skin?"

"Uh...no," says McSpadden.

"Speak English?"

"Yes," says McSpadden.

"Do you have a picture?"

"On my phone, sending it now," says McSpadden. He actually took it by accident when they first brought Thor and Miss Lewis into the station. Damn camera button was too easy to hit — he has hundreds of pictures of the inside of his pocket.

"Got it," says Laura, "Sending it through the proper channels. Now tell me everything that happened."

When McSpadden is done, Laura says, "Get his signed statement and go through the usual rigmarole. I'll be back to you within a few hours. Don't treat him like a criminal...he may be one of the good guys, and even if he's not, you really don't want to tick him off."

"What?" says McSpadden, but Laura's already gone.

Loki sits in a small room in the sheriff's station. Next to him is the comely wench of the extraordinary bosom who he had rescued — and the dog inaptly named Fenrir. At his feet is the knapsack. His sword is invisible at his waist. Killing the man-beast they've identified as Ed Malson would have been far cleaner with his sword, but since swords have fallen out of fashion here on Earth, it raises too many questions. Hence he settled for beating him to death with a small log.

The snake venom and hunger made him irritable, and he'd slipped out of character right after rescuing Miss Lewis. But now he sits with his shoulders slightly slumped, his face schooled into an expression of solemness and a bit of intimidation — just like a 25ish year old man who had never killed someone and found himself in a police station would look.

He's not sure a human 25 year-old would be eating from a bag of Ghirardelli 60% dark chocolate chips — a gift from Miss Lewis — but he is so very hungry and these chips are so very good.

He looks over to Miss Lewis. Her knuckles are bandaged, but she still is tapping away at the little device called an iPhone. She's called her grandmother in Chicago and is now "texting agents of insurance." He's learned a lot about her from the things she's babbled to the police so far. Primarily that she is of no import to this world whatsoever.

But he heard her praying, three times. Before he killed Malson when she was begging for help, when she commanded Fenrir to distract him, and afterwards, when he wanted to leave before the police arrived — he heard her asking him not to go, and telling him how afraid she was.

He understands her fear. He thought the memories of Cronus were buried deeper, but something about Malson — his sadism, his white hair, even his baby like features, brought the memories to the surface.

He shakes his head. He hates remembering himself as so helpless and vulnerable.

Scowling, he pops another chocolate chip in his mouth. Why did he hear her prayers? None of the Aesir, or Loki, for that matter, hear all the prayers sent to them. Only some filter through. Odin believes that only requests relating to the receiver's higher purpose are heard. So she's important to Loki, in some unfathomable way. Maybe just to see that he eats something?

He looks down at the chocolate in his hands. He's too weary to World Walk right now. He might as well be here. Maybe he'll learn something about how their latest technology impacts criminal investigations. It will be very helpful if he and his boys are forced to stay on Earth for a while and need to rob banks to support themselves. Bank robbing was very lucrative for Loki in the 1940s. Granted, it was more bank burglary — no humans were harmed, or even noticed his presence. Hoenir is fond of humans, and Loki wouldn't purposely upset Hoenir.

But would his sons even accept burglary? Valli might... he is a bit twitchy, but since Nari infected him with his idealistic zeal for political reform even Valli might be repulsed by the idea of a life of crime...unless Loki somehow managed to convince him it is for "the greater good." How could any children of his be so fatally idealistic? Where did he go wrong? He warned them Odin would turn a blind eye to all sorts of mischief unless it threatened the throne.

For a moment his boys' faces, frozen in that instant in deep space, hover before his eyes and he blinks. He can do nothing right now.

To distract himself, he looks over Miss Lewis' shoulder. The small device called an iPhone has no resemblance to a phone at all. It is, in fact, a small computer that has phone-like capabilities — it doesn't work everywhere, apparently. Last time he was on Earth, computers occupied whole rooms and had to be tediously programmed with punch cards. The boxes on the sheriff's desk are impressive enough, but this one fits in her palm. It has a calculator in it, a location device, a camera, music, flickering little games, and a way of connecting with other computers all over the world through a thing called the Internet. All these "apps" interface with a tiny keyboard that disappears and reappears at her touch. It's fascinating, and the sort of thing he could ordinarily be very distracted by.

A noise at the office door catches his attention. He looks up to see Deputy Colbert walk in. "Here's your driver's license...Thor," he says handing Loki a little card. Loki takes it and taps it against his knee; he can feel the deputy's suspicion in the air. It's actually Miss Lewis' card; Loki has made it look like it belongs to his current alias: Thor Odinson. Choosing the name of his sons' betrayer was just a little game — to tick Odin off, to test the humans, and to give himself a quiet laugh.

It turned out to be not such a great idea. Thor Odinson, that bastard, is apparently a hero in a "comic book" and "movie franchise" and they thought he was lying. Hence, stealing Miss Lewis' ID after they'd "photocopied" it — whatever that meant — and proffering it to the sheriff with an apologetic smile and a smooth excuse of "thought I lost it in the scuffle." The fake social security number he gave them wasn't enough.

They ran the license and the social security number he provided through their computers. It was an interesting challenge, making the computer screens appear as though his alias' info checked out. Fortunately, Loki can project his consciousness — even create immaterial doubles of himself if he wishes to. He hovered over their shoulders while they used their devices to pull up Miss Lewis' info. He was able to create the same screens for Thor Odinson. The magic involved put the station's cat in a happy tizzy, but he's sure the humans are oblivious to the reasons for the cat's joyful frolics.

As Colbert leaves the room with a small nod, Miss Lewis turns to Loki. "I heard you tell them that you..." Taking a breath she licks her lips. "...don't have a permanent address. And I want you to know, if you need it, my grandmother has an apartment over our garage that isn't occupied. You're welcome to it...until you get on your feet."

Loki blinks. What an utterly naive, far too trusting offer. For some reason it puts to mind a childhood story about a wolf, a little girl and her grandmother.

...But he isn't really the wolf, is he?

Trying to keep the bemusement from his features, he says, "Thank you... Miss Lewis."

She flushes, and looks down at her phone. "You can just call me Amy."

Loki raises an eyebrow. And then, taking a purposefully loud breath, he says, "I will consider it." Smiling softly and as non-threateningly as he can, he adds, "Is there food there?"

Glancing back to him, Amy smiles...just a little, and says, "My grandmother will feel it's her duty to make sure you're positively stuffed."

Well, that sounds promising. But he doesn't want to seem too eager. He looks at the device in her fingers. "What are you searching for on your iPhone?" he asks.

"Oh," she says, turning to it. "I'm trying to find bus schedules. My car isn't going to be repaired for at least a week, and I can't stay here."

What a wonderful device! "That information could be useful to me as well," says Loki. "Perhaps I can lean over your shoulder?"

"Sure," says Miss Lewis — Amy — and Loki watches with fascination as she navigates through the iPhone's many screens.

He jerks his head up with a start when Sheriff McSpadden and Deputy Colbert come back in. Colbert has the cat in one arm.

"We're going to need to get your statements. Miss Lewis, you can stay here. Mr. Odinson, will you come with me?"

They're going to question him. He isn't surprised by this; he spent a little time with the police in the 1940s. Humans have fallen so far since the early days when they'd just throw you a party when you killed a monster. But it can't be helped.

Nodding, he scratches his leg and uses it as a distraction to grab his knapsack. Cradling the chocolate chips in the other hand, he stands. "Of course."

As they leave the room, the cat perks its ears in Loki's direction. Walking down the hall, he hears Amy say, "He's not going to be in any trouble, is he? He saved me." It's a bit touching, actually.

The room he is taken to has no windows, only a single table with a small gray mechanical box on it, and a mirror that undoubtedly is a window to another room. McSpadden inclines his head towards a chair, and Loki sits down. He's not afraid. The sword is in easy reach, he has enough magical energy left to make himself invisible if he needs to, the lock on the door is a non-issue; and actually, he's very curious.

Before they begin to talk, the sheriff presses a button on the small box on the table and says, "We'll record this whole conversation." Loki watches with fascination as two little wheels in the box start to turn, and the man says, "You kids, never seen a cassette recorder before..."

The question and answer session that follows goes as well as these things can. Loki fabricates details of "Thor's" past from his last journey to the realm.

And then they get to the immediate present.

"So, after the trucker you were hitching a ride with kicked you out of the cab, you heard Miss Lewis call for help?" says the Sheriff.

"Yes," says Loki.

"She says Malson said he'd kill her if she opened her mouth," says the Sheriff.

For a moment, Loki thinks he's being cross examined and feels the corner of his lip start to tug upward into a cruel smile. But then he realizes McSpadden's body language is still non-confrontational. He seems almost...confused.

Loki schools his features into a look of sympathy. "Yes." He blinks. "She thinks she saw a wolf, too. But..." he shrugs. "There was only her little dog. She is understandably distraught."

"Yes," says McSpadden. "The wolf..."

There is a knock at the door, and McSpadden excuses himself from the table. The door opens and Colbert is there with the cat. "She's clean, but Patches didn't like the dog. Thought you might like her..."

Before Colbert can finish the sentence, the cat launches itself out of his arms and walks over in Loki's direction, tail swishing madly back and forth.

Loki's eyes go up to the two men in the door. Both of their mouths are slightly agape.

"Do you want me to stay?" Colbert whispers.

They know the cat senses magic! But how have they even

come in contact with magic before? Loki closes his eyes a moment. Of course. The same branch of the World Tree that sucked him here from the Aesir magical dump. They've had other things drop in...possibly very unpleasant things.

Loki looks back to Patches. Holding out a finger, he says, "Here, Patches, no need to worry. The Sheriff and I are just having a little chat." Patches approaches Loki slowly. She sniffs his finger carefully, and then rubs her head against it.

Loki looks up to McSpadden. The Sheriff straightens. Loki restrains a smile.

"I'll be alright, Colbert," says McSpadden.

Loki tilts his head. As the door closes and McSpadden sits down again, Loki projects a warm cloud of warmth around his hand. As he expects, Patches' caution quickly evaporates. She begins purring and rubbing her head and body against his fingers.

With a smile Loki reaches down and puts her on his lap, settling another warm bubble of air around her. Patches lies down on his knee and begins purring loudly, kneading her claws, and staring in McSpadden's direction. Cats are utter whores for a warm lap.

Loki can't restrain his smile. "You have more questions?"

In the interrogation room McSpadden's phone buzzes with a text message. He looks down. It's from Laura Stodgill. He carefully peeks at it beneath the table.

Positive match. In discussion as to what to do. Don't make him angry.

Well, that's comforting. Tilting his head, he looks back

up to Thor.

"...and so you are on your way to the Dakotas to take part in the oil boom," says McSpadden. It's plausible; in fact, out in the main lobby CNN has been running a show about just those very jobs this evening. McSpadden scowls — is that a coincidence?

"That's right," says Thor. Popping a chocolate chip into his mouth, he smirks slightly. It's a smirk that says, I know you know I'm lying, and it doesn't bother me at all. In Thor's lap Patches is rubbing her head against his stomach, purring so loudly that McSpadden knows the tape recorder is going to pick it up.

On the one hand, he's glad she's not hissing. On the other hand, he can't even imagine he's in charge of the situation here.

Before Patches came into the room, Thor had every appearance of a vaguely disoriented, slightly frightened young man who had almost inadvertently saved a young woman from terrible tragedy. As soon as Patches started acting up, he seemed to pick up exactly on what was going on. Apparently he decided a facade wasn't worth maintaining anymore.

Now Thor sits straight up, eerily light blue eyes focused down on McSpadden. McSpadden isn't a small guy at 6' 2", but Thor's got a couple of inches on him. Thor isn't cocky, not like a petty thief. No, he's confident, like he knows he can get up and leave at any moment; he's just playing along because this is some sort of amusing game to him. Before the weirdness in McSpadden's neck of the woods he would have written Thor off as crazy. Now with Laura's response, and Patches' response...McSpadden sighs. Ah, for the good old days.

"I don't suppose you have any idea how the pictures

caught on fire?" McSpadden says.

Thor's jaw goes hard. "They were very disturbing."

Which isn't an answer but is definitely true. McSpadden had gotten to the point in his job where he thought he couldn't see anything worse than he already had. He'd been wrong.

"Well," says McSpadden. "We'll need to type this out, and then have you sign it and then..."

Thor raises an eyebrow.

...and then normally it would be McSpadden's call to decide whether the guy should stay or go.

Frustrated, McSpadden turns off the tape. Thor blinks and bends over to look closer at the cassette player. It's the first time since Patches came in that he looks even slightly less than in complete control.

Thor looks up at McSpadden and straightens. "You have no say over my being allowed to stay or go, do you?" says Thor.

McSpadden rubs his eyes. He should lie, but frankly, he's a little fed up — fed up with not being in charge of what went on at his station, and fed up with the Department of Anomalous Devices of Unknown Origin for not filling him in on what the Hell is going on.

"Nope," McSpadden says.

Thor cocks his head. "Thank you for that bit of honesty." He reaches a hand into the bag of chocolate chips, and then scowls down at it. Picking it up, he peers inside and the scowl intensifies.

And suddenly McSpadden has a bit of a quantum leap. Maybe The Department of ADUO won't talk to him, but maybe Thor will.

"I was told to be nice to you, though," McSpadden says.

Thor looks up.

Standing up, McSpadden says, "While we get this and Miss Lewis' statement typed up, you're welcome to have breakfast with us."

Thor's eyes widen. "I would appreciate that, Sheriff."

McSpadden smiles at his own guile. "Just bagels and cream cheese — maybe some lox if Sherrie is feeling like going all out." Patting his stomach he says, "Gotta fight the stereotypes."

Thor just blinks at him.

"Come on," says McSpadden, opening the door.

Thor puts Patches down and walks with McSpadden towards the break room, Patches at their feet.

"I don't suppose you can tell me where you're really from?" McSpadden says.

A mischievous smile comes to Thor's lips. "I already have."

McSpadden can sense he's not going to get any more of an answer than that. Instead of pressing he says, "Could you at least tell me when the weirdness will stop? The carpet was kind of funny, but the monkey's paw..."

Thor stops walking, and his eyes widen. "You found a monkey's paw?"

McSpadden nods.

Shaking his head, Thor says, "I knew there had to be at least four of them..." He eyes McSpadden. "What did you do with it?"

"Gave it to the proper department," says McSpadden.

Thor's jaw goes hard. "And you'll give me to the proper department?"

McSpadden's stomach drops. He swallows.

Thor's eyebrow quirks. "You mentioned breakfast?"

58 C. GOCKEL

McSpadden nods and starts leading him down the hall again. "I suppose I shouldn't worry about the unicorns..."

"Unicorns? There shouldn't be unicorns." Thor says.

McSpadden shrugs. "We've had a couple of sightings. I suppose they are harmless enough."

Thor stops abruptly and takes McSpadden's arm so quickly McSpadden spins around. Expression very serious, Thor says, "Sheriff McSpadden, in deference to your honesty with me I will tell you this. Unless you are especially pure, never, never, think a unicorn is harmless. If you value your life."

"Uh...." says McSpadden looking at the hand.

Dropping his arm, Thor turns his head and sniffs. "Do I smell smoked fish?" Without waiting for McSpadden to take the lead, he heads straight to the break room and McSpadden jogs to keep up. Miss Lewis is already sitting there with Colbert. She's reading over a statement in front of her. Her dog, Fred, or something, starts growling at Patches and the cat takes off. Amy looks up at Thor. The man's face suddenly takes on the look of bewildered young man again and he nods at her. "Are you alright?" he asks.

"Yes," she says, smiling softly and then turns back to her statement.

"I'll get your statement for you in a few minutes," says McSpadden.

Thor looks at McSpadden and gives him a wink.

McSpadden blinks. Thor is definitely dangerous. Clenching his jaw, McSpadden remembers the half burned pictures from Malson's van...and other things they'd found in the back.

Being dangerous isn't the same as being evil. Turning on his heel, he leaves the room.

When he comes back Colbert and Miss Lewis are gone. Thor is sitting with his feet up on the table, munching on a bagel with lox. Patches is on the ground, pawing at his lap.

"Where — " says McSpadden, looking around the room.

"Miss Lewis had a bus to catch," says Thor.

"Well — " McSpadden starts to say, when his phone starts to buzz with another text.

He picks it up. It's from Laura. He clicks on it.

Word on high is he's the good guy. He's free to go. Jameson furious.

McSpadden scowls. Jameson is the director of ADUO — how can anyone be higher than him?

Thor's voice comes from just over McSpadden's shoulder. "Well, that is interesting."

McSpadden jumps away fast and turns. He almost draws his gun.

Thor takes a bite out of his bagel and looks towards the window, his face vaguely contemplative. "The good guy," Thor muses aloud.

McSpadden goes over and picks up Patches. She is utterly uninterested in his phone — so the message from Laura is not just enchanted...or magical...or whatever. Wiggling out of his arms, she hops to the ground and runs over to Thor.

Smirking at McSpadden, Thor picks up a bottle of water off the break room table and takes a swig. "Sheriff McSpadden, I thank you for your hospitality, but waiting for my statement at this point would be superfluous."

"Uh, I gotta keep you here until you sign it," McSpadden says, straightening. "Procedures and all that."

Rolling his eyes, Thor says, "Remember what I told you about the unicorns."

And then he disappears. McSpadden looks around the break room. The bagels, cream cheese, and lox are all gone, too. For a brief few moments Patches does an impression of a whirling dervish, running like mad in circles. Then she stops abruptly in a beam of morning sunlight, licks her back once, and promptly lies down and goes to sleep.

Loki makes himself and all the food in the break room invisible. Holding the bagel he is eating between his teeth, he stuffs the rest into his knapsack, right in front of McSpadden. Patches hops madly around his feet. He's a little worried she'll try to follow him, but when he runs for the door she doesn't pursue.

He exits the station, the door swinging on empty air behind him. He glances at the sky. Not a raven in sight — Odin's messengers or otherwise, but he remains invisible anyway. Seeing Amy and Deputy Colbert in the distance, he runs to catch up. His hunger is nowhere near sated, and it takes more effort than he expects.

Amy is just stepping up the bus' steps when he can't bear the strain anymore. He drops the invisibility and gasps for breath. Fortunately, he's behind Amy, the deputy has already turned away, and the bus driver's facing away.

Amy spins with a start.

"Thought I'd take you up on your offer," he says, swallowing and trying to appear pathetic and non-threatening. The effect may be slightly undone by his heavy breathing.

Her mouth opens. For a minute he thinks that maybe his illusion of Earth fashion has dropped, but he looks down and it's still there. Then in his mind he hears, Please don't be a bank robber or anything. The fact that he hears her is disturbing; the fact that she's praying that he doesn't rob banks is very disturbing.

"All right?" he says slowly, not sure if he is agreeing not to rob banks, or asking if her offer is still good.

She swallows. "Do you need me to buy you a ticket?"

He winces.

The bus driver says, "Buy it for him online when you sit down! We've got to get a move on!"

"Okay," she says. From a shapeless bag on her shoulder, Fenrir gives a happy yip.

"Is that a dog in there?" says the bus driver.

"No!" say Amy and Loki in unison, quickly hurrying up the steps.

As they settle into their seats which are a might bit cramped, Amy complains about being in a "cattle car." Loki says nothing. He actually thinks the vehicle is fairly amazing. It's not one of the litters of Odin's wife, Frigga, and the seats are not proportioned for someone his size, but even with his legs splayed wide, one knee awkwardly out in the aisle, it is much more comfortable than a horse.

His brain churns with questions. Why did Odin's spell leave him so drained? And how did he escape it? How is he the good guy? Could they possibly mistake him for the real Thor? And unicorns... How in the nine realms are they slipping over here? They certainly didn't come from Asgard's orbiting garbage heap.

He closes his eyes. He should pull out his book and look for branches of the World Tree in the vicinity of Chicago.

Instead he falls asleep.

CHAPTER 4

Maybe it is the steady hum of the engine. Maybe it is that there are people all around. Or maybe it is just exhaustion. Whatever, even though Amy wouldn't think it possible, in the bus, just a little before St. Louis, she dozes off. She wakes up with a start, vague memories of darkness and Ed Malson in her mind.

She takes a breath. Fenrir pushes her nose out of the bag in Amy's lap and licks her hand. Amy pats the dog's head. She is safe. Thor Odinson saved her. She rubs her eyes. His parents must be lunatics for giving him a name like that. Lunatic parents may be something they have in common. Thinking about Thor, she blinks. Wincing from the pain in her neck, she rolls her head to look at him across the aisle. Her eyes widen. Thor's head is bent down against his chest; his eyes are closed. He's shivering, his lips are moving, a scowl is on his brow. She can tell instantly he is having bad dreams, too.

But that isn't what's making her eyebrows touch her hairline.

He's wearing armor. What looks like the handle of a sword is poking out of the knapsack that sits on the floor between his feet.

Another passenger walking by looks down at him and blinks and then walks back to his seat, a confused expression on his face.

Amy's heart starts to beat fast. This is too weird. Not just that he is wearing armor, but that he was dressed like a rock-a-billy, hipster, wannabe when he got on the bus. Where did he stow the extra clothes? Not in the little bag. But she saw the armor before, didn't she, when she hit him with pepper spray?

Her train of thought is interrupted when Thor whispers something strange and guttural. Fenrir pushes herself out of the bag, runs across the aisle, and hops into his lap.

Amy looks up and down the aisle. No one seems to have noticed. She looks at Thor. His eyes are blinking open. Fenrir pants on his face and his head jerks up, in surprise or because Fenrir's breath has been especially bad since the road kill incident.

Raising an eyebrow, he puts a hand on the wiggling Fenrir. "Hello beast that looks like a dog," he says in the proper East Coast tones she first noticed in the police station, when the shock of everything had started wearing off.

...or maybe the shock didn't wear off. He's wearing armor.

The Art Institute of Chicago has some suits of armor from the middle ages. They look like barrels with metal tubes for feet and arms. What Thor is wearing is very different. It fits like a second skin. It seems to be a dull metal that picks up the colors around it — it almost blends into the seat. There is a chest plate, and some interlocking horizontal strips about the width of a finger that fall to his belt. The same thin strips rise up his neck. There are more plates around his legs and arms, between them more of the interlocking finger-width pieces of metal.

Thor glances at her. His eyes open a little bit when he sees she's awake, and then he looks back to Fenrir, who has rolled over on his lap. Wrinkling his nose and scowling a bit, Thor gingerly scratches Fenrir on the chest with a finger.

Thor is very pale, and at the moment very scruffy, his hair is disheveled, and it looks like he hasn't had a shave in days. His face is narrow, and his features are somewhere between sharp and delicate. He's definitely not unattractive, but you wouldn't mistake him for the rugged actor who plays his namesake in the "Thor" movie franchise.

She stares at him. As he scratches Fenrir, the armor makes no sound at all. She would expect the metal to clink or something.

Turning to her, Thor scowls a little bit. "Is something wrong?"

Amy opens her mouth, but no sound comes out.

"Yes?" he says tilting his head.

Biting her lip, she points at him. "Ummm..." she says. "You're wearing...armor. Kind of weird SWAT meets elven Lord of the Rings armor."

His eyes go wide and he looks down. Almost to himself he says, "Well, that's never happened before.."

"Am I still asleep?" Amy says. "Is this a dream?"

He looks at her and the corner of his lip twitches. Tilting his head he says, "You are dreaming." Reaching down into his knapsack and pulling out a bagel, he says, "Close your eyes.

Enjoy the comfort of this magnificent vehicle."

That doesn't help the moment feel real. "It's a bus," she says.

He scowls a little. "I know that."

"It isn't magnificent," she says. And it brings back bad memories of other bus rides she's had to take.

He blinks. "Go to sleep. When you awake, I will be wearing the normal attire you saw me in earlier."

"It wasn't normal."

"What?" he says, brows rising.

"It was totally retro, 1950s-esque," Amy says.

His mouth twitches. "Was it really so conspicuous?"

"Well..." Amy says. "Sort of... I mean some people wear that kind of thing, but it isn't precisely normal."

He stares at her a moment, and then he says, "Go back to sleep. When you open your eyes I'll be totally retro again."

Amy settles back against the seat, takes a breath, and closes her eyes.

Someone says, "Is that a dog?!" in a very accusatory tone.

Amy's eyes bolt open to see an older man glaring down at her lap. Her fingers tighten around Fenrir. "Ummmm..." she says.

The man backs up. "Oh, I must have been mistaken."

Amy looks down. In her lap is a shaggy gray teddy bear that looks immobile — but she feels a wiggling Fenrir in her fingers.

Amy looks across the aisle. Thor is wearing retro clothing again. "You are dreaming," he says softly.

Staring at the seat in front of her, Amy scowls. "That is the logical explanation."

She doesn't feel safe anymore. She has this horrible feeling that she didn't escape Malson, that she is dying in a ditch somewhere and her brain is making up this long dream to save her from the pain.

"Close your eyes," he says.

She doesn't want to know if this is real or not. Squeezing her eyes shut, she says, "I'm not opening them until we reach Chicago."

"Shhhhhh...." he says softly. "When you wake up, things will return to normal, and when they're normal you'll know you're safe."

His voice sounds so confident, so sure, as though he knows exactly how she's feeling.

The villagers pick up the pieces of Cronus' body. They laugh and smile. Loki is still sitting on the floor of the boathouse, arms wrapped around his knees. Hoenir and Mimir haven't entered yet. Both of them would have been useless, of course.

A villager comes up and hands Loki a flask of something. Patting Loki on the shoulder, he flashes a smile missing several teeth. "Well done, Loki! Drink this."

Loki takes the flask; it smells strongly like alcohol. Loki's had watered down mead before, but not often. Frigga's handmaiden, Eir, is talented in the healing arts. Eir has Frigga convinced that alcohol is particularly harmful for young developing minds and livers.

Odin says in his day everyone drank. Brusquely taking the flask, Loki takes a long swig.

It burns, and he has to fight hard to keep it down. The man laughs again. "We are burning his body, building you a throne, and will kill a calf in your honor! Come! Celebrate with us."

He pats Loki on the shoulder and offers him a hand up. Loki accepts and tries to hand back the flask.

"You keep it!" says the man. "You've earned it."

Loki looks down at the flask. He knows as soon as he exits the boathouse, Hoenir will take the drink from him. That seems unmanly. Tipping the flask back, he proceeds to drain it, even though tears run down his cheeks and some of the liquid runs down his chin. When he's done, he wipes his chin and hands the flask back to the villager.

Eyes wide, the villager says, "You are a god."

Loki smiles triumphantly. Suddenly humans are streaming into the boathouse, men, women, and children. They throw their arms around Loki and then hoist him onto their shoulders. Warmth spreads through Loki, and he sees Hoenir and Mimir over their heads and waves happily.

Soon the bonfire is roaring, and Loki is sitting on a rough chair that is too wide for him. They call it a throne. He would call it branches, but he smiles, and the villagers smile, and it's all like a wonderful dream. He calls the little boy Jonah over to sit with him, and the villagers seem to think that is hilarious and fantastic. They bring over some weak beer; Jonah accepts it readily, so Loki does too. Nearby Loki hears Mimir say, "Well, I suppose one little drink won't hurt him..."

Soon after, there is food and more beer, and then there is music and dancing around the fire. Hoenir and Mimir try to pull Loki away, but Loki tells them something to the effect of, "in just a minute," and dives into the dance with the villagers. Someone must have thrown some new kindling on the fire just then because the flames seem to rise halfway to Asgard. Or maybe he is just drunk. But he is happy. And after today, and the boat, and Cronus, and staring into the faces of the humans around him who are so kind, so fragile, so mortal, and who love him so much it is almost a physical pain...

Someone hands him another flask. Hoenir is nowhere in sight and he takes a long swig. He spins around the fire with the humans and the flames leap.

It is dark when someone says, "Loki, our God of Gods!"

Laughing and quite drunk, Loki stands upon the throne. "No!" he shouts. " I am the God of Fire!" The fire chooses that moment to send a shower of sparks into the air. The villagers howl in delight. "The God of Spirit," he says, shaking the flask. The villagers laugh again. "And..." A group of three young girls standing near him giggle. It's not like Loki hasn't noticed girls before, but at that moment it seems for the first time he really sees them. They look so soft, so inviting...and what they are inviting him to isn't so vague and abstract anymore. "...girls," he says. Jumping from the throne, he takes a spinning step in their direction. A piece of wood in the fire breaks with a thunderclap, and the villagers gasp.

A heavy hand comes down on Loki's shoulder, stopping his spin. Somehow he knows without looking who it is, and the dream-like quality of the night comes crashing to an end. He feels his cheeks going red with embarrassment. He also feels an odd sense of relief, as though if that hand weren't there he might spin so fast he'd leave the ground.

The music stops. A hush comes over the villagers. Only the fire is still crackling. Odin's voice rings through the night. "The God of Mischief is more like it!"

Loki's legs crumple beneath him, and there is some laughter from the villagers that sounds far off and uncertain. Before he hits the ground, Odin catches him. Hoisting Loki up in his arms, Odin cradles him like he would a babe, or a woman. Loki scowls.

And then he realizes if Odin did throw him over his shoulder like a proper warrior, he would probably throw up.

"Come on, Loki," Odin says, not unkindly. "We're going home."

Loki smiles and waves at Jonah, and the villagers, and the girls. He is embarrassed. A little. Or maybe a lot. He is too drunk to properly gauge the emotion.

And Odin coming to spoil his schemes is so normal...he suddenly knows at last he is safe.

When the bus drops them off at the intersection of Canal and Lake Street, Loki's head immediately turns to the south east and downtown. Chicago is hot, sticky and tall. Very, very, tall. Across a dreary parking lot and the river, skyscrapers tower. It's all he can do to keep from gaping. Every single building seems to be as tall or taller than the Empire State Building. And nearly all of them seem made of glass. Some of the windows are darkened, but others are bright mirrors that reflect the large white clouds in the Midwest sky — they seem to Loki to be gigantic moving canvases. And to think they're all solid, and real, not dependent on illusions like the buildings of Asgard.

"Yes," says Amy. "Lovely parking lot. You can see the pollution on the horizon. But it's Chicago. What can you do?"

Loki blinks. There is a bit of haze low to the ground, but... "It's cleaner than I remember," he says. And it is certainly cleaner than Victorian England. For a place that doesn't have a Void to dump the garbage from their misspent magic, Chicago is doing rather well.

"Huh," says Amy. "Let's catch a taxi."

She holds out a hand, and a white vehicle that is very similarly shaped to the chariot of her would-be-abductor screeches to a stop.

As Amy and the driver wrestle her bag and a rather large trunk into the back, Loki slips into the interior. It is blessedly cool inside. He stops and peeks between the seats to the front. The dashboard is alight with glowing numbers. One is clearly the time, another is the temperature, but all the others are completely incomprehensible. He blinks. Computers are everywhere.

The buildings, the computers — Earth is turning into a place that is almost magical. It temporarily makes him forget about the hunger that is beginning to gnaw at his stomach and the exhaustion tugging at his limbs. Odin's spell to stop time drained him more than he thought possible — how Loki resisted it is a mystery.

He shakes his head. He won't solve that puzzle now. Leaning forward, he tries to get a better view of the numbers on the dashboard.

The driver and Amy slip into the car and put on their seat belts. "814 N. Hermitage," Amy says and the cab driver steps on the gas so fast Loki falls backwards in his seat. Out of the corner of his eye he sees Amy staring at him with a look of pure confusion on her face. Even Fenrir is cocking her head in his direction. For a moment he thinks that his illusion of totally retro clothes has fallen again, but he checks, and it's still there.

As they speed away from the center of the city along Chicago Avenue, the buildings get noticeably lower. Many are also noticeably older — two and three story row houses of stone and brick that are visibly sinking into Chicago's soft soil. These familiar buildings are interspersed with newer abodes with tremendous windows that can't be sensible for temperature regulation or for warding off potential intruders. It really is a good thing that Asgard put a stop to the Jotunn plans for a new ice age on Earth — and took care of the troll situation.

As they drive further west along Chicago Avenue, shops and restaurants begin to appear. Many of the names are in Spanish, and Loki notices a great many people who seem to be of South American descent walking among the natives of European and African origin.

They turn up a green, leafy street. About a third of the houses seem to be very new, a third are old and decrepit, and a third look old but lovingly maintained.

Amy says, "This is good," and the cab stops so fast that Loki braces his hands on the front seat.

The cabbie, who had been so solicitous when Amy got into the cab, doesn't do much more than throw Amy's bags on the street after she pays him. As he speeds away, Loki watches as she tilts the trunk up and tries to drag it while simultaneously trying to heave a large cylindrical cloth sack.

It occurs to him that he's probably supposed to help. He is from Asgard. Centuries ago, Asgardians would occasionally take humans as servants. It never works the other way around... But plenty of Asgardians have mocked Loki for his lack of pride before.

"May I help you?" he asks solicitously.

Shaking her head, she says, "No...that's okay...I can manage it." Dragging the trunk along the ground, she bumps into the curb and nearly topples over. The trunk and the bag fall to the street.

He tilts his head. She seems to know her Norse mythology, so he says, "Don't be such a Valkyrie." The winged warrior women are always so touchy.

"What?" she says. Apparently his gentle jibe didn't translate well. Rather than explain, he just bends down and grabs the trunk by both ends.

"Don't..." she starts to say, coming forward.

He swings it over one shoulder with ease.

"It's heavy," Amy says, touching his free arm before he can move away.

She stops and looks down. He looks where her hand is. She feels his armor, even if she can't see it. Her gaze meets his and her brows come together.

He's saved from having to say anything by the sound of a woman's voice. "Amy! Amy!"

They both turn to see an old woman coming down a narrow walk from an old brick two-story house of the lovingly maintained variety. Ivy climbs nimbly up the walls and spills out over the yard.

Loki tilts his head. He isn't used to the elderly. Their wrinkled papery skin and white hair remind him pleasantly of gnomes, but the old have a brittleness to them that gnomes don't share. Aging seems such a terrible affliction.

The old woman is wearing a dress that wouldn't be out of place last time Loki was here, but she wears the same leather-like shoes with stripes and laces that Amy wears.

She wraps her arms around the girl and Fenrir begins yipping up a happy storm.

"I'm so glad you're home! Don't ever travel alone again! Take a plane, take a train, take a bus!" the old woman says.

"Oh, grandma, it was a freak incident..."

Pulling back, the woman says, "Don't go quoting me statistics about lightning strikes and how unlikely this is ever to happen to you again. It happened once! That's enough."

"Grandma..." says Amy.

But the old woman is coming towards Loki, arms outstretched. "You're the man who saved my darling granddaughter!"

Loki's eyes widen. She'll embrace him. Loki's not squeamish about physical contact with humans, unlike some Asgardians...Asgardians like Heimdall, that stuck up stickler for protocol and station, but she'll feel Loki's armor. Picking up Amy's remaining bag, he says, "Careful, I don't want to drop these on you."

She stops and closes her hands together. She beams at Loki. His head roars with the sound of *She's all I have left in the world, thank you, thank you, thank you.*

Loki blinks. More human prayers in his head? But the saving of lives is done. This is so very odd.

Despite the torrent in Loki's mind, all the old woman says is, "Oh, yes, of course." But she continues to smile at him, and something in his gut constricts. He's always thought of prayers as a weak trick, but he's beginning to think they're deceptively powerful. He's not sure he likes it.

"Thor, this is my grandmother, Beatrice," Amy says.

Shaking her head, Beatrice says, "Such an unusual name. My late husband would have loved it." And then turning she says, "I hope they lock up that horrible Malson man and put him away forever."

Loki looks at Amy. Apparently she hasn't been entirely truthful with Beatrice. Catching his gaze, Amy winces and holds a finger to her lips. Loki raises an eyebrow. There was a time on Earth when even grandmothers would have reveled gleefully in stories of heroics, no matter how gory.

Up ahead Beatrice says, "Come inside out of the heat!" and waves them both up the narrow walkway. "I can have food on the table in thirty minutes. Everything's ready; I just have to heat it up."

Mouth watering at the word food, Loki follows them in. Looking very uncomfortable, Amy says to him, "Um, if my bags are too heavy you can put them down..."

He's tired. He's hungry. But they're not heavy. "Where do you want them?" he asks.

Amy jumps a little at the sound of his voice. Being hungry always makes him cranky; it's beginning to show, evidently.

"This way," says Amy. He follows her up a narrow staircase to a small sleeping room.

Setting them down on the ground, he says, "Whatever your grandmother is cooking smells deli— "

A tiny ping rings through the room.

He stills at the sound.

Ping.

There it is again, and the most infinitesimal of pressures on his back. Scowling, he spins around. Amy has her fingers outstretched, a guilty look on her face. It takes him a moment but he puts it together — she pinged his armor with her finger.

"What do you want?" he says, the words coming out harsher than he intends.

Backing up a little, Amy looks down. "To know I'm not dreaming."

Loki sighs and rubs his eyes.

Ping. Ping.

He feels a light pressure now on his lower arm.

He opens his eyes and Amy has her fingers outstretched again. This time she doesn't look guilty. Just confused.

"You shouldn't go ping," she says. "I have to be dreaming."

He stares at her a moment, beyond irritated. He's saved her life, sat through a tortuously long questioning session, carried her bags for her — and he's hungry. Yet she has the gall to question her good fortune, to question him, and to ping his armor.

He suddenly has the desire to be a little cruel. "You're not dreaming," he says. Dropping the illusion he stands before her in his armor. "Does this help?" he says with a smile.

"No!"

The sound of footsteps on the stairs makes the girl turn her head. "Change back," she says. "Don't frighten my grandmother."

Loki would rather not frighten anyone who will feed him. He slips back into the illusion of "totally retro" clothing.

Beatrice comes around the corner, a stack of linens in her hand. Loki smiles benevolently at her.

"Amy, why don't you show him the spare room?" Beatrice says.

Taking the load from from her grandmother, Amy says, "This way."

As she leads him out of the house, Loki looks up at the sky. He sees no sign of ravens, the spies of Odin. He doubts Heimdall can see him. Heimdall has to know where to look first. Just in case he puts on his helmet, disguised as a fedora, before he follows her across the tiny lawn and into an alley behind the garage. Amy unlocks and lifts the garage door. Inside, off to one side, is a large vehicle. It reminds him vaguely of a Jeep.

Amy leads him past the vehicle to a door. She unlocks it and says, "It's a little inconvenient," and then leads him up a flight of stairs. Every step upward the heat becomes more and more oppressive.

Loki lets the illusion of Earth clothing drop again. It's a game, and she started it.

At the top of the stairs she turns around and jumps at the sight of his armor. She does have one of the lovelier bosoms Loki has seen on this or any other world, and the bounce does rather nice things. He smirks.

Thrusting the pile of linens at him, she says, "Here." And turning around again she walks into a medium-sized room. There is a bed in one corner, and a couch. "The shower is that way," she gestures towards a door, "And the swinging door takes you to a kitchenette. I think there are glasses. There isn't any food, though. Do you need me to show you how to turn on the air conditioning?"

That's it? No more questions?

...Air conditioning?

He is a Frost Giant, and the room is rather uncomfortable, even if his armor does have some temperature control.

"I would like help with the air conditioning," he says.

She walks over to a boxlike thing in the window, plugs it into the wall, and shows him how to operate the dials. And she hands him some keys, and walks towards the door. Just before leaving she turns. "See you in about 20 minutes."

He tilts his head and looks down at his armor. He blinks. "You're not bothered?"

Her eyes go wide, and she looks down. "I'm probably going crazy and dying at the bottom of a ditch somewhere, but you know, this is an interesting dream, a better dream than that reality, and you're responsible, so I'm grateful and I'm just going to go with it until I wake up..." She swallows. "Or not wake up...or whatever."

Well, now he actually feels like a heel. And a little foolish. Really, she's quite lovely and just his type. Although he's currently not in the mood, he certainly has no issue with indulging in passing carnal pleasures with a human. No use burning bridges.

Going forward, he takes her hand. "Miss Lewis," he says in his calmest, most reassuring, most courtly tone — he is in armor, no use disguising his origins anymore. "You are not dying. You are home, you are safe, and the gentleman from the forest is no more. I do regret that my lapse in control has caused you to doubt this. If I believed it were prudent, I would offer to erase your memories and allow you to forget seeing Fenrir as a wolf, the portfolio pictures bursting into flames, and my armor. But memory erasing is a tricky business, and..."

He looks down at her hand. It is shaking. Pursing his lips, he says, "This is not reassuring you."

"Not at all," she confirms.

"Damn." With a sigh he makes to kiss her hand. It is a courtly gesture, one he would bestow on a lady in Asgard had he distressed her accidentally.

To his shock, she rips her hand away before it even touches his lips. "That really doesn't help," she says.

Eyes wide, Loki holds up his hands. "No offense meant."

Scowling and looking away, she says, "See you in a few minutes." And then she turns and disappears down the stairs.

Tilting his head, Loki turns in the direction of the shower, thankful that he knows what one is.

He's just rinsing his hair when he sees the red mist again. It wraps around him in the shower, and the hair on the back of his neck stands on end. The child's voice comes again in Russian. "The petty bourgeois are keeping the grander house to themselves and leaving you the meaner accommodation."

Blinking the water from his eyes, Loki restrains a shudder. "I'm grateful I don't have to rob banks again for food and a place to stay," Loki says. Stepping through the red mist and out of the shower, he grabs a towel.

"My Josef robbed banks, too," says the child voice. "For the revolution." In a voice that sounds slightly ashamed, it adds, "And food...and soft ones."

"Josef?" says Loki. Obviously, the mist wants to talk to him, and Loki isn't so foolish as not to comply.

"He woke me. He touched me. But he wasn't like you. He couldn't hear me."

Slipping on his breeches, Loki says, "You have a corporeal form?"

"Yes," says the mist, its voice sounding fainter, the red magic ceding to pink.

"Where are you?" Loki asks.

"It is impossible to know position or momentum with certainty," says the voice, barely audible now, the mist almost invisible.

Leave it to a magical creature to stumble over the Heisenberg uncertainty principle. Magic really was just expanded quantum theory.

"Yes, that's true," Loki says, trying to remain patient. "But you can think of your position in relative terms to mine and then give an estimate of location..."

There is no response. Loki exhales heavily in frustration.

He is very curious. But he doesn't have time for this right now. He needs to eat and sleep to give himself enough energy to open a gate to the World Tree. He needs to find Valli and Nari.

He slips on a shirt that was in the pile of towels and sheets. Stepping out of the bathroom, he looks at his armor and sword laid out neatly on the bed.

Beatrice is going to touch him. He just knows it. He goes to his knapsack, pulls out his book and slips it into his pocket. Closing his eyes, he briefly projects his consciousness out of the small room, through the roof, and into the sky. There are no ravens in sight.

Jaw tight, he heads for the stairs.

CHAPTER 5

Thor, the weird maybe figment of Amy's imagination, shows up for dinner wearing a chambray shirt that used to belong to Amy's grandfather. Her grandfather was a tall man, but it still barely comes to Thor's waistband. He's rolled up the sleeves so they don't look too short.

He's shaved and his hair is clean and combed back from his eyes. It's disturbing, but he of the inappropriate King-Arthur-esque come-ons cleans up nicely.

She shakes her head. Remember the armor, Amy. Remember the ping when you flicked his back.

Remember he saved you...

She sighs. She is probably just imagining all of this. It's too much to think about, so she focuses on the spread on the table.

Beatrice has pulled out the stops for Amy's rescuer. Amy's grandmother is of Ukrainian descent, and the table shows it.

Stuffed cabbages, sausages, boiled potatoes, and homemade sauerkraut. Amy prefers to eat vegetarian, and in deference to that her grandmother has also laid out some cheese sandwiches and mushroom soup with dumplings.

Thor sits down with a big smile and proceeds to eat everything. He doesn't eat fast, doesn't shovel food in his face, but he's like a machine. He just keeps going, and going, and going.

Her grandmother asks him questions, and he answers quickly and vaguely and turns the conversation back to Beatrice. He asks all the right questions about the neighborhood, and Beatrice is happy to expound on how it had once been predominantly Ukrainian but now is filled with yuppies and Mexican "foreigners" — Beatrice doesn't quite catch the irony in her being from the Ukraine and a foreigner. Thor doesn't comment.

He seems so much like the nice, kind of shy awkward guy she remembers from the police station. Beatrice seems utterly enchanted by him. It takes nearly half an hour for her to turn to Amy and say, "How did your final exams go, dear?"

Putting down her sandwich, Amy says, "Oh, great, Grandma. I think my exam for Equine Theriogenology went really well." Her grandmother looks at her pointedly, and then tips her head in Thor's direction. Amy belatedly remembers it's not nice to use words people probably don't understand. Licking her lips she prepares to explain theriogenology is the study of animal reproduction when Thor says, "Oh, really? Was the curriculum theoretical or practical? I'm no expert on theriogenology myself, equine or otherwise, but I have had the opportunity to be present for a foaling here and there. And my friend...Homer...was always hatching odd things."

Amy blinks. "The class was theoretical and practical..."

"Oh, excellent," says Thor. "It's so lovely watching foals clamber up on their wobbly little legs, isn't it?"

"Yes," says Amy, her mouth threatening to pull into a smile.

"Did you grow up on a farm?" Beatrice asks Thor.

"No," he says. "But there were stables nearby." Helping himself to the last of the stuffed cabbages, Thor says. "What are in these cabbages? They are delicious!"

Beatrice giggles like a young girl and Amy restrains a sigh as her grandmother begins to tell Thor exactly what's in them. Instead, going to the stove, Amy ladles another bowl of mushroom soup for herself. Actually, listening to her grandmother talk about ground pork and seasonings is beginning to make her feel like this isn't a dream.

Didn't Dream-on-the-bus Thor tell her she'd know she was alive when things became ordinary again? And maybe Armor-in-the-garage-attic Thor was just another dream? She hasn't gotten a good night's sleep in days now. Maybe she drifted off to sleep when she came out of her shower and lay down on her bed? Of course! That must be what happened.

She's just going back to the table when the CD player, which had been playing some mellow shoe gazing electronica, switches to her grandmother's Glenn Miller CD.

Thor sits up straighter as the opening bars to "In the Mood" comes on. "I know this song," he says.

Sighing, Beatrice says, "I learned to dance the Swing with this song."

Thor grins. "So did I!" Setting his napkin on the table, he stands, bows slightly and holds out a hand. "Beatrice?"

Beatrice puts a hand to her mouth. And then she smiles

and says, "Oh, why not? But let's go to the living room. There's no space in here."

Taking Thor's hand, she leads him to the other room and Amy follows.

"No dipping or throws!" Beatrice says, "Remember, I'm old!"

"Nonsense," says Thor, putting a hand on her back as they step in front of the fireplace. "You don't look a day over 65!"

Beatrice laughs and holds up her hand for him. "I'm closer to 85, young man!"

Taking her hand in his, Thor pauses. "No, really, I meant it, you don't..." The look on his face is genuinely perplexed. But then he blinks, says, "Good on you!" and they begin to dance. Thor is very gentle for such a huge guy and Beatrice smiles from ear to ear — if she feels anything weird beneath Grandpa's old shirt Thor's wearing, she's not showing it. Amy leans against the mantle and just watches. She hasn't seen Grandma this happy since Grandpa died, and it makes her a little misty eyed. Even if this is all in her head, for Beatrice's sake, she doesn't want it to end.

And then it almost does. The light in the living room flickers and goes out, and there is an instant of darkness. But then, all at once, every single candle on the mantle lights up. Amy jumps, as her hair nearly catches fire.

"Oh, candles! Lovely!" says Beatrice.

Thor smiles at Amy. "Thanks for lighting those!"

Amy decides not to say anything. Aren't hallucinations part of sleep deprivation?

As the music winds down, she just follows her giggling grandmother and Thor back into the kitchen.

Breathing a little heavily, Beatrice sits down and smoothes

her hair.

Thor slides into the seat across from her and starts helping himself to the last of the boiled potatoes and sausage.

"You are too much fun to be Thor!" Beatrice declares.

Thor's body stills, a spoon full of potatoes hanging in the air. "Oh?" he says. His voice has just the barest hint of an edge to it, and Amy tenses. "Who am I then?"

Something mischievous enters Beatrice's eyes. "I'd say you're more a friend to Hoenir than you are a Thor."

Thor puts the potatoes down. "Friend to Hoenir..."

Winking, Beatrice says, "It's a kenning, young man. You can Google it later."

"Google?" says Thor.

"I'm a very tech savvy Grandma!" says Beatrice. "I email my granddaughter every day! It's so wonderful."

"Email..." says Thor.

"Kenning?" says Amy.

Looking at Amy, Thor says, "A kenning is a conventional poetic phrase used in place of the name of a person or thing. For instance, storm-of-swords means battle."

Beatrice blinks, "Very good! How about whale-road?"

Putting a potato in his mouth — the whole thing, but it really isn't that big a mouthful for him, Thor smiles, chews a moment, swallows, and then says, "The sea!"

The next half hour or so consists of Beatrice throwing kennings at Thor. Thor gets all the old obscure ones, like gore-cradle for battlefield, and battle-flame for the light on a sword, but he misses the new ones, like beer-goggles. When Amy explains it he laughs heartily. He doesn't get surfing-the-net either; when Amy tries to explain that one, he only looks befuddled.

Thor's cleaning up the last of everything on the table when Beatrice says, "Well, I think I'll offer you dessert and then call it a night." She looks at Thor's plate. "Unless, of course, you still would like more meat and potatoes..."

She's just being polite, of course; anyone can see it.

But Thor nods vigorously. "I could eat more meat and potatoes if you've got them."

Beatrice blinks at him. "Well...I do have a cold smoked ham in the fridge I was thinking of serving my church group..."

Smacking his lips, Thor says, "That sounds delicious! I love ham!"

Beatrice stares at him, then shaking her head, gets up and says, "I forget how much young men can eat!"

Amy helps her grandmother put a huge ham on a serving plate in the middle of the table. Beatrice hands Thor a carving knife — and a loaf of bread for good measure, and then excuses herself. As she is leaving, she turns and says, "Friends of Hoenir are always welcome in this house."

Thor smiles. "Well, Hoenir is a lovely man. I'm sure any friend of his is exceptional."

Beatrice laughs. "Hoenir's friend did put the gods in their place on more than one occasion," and Thor looks absolutely befuddled again.

Beatrice leaves the room, the old floorboards, and then the stairs, creaking as she goes up to her room.

An awkward silence settles on the table. Thor rips off a piece of bread, looks down at his plate and says, "Friend of Hoenir..."

Amy whips out her iPhone and Googles it. She sits up straighter. "It's Loki," she says. She swears the lights flicker

just a bit. At her feet, Fenrir makes the same noise she makes
when she spies a rabbit.

She looks up and sees Thor staring at her, as though gauging her reaction.

Amy doesn't move. She feels like pieces of a puzzle in her
brain are falling into place, but the picture that is forming is
too weird and too impossible to be real.

He looks down at his plate. "Hoenir was a good friend.
From the beginning...even willing to risk his life..." Thor stirs
the food on his plate, but says no more.

*Loki is 12 years old. A mist is settling over the gardens outside
the palace in Asgard. It is early evening, and he runs as fast as
his legs can carry him down dark garden paths, his breathing
loud in his ears.*

*He doesn't stop until he gets to Hoenir's hut. As he bangs at
the door, a little gray mouse with eight black insect legs and no
tail drops down from the eaves on a silvery trail of spider silk.
Loki loves spiders. Ordinarily he'd pet the little creature, but now
he's too flustered to even raise a finger to it.*

*The door opens and golden light spills out. Hoenir is wearing
an apron and gloves of the kind falconers wear. He steps silently
aside and Loki bolts in.*

*Loki never knows what he'll find when he comes into the
hut. On the outside, it looks like a single room just a few paces
wide, but on the inside it has many rooms, and is much larger
than it looks from the garden. He never knows which room he'll
step into. Sometimes it's a sitting room with comfy chairs and a
roaring fire, sometimes an enormous library grander even than*

Odin's, sometimes a kitchen, or sometimes, like tonight, he enters a workshop. There is a long workbench as high as Loki's chest and some tall chairs next to it. From the ceiling hangs a large lamp-like thing that glows orange and nearly touches the bench top.

Mimir is standing on his neck by the lamp. "Ah, Loki, we were just about to do a hatching. Would you like to select an egg for us?"

Hoenir gestures towards an enormous basket, as big as Loki, filled with eggs, all rather long and oblong instead of the regular shape of a bird egg. Loki finds one that is about twice the length of his outstretched hands and about half as wide. It is leathery and soft.

"Excellent," says Mimir. "Why don't you bring it here and set it beneath the lamp."

Hoenir leads Loki to a tall chair close to Mimir and the lamp. Loki climbs up on it and puts the egg beneath the light. The lamp gives off a lot of heat.

The three of them sit staring at it for a long time. At last Mimir says, "So, Loki. What brings you to our hut at this time of night?"

Loki shrugs.

For a few moments Mimir says nothing, and then he says, "So have you seen baby Baldur? I'm not such a fan of babies myself, but Odin and Frigga's child...why I've never seen such golden curls on a newborn. And even his cries sound musical."

Loki scowls. "His curls aren't golden. His hair is thin and black and straight. And his cries sound just like every other baby's cry. They're loud and I wish he'd shut up."

"Now, now," says Mimir. "I've seen Baldur, and he most definitely has golden curls, and rosy cheeks and..."

"No," says Loki, staring at the egg. He thinks he sees it

moving. "*His hair is black. And his skin is pale and nearly blue... like mine. He looks more Jotunn than Aesir. And there's magic all around him...gray magic, so dark it's nearly black.*"

What Loki doesn't say is how just being around Baldur makes the hair on the back of his neck stand on end. How he feels a chill just being near the baby.

"Did you tell Odin what you see?" Mimir asks quietly.

Loki can only swallow.

"Oh, dear," says Mimir, and Loki glances up to see Mimir looking at Hoenir. Hoenir looks very distraught.

"I'm afraid to ask..." says Mimir.

Loki stares as the surface of the egg rips apart and a tiny hole appears. "Odin told me to leave the palace and never come back."

It was the only time Odin has ever screamed at him — usually there have been maids and governesses for that. Loki has taken his designation as "God of Mischief" rather seriously. Mimir and Odin have stressed the Aesir aren't really gods — more gardeners of the World Tree, but Loki likes his moniker. It's great fun to make an illusion of a snake in a laundry basket and then explain it to Odin as his "sacred duty." Such things never fail to make Odin chortle.

But telling Odin what Baldur looked like to him...that had not gone so well.

Beside him he hears Hoenir scoot back in his chair. The egg starts to shake.

"What sort of creature's in the egg?" Loki asks. He doesn't want to talk about Odin or his exile from the palace.

"A hadrosaur," says Mimir, his voice soft.

"One of Hoenir's creations?" asks Loki.

Mimir raises his eyebrows, "No, well, only distantly. It was created by evolution."

Loki wonders who Evolution is but asks the more pressing question. "What is a hadrosaur?"

"It is a sort of herbivorous dragon," says Mimir.

Loki puts his hands down on the counter and rests his head on them. The egg starts to shake some more; a tiny hole splits into a tear.

The tear splits down the side of the egg, and then a tiny dark green head peeks out. The creature has eyes set in the side of its head; its mouth is slightly agape. Its teeth look strangely sharp for a herbivore — maybe they're just baby teeth, sharp for splitting the egg's leathery shell?

"Wait a minute..." says Mimir.

Loki and Hoenir lean closer.

Blinking hawk like yellow eyes, the head emerges on a long ungainly neck, followed by two tiny little arms with little hands and long sharp claws. Powerful hind limbs follow and a long thick tail.

"That isn't a hadrosaur," says Mimir.

The little creature tilts its head towards Mimir, then catches Loki's eye. Seemingly changing its mind, it looks back to Hoenir.

"No!" Mimir screams.

Hoenir backs up, but too late. The creature springs from the counter and sinks its claws and teeth into Hoenir's arm. Hoenir stares at it wide-eyed as though in shock.

"Loki! Stop it! Stop it! " Mimir shrieks.

Jumping forward, Loki grabs it by the neck like he would a snake. He pinches its jaws on either side, pushing the gums into the creature's own sharp teeth. It releases Hoenir with a hiss and thrashes in Loki's hands.

Mimir sighs. Loki holds it at arm's length. "What should I do with it?"

Putting a hand on his chin, Hoenir looks around the work-shop, seemingly unconcerned with the blood dripping from his arm.

Loki readjusts his grip so one hand is on the neck and the other is wrapped around the creature's writhing torso. It really is quite interesting. He squints to get a better view of its tiny, razor teeth when the door to the hut bursts open.

Odin stands in the door frame for an instant. Then he walks over to Loki with quick strides that leave Loki paralyzed with fear.

Ripping the little dragon from Loki's hands, he wrings its neck and throws the lifeless body across the room. Hoenir's eyes open in horror. When Odin speaks, the hut's windows rattle. "A velociraptor! I thought we discussed this. Never. Again!"

"We thought it was a harmless hadrosaur," Mimir says. "We were hatching it for the elves —"

Odin grabs Loki by the collar and shakes him so hard his teeth rattle "It's your fault," he says. Heaving Loki against a wall, Odin says, "What did you expect, Hoenir, inviting this little agent of chaos into your workshop? He should never come here!"

Loki can only gasp for breath. With a sneer Odin tosses him to the side.

"He can't help what he saw!" Mimir shouts as Loki falls to the floor.

Hoenir runs between Loki and Odin, and Mimir says, "You can't kill Loki, Odin. Not really. Not without killing Hoenir, too."

With a cry, Odin tips over the workbench. Mimir's head lands with a crack and then goes rolling across the floor. Laughing maniacally, Mimir says, "Oh, come now, don't be paranoid of Hoenir and Loki's friendship! They can't help it."

"Shut up, Mimir!" Odin roars.

"I won't shut up! We don't agree with how you treat him! Calling him the God of Mischief! You trivialize him!"

"I'm trying to give him a childhood! Doesn't he deserve that?" Odin yells.

"You're trying to control him!" Mimir shouts. "But as soon as he sees something you don't like..."

Odin goes stomping in Mimir's direction. Next to Loki, Hoenir meets Loki's eyes and then looks towards the door. Loki nods. As Hoenir runs between Mimir and Odin, Loki darts out into the night.

The last thing he hears as darkness falls upon him is Mimir saying, "It's not just chaos that gives birth to monsters."

Hours later Hoenir comes for him. In one hand he carries a lantern with a flame that he holds aloft. In the other hand he has a lantern hanging at his side, but where the flame should be is Mimir's head.

"Come with us," Mimir says. "Odin will recover, but you'll be staying with us for a while."

Loki scampers up from where he'd been huddled on the ground. He's relieved, terrified, and confused. He says nothing that night. But a few days later, when he is sitting in Hoenir's kitchen, he says to Mimir, "What did you mean, Odin trivializes me?"

Mimir sighs. "Nothing, Loki. I said it in anger. Odin is very good at what he does...tending the branches of the World Tree, and keeping things running smoothly. I should not have questioned him in that way."

"I like being the God of Mischief," Loki says. He does. There is a freedom in being a mischief maker; he can skirt rules and expectations. Sometimes he does it for fun, but sometimes he does *it because it feels right. Like when a group of boys were saying cruel things to Sigyn, a girl Loki fancies. He sidled up beside her and made it appear as though both he and Sigyn were Valkyries with wings and flaming spears. To most male Aesir pretending to be female, even a Valkyrie, would be shameful. But it was so much fun as the boys ran away to shout, "What's wrong! Afraid of girls?"*

Mimir says nothing for a few moments. But then he says, "Loki, about Baldur...It is alright for a man to be enchanted by his newborn baby." Sighing, Mimir says, "And...Odin grieves for him."

"But he's not dead," says Loki.

Mimir does not respond.

"I don't remember doing anything for Hoenir except causing trouble," Thor says, the words tumbling out suddenly after a long silence. His eyes flick up quickly to hers.

"You don't remember doing anything..." Amy blinks. The puzzle pieces that fit together in her head, they're just crazy. He isn't Loki. The police let him go, he has a clean record, he's got a social security number that checks out, for heaven's sake. They're obviously playing a little game here. She can play along. Raising an eyebrow, she says, "You're Loki now, not Thor?"

He shrugs nonchalantly, but his eyes are glued to hers and there is a wicked glint there. "So you say," he says.

Shifting her eyes back down to the iPhone she says, "Here it mentions you saving Hoenir while he was held captive by some dwarfs."

"That never happened — it was Lopt who rescued Hoenir," he says, too forcefully to be funny.

Tapping her screen with her thumb she says, "According to Wikipedia — "

"Wikipedia?"

Amy feels a chill go down her spine. "How can you know what a kenning is and theriogenology and not know what Google or Wikipedia are?" She shakes her head. He is really good at this game. She blinks.

Or wait. Maybe he was raised by one of those fundamentalist religious groups that home school and don't allow modern technology? She remembers how shy and polite he was at the police station. Even his awkward clothes. Yep. Rural religious fundamentalist home school escapee. It all makes sense.

Smirking at her he takes another bite of ham. "We don't have Google or Wikipedia in Asgard," he says.

Okay, now the game is funny again. "Uh-huh," she says.

"So really," he says leaning toward her from across the table. "What are they?"

Amy smiles. "Wikipedia is an online encyclopedia that everyone can contribute to."

His eyes widen and a happy smile plays on his face, as though he's just worked out something monumental. "Online means the internets?"

She does not snort. But it is a near call. "Yeah, the internets."

Brow furrowing, he says, "If anyone can contribute, doesn't that put the authenticity of the information in question?"

She smiles and looks down at a picture captioned, Loki as depicted on an 18th century Icelandic manuscript. "Yeah, you wouldn't believe how unflattering the first picture of you is." It really is hideous.

With a scowl he holds out a hand.

She passes over her iPhone.

His scowl deepens and he says, "The artist makes me look like a dwarf!" His irritation seems so genuine, she almost laughs aloud.

"And they gave you such a big nose."

He pushes the iPhone back to her. Without taking it she says, "The picture of you and Sigyn isn't so bad." It isn't a good likeness of the guy in front of her, but at least it isn't ugly.

He stares down at the iPhone.

"Scroll with your finger," she says.

He blinks. "Is any sort of special concentration needed?"

It takes her brain a little while to comprehend the randomness of the question.

Leaning forward, he says, "It's like magic, isn't it? Don't I have to picture what I am doing in my mind?"

She purses her lips. "No," she says softly. "You just have to move your finger."

Swallowing, he gingerly puts his finger on the surface of her iPhone and then drags it down. Smiling, he says, "It works!"

His joy seems so real, it makes Amy's eyes widen.

And then his smile vanishes. "Ah," he says. "My 200 year imprisonment. It wasn't as bad as depicted here. There was snake venom, but no snake, and I was shackled but could walk around a bit." Squinting at her phone he says, "This looks nothing like me. Nice likeness of Sigyn, though...although I don't remember the Bible-esque robes being in fashion then..."

Holding the phone up he smiles wryly at it and says, "Ah, yes, memories."

And that's a little too much. Who knew homeschoolers could be such great actors? She takes the iPhone from him. "Okay," she says. "Enough of this game."

Shrugging, he says, "You started it." And then he picks up his fork and starts to eat again.

Amy looks down at the iPhone and the Wikipedia entry on Loki. "Says here you are a shape shifter."

"Um..." he says.

She glances up and he looks distinctly nervous.

She grins and reads aloud, "Loki gave birth—in the form of a mare—to the eight-legged horse Sleipnir. Says the dad was some special stallion..."

Putting his fork down hard, he says, "Now, how can shape changing even possibly work? We are all formed by immensely complex instructions coded into our cells and by the environment. It's hard enough to just create simple elements, and so energy consuming. But for living things, the concentration, the imagination involved...How could anyone — well except maybe Hoenir and I'm not sure about that — ever hope to match the splendid complexity of all the subtle interactions — "

Grinning wider, Amy says, "I'll say you have a little experience foaling."

He rolls his eyes and she snickers.

Glaring at her he says, "It's not true."

Amy snickers, "Of course it's not true."

Narrowing his eyes, he says, "I can only create illusions of other forms."

Amy blinks, Fenrir barks, and across from her is a woman with Thorish strawberry blond hair wearing Amazonian-esque armor that is more of a glorified girdle squeezing in an impossibly small stomach and supporting enormous breasts.

The woman gestures to said breasts and says in a voice that sounds exactly like Thor's, "I mean, if I had these, would I ever leave the house?"

Amy stares at her hallucination for a fraction of a heart-beat, and then she bursts out laughing. She laughs so hard she convulses around her middle and hits her head on the table.

"It wasn't that funny," says Thor.

Rubbing her sore head she says, "No, no, no, it's just, this dream is too wacky happy and unoriginal for me to be dying in a ditch somewhere. I'm at home and I'm hallucinating and I'm going to be fine."

"Unoriginal?" says Thor, back in his more Thor-like form.

Snickering at how scandalized he sounds, Amy stands up and stretches. "I'm going to go to bed, or slip from REM to Stage 1 sleep. Why don't you go now...if you're even here."

He stares at her a moment. Turning to the food on the table, he says, "May I take the ham?"

Shrugging, she says, "Go ahead." She looks towards the living room. Flickering light is coming through the door. "I should put out the candles even if I am only dreaming." Just to be on the safe side.

"Good idea," he says. "How did you light them so quickly? Electricity?"

Turning back, she points at her head. "With the power of my mind."

Brow furrowing, he says, "Don't toy with me," and waves a hand. Beneath the table Fenrir barks.

Amy turns around; the other room is dark. She peers around the corner; all the candles are extinguished. She's not even bothered anymore.

She looks back at the table. Thor is already standing up with the plate of ham in one hand, and the loaf of bread in the other. He's not smiling.

"Pleasant dreams!" she says.

He nods at her. "Likewise."

She shrugs. "They already are!"

After Thor's out the door, she heads up the stairs to her bedroom. To her surprise, her grandmother is standing on the landing in her pink nightgown, looking towards the door Thor just exited.

"Sounded like you had a lot of fun chatting with Hoenir's friend," she says, eyes narrowing to slivers.

Amy just snorts.

CHAPTER 6

Amy has more dreams later that night. They aren't as pleasant and she has trouble falling to sleep again. In desperation, she pulls Fenrir up near her pillow. Still, she doesn't go to sleep until the very early morning. When she wakes up, it is to Fenrir whimpering by the door. She blinks at the light and then does a double take. It must be nearly noon.

Amy gets up quickly, dresses, and heads down to the kitchen. Beatrice has her apron on and is leaning over the sink washing dishes. She smiles up at Amy. "Good morning, Dear."

Thor is sitting at the table, in his retro outfit, a Chicago Transit Authority map spread out in front of him. How did he get invited to breakfast? Or brunch, or whatever.

"Good morning," he says. He looks like the guy she remembers from the police station. A little rumpled, shoulders not quite square, expression soft. The sort of shy guy who filled her with trust. He doesn't look like the mischievous guy in her dream last night, the one who turned himself into an Amazon, or the guy in the armor.

She blinks as she lets Fenrir out the back door. The kitchen is flooded with warm yellow light. Thor is complimenting Beatrice on her cooking; there is a bowl of freshly scrubbed strawberries on the table; the room smells like coffee, bacon and toast.

...and it feels even more dreamlike than Amy's dream of Thor the Amazon.

"Amy? Amy?"

Beatrice is suddenly standing very close to her.

"Are you all right?" her grandmother says.

"Yes," says Amy.

"Sit down," says Beatrice. "I'll get you some coffee."

"No," says Amy. "I'll make some myself."

She goes to the cupboard and takes out a cup. It crashes to the counter but doesn't break. Amy shakes her head and rights it. She lifts the coffee pitcher off the base and starts to pour. The stream of hot fluid bounces around, some spilling on the counter. She wipes it up quickly with a dishtowel and goes to sit at the table.

Taking a sip, she notices that her grandmother's and Thor's eyes are on her.

"I'm alright," Amy says.

Her grandmother tilts her head. "You've had quite a shock."

"I'm alright," Amy says again, more forcefully this time.

"I'm sure you are," says Thor. Turning to Beatrice he says, "Thank you for the map — and of course, for breakfast."

Picking up a cup Amy knows contains chamomile tea, Beatrice nods, "You're always welcome at this table, of course."

There's something about the way her eyes are narrowed and the way she peers over the cup that tells Amy something isn't quite right.

Thor doesn't seem to notice. "I think I better go now," he says with a warm, sunny smile. He stands up from the table, the Chicago Transit Authority map and a tiny white book in one hand. "Oh," he says suddenly. "You must have dropped this last night. I found it on the floor." He puts her driver's license on the table and slides it towards Amy. She doesn't remember taking it out of her wallet since the police station.

A few minutes later he's gone. Amy scowls. "Did you invite him in?"

Beatrice nods and looks towards the door. "It's better to make sure he's always invited."

Amy stares down at her coffee. What does that mean?

Tilting her head, Beatrice pulls the tea bag from her cup. "Of course, it is nice to be able to cook for someone again," she says brightly.

Amy reaches over and grabs her license. "I need to get ready for an interview at a new temp agency." The one she used to work for went out of business.

Beatrice blinks. "Are you sure that's wise? You don't seem quite yourself."

Amy stares at her coffee. She isn't herself. But she just has to get over it. It's not like this experience is completely new; it is just extreme. She's dealt with creeps before. What woman hasn't? She'd been felt up on the 'L' one time — and had elbowed the guy so badly he'd sputtered and nearly puked. Some really lovely gentleman had followed her home from the bus stop one night and she'd unslung her backpack, screamed at him like a banshee, and chased him away.

She puts her head in her hands. She didn't escape this time. She was rescued. It turns out maybe there is a big difference. And if she hadn't been rescued...She screws her eyes shut and starts to sob.

"There, there," says Beatrice.

"Grandma," she says. "If it wasn't for Thor..." she can't talk about the pictures, can't say what she saw in them — or them bursting into flames. That part was real, the fire, wasn't it?

She takes a big gulp of air. She isn't sure of anything anymore. "Should I have invited him home?" she says. "He, he, he..." What? Has featured prominently in some weird dreams, or... "Maybe I trust him more than I should because he saved me, but he could be crazy, too." She shakes her head.

Beatrice's hand stops. "Oh, I don't think you or I have anything to worry about from our guest." She looks around the kitchen, "Other than that he might eat us out of house and home. Always better to invite him to the party, though..."

"Grandma?" says Amy.

Beatrice blinks. "Oh, nothing."

Amy stares at her grandmother for a few moments. She looks tiny and frail. But she's not — or she wasn't.

Beatrice's parents put Beatrice and her two brothers on a boat to the free world back in 1940, just before the Nazis invaded. Before they left they'd already lost family members and friends under Soviet rule — some disappeared in the middle of the night, others simply died in the great famine of the early 1930s.

Beatrice lost her entire world. Amy feels like her world has changed forever, that she's lost something precious — but compared to Beatrice, Amy has lost nothing.

"How did you do it, Grandma? When you got on the boat..."

Beatrice blinks. "What?"

Swallowing, Amy looks down at her hands and plays nervously with her fingers. "I was just wondering how you kept going...after you lost everything."

Beatrice sighs and looks down at her tea. "You just do."

Standing up, Amy wipes her face. "I'm going to get ready to go."

Beatrice looks at her for a moment and then nods.

Amy manages to get ready for her interview, and she gets out of the door with plenty of time to spare — even though leaving her home shatters her sense of security.

What she doesn't manage to do is drive. She stares at her grandmother's Subaru Forester, keys in hand, and decides she'd rather take the bus. She's not sure if it's because of the rollover, or if she just wants to stay around other people.

As she walks out to the front walk and heads towards the 'L', she sees an older man, perhaps in his 50's, buying an ice cream from one of the Mexican ice cream bicycle carts that frequent her neighborhood. He's got a stern square jaw and is completely bald on top. Amy notices him because he's wearing a gray suit despite the heat. The suit looks too nice to belong to an old timer from the neighborhood, but he isn't young enough to be a yuppie. As she walks by, he tips his head at her over his drumstick ice cream cone. Not wanting to be rude, she nods back.

Loki consults the CTA map and his book. The location is right.

The building in front of him looks to be about 100 years

old. It has not been maintained very well. The facade of brick and cement is crumbling. Cutting straight through the heart of the building is a covered brick alleyway that leads to a dismal inner courtyard. There is a decorative iron gate that is rusted and blood colored. Loki scowls — it is strange that mortals tend to erect physical gates where World Gates reside. Another strange bit of human magic? He tilts his head; fortunately the iron gate is now open and won't be in his way. Beyond the iron gate, on the far wall of the courtyard in peeling paint, are the words, "Graphic Arts Co." Set into the walls are boarded up doors and windows covered with graffiti.

Loki looks around. He sees a few men down the street unloading a small van. They don't seem to notice him. Loki has altered his Midgardian attire considerably. As he walked here — only a few short miles — he observed the natives and gradually modified his clothing. He now appears to be wearing a gray tee shirt, breeches of a thick blue fabric, gray shoes with laces and stripes, and dark glasses. And he appears to have a black rectangular bag slung over one shoulder.

He is actually wearing his armor, with his helmet on, visor down. Over one arm he's slung his army knapsack filled with the two remaining grenades, some of last night's ham and bread, and a large bottle of water he nicked from a store on the way.

Moving beneath the overhang towards the iron gate he closes his eyes. An instant later he is invisible to anyone who looks in his direction.

Loki walks until he feels a shiver snake its way up his spine. The World Gate is here. He can feel the tug of magic in the place where time and space are weakly defined.

He begins to murmur a childhood rhyme he used to recite

to his children. It isn't a spell, per se; but it helps him focus his mind. Lifting his hands, he closes his eyes and begins to imagine pulling back a heavy curtain. The gate opens surprisingly easily, and a swirling vortex of color spins before him.

Loki steps forward...

...and feels stone beneath his feet. He takes a deep breath, drops the invisibility spell to conserve magic, and opens his eyes to the bright white-blue sunlight and silvery hues of Alfheim, land of the Elves. He looks down; beneath his feet is a silver road. That is right. The realm is right. But...

Scowling, he spins around...On both sides of the road is dense forest. On one side of the road the tree trunks are light lavender; the undergrowth is sparse and dotted with blue and yellow flowers. On the other side the trunks are deep indigo and nearly black; the undergrowth is dense and dark. Above the dark trees is an ominous swirl of dark gray magical clouds. He is certain he sees eyes peering at him from beneath the dark branches.

Unsheathing his sword, he switches to the tongue of the Dark Elves and says, "Don't even think about it." Just to be on the safe side he concentrates his magic towards the undergrowth and imagines the molecules there swirling and dancing together. There is a burst of flame, just as he intends, and a curse from his onlooker. He hears stirring in the undergrowth as the Dark Elf disappears into the forest.

Letting the flames dissipate, Loki consults Lothur's journal. His jaw goes tight and his brow furrows. It's colder here than in Chicago, but he feels himself getting hotter beneath his armor. He should be so close...but the entrance point is wrong.

Narrowing his eyes, he lets his consciousness fly to the air.

He sees what he is looking for, the palace of the queen of the Light Elves about 100 miles down the road. Once this World Gate would have dropped him right outside her door, but the branches of the World Tree grow, and as they grow, they shift.

It is said the elf queen, like Odin, Heimdall, and possibly Hoenir, can see all that happens in the Nine Realms if she wishes. She may be able to tell him where his sons were deposited. Since Heimdall and Odin aren't likely to be helpful at the moment, and Hoenir will be difficult to reach, the elf queen seems like Loki's best option.

Most of the way the road abuts the dark forest. The Dark Elves won't harass travelers on the road by day; but by night it will be another matter.

There are other ways to get to the elf queen's palace besides the road. If he takes those ways, when he emerges on the other end, he won't be helpless, but he will be much weaker, very tired, and ravenous. Not a way to make a good impression, and definitely not good if his reception is less than welcome.

He lets his consciousness sink back into his body. There is a part of him that wants to instantly go forward. The information he needs is so close...and he is strong again. Yesterday it was easy to be patient, he was too weak to be otherwise. But now, it is a struggle not to be impetuous.

He takes a sharp, frustrated breath and considers his situation. If only he had a carpet or...

Sheathing his sword, he turns and steps back to where the World Gate has shut. Closing his eyes he begins to tug at the gate again until it is open as wide as it will go. Furrowing his brow and concentrating to keep it open, he quickly measures the width by pacing the length. It is just wide enough.

Nodding to himself, he is just about to leave Alfheim,

when a flash of something white on the light side of the road catches his attention. Turning towards it he scowls.

Sure enough...

Unsheathing his sword, Loki stands before the semi-open World Gate and glares at the unicorn emerging from the wood. What it wants in Midgard Loki can't imagine, but it's not coming through Loki's gate. Hoenir would never hear the end of it if he let such a vicious temperamental creature loose in a major Midgardian metropolis. Lifting his sword high like a spear, Loki says, "Don't you think about it either."

The beast lowers its head and snorts. The air between it and Loki shimmers with heat. With a curse, Loki forces the excited molecules to quiet. Lowering the sword, he pulls a knife from his belt and hurls it in the beast's direction, but the monster vanishes and the knife explodes harmlessly against a tree.

Narrowing his eyes, Loki shouts, "You'd taste good on an open spit!"

There is no sound. Loki doesn't turn his eyes from the forest. Rather than risk being gored in the back, he makes himself invisible, carefully backs up through the World Gate... and promptly collides with the iron gate on the other side. He feels like Thor has just heaved him against a wall — in anger, or worse, enthusiasm. Loki doesn't curse, but it's a near call.

He lets the World Gate dissipate, turns around and surveys the situation. There is a plate on the gate that looks like it may have had a locking mechanism at one point, but now it's partially rusted through. Instead, the gate is held by a simple padlock on a rusty chain. It takes hardly a thought to make the padlock spring open. He pushes at the gate gently, but it's hanging so low on its hinges that it scrapes the ground. A tiny push isn't going to do it. Loki grasps the metal plate and lifts. Pain shoots up his hand and he lets go. There is a loud clang as the last bit of the ancient plate falls to the ground. He does curse.

Someone shouts something from an open window.

Scowling, Loki lifts the gate again — this time using one of the great rusting vertical iron bars. It opens easily enough and he slips out of the alley and onto the street.

He walks down the block until he finds a vehicle that he thinks will suit his purposes. A Mercedes-Benz emblem is on the hood; he recognizes it from his journeys through Nazi Germany. What's more important is that, as odd as the shape is, sleek and low to the ground, it has a visible stick shift. Most of the cars don't. Loki's last attempt at navigating a human vehicle didn't end well, and he's afraid of trying to master a new and more difficult technology on short notice. He puts a hand towards the lock, reaches out...

The car begins honking. Loudly.

From down the street he hears a man's voice. "That's my car!"

The car is calling to its master! Humans have crossed the divide between makers of machines to makers of living things!

A window opens. "Shut it up!"

Loki is invisible. He does not need to run. But he does anyway.

When Amy turns up Beatrice's front walk it is still light out and the Mexican ice cream bicycle cart is still wheeling up and down her block, its bell ringing cheerfully.

She really should have stopped by the vet clinic and the restaurant where she normally hostesses over breaks. She doesn't want to risk coming home after dark though. Not yet.

She feels like she is covered with a second skin of pollution, dried sweat, and grime. Chicago in summer. She sighs.

As soon as she is inside, she heads to the shower. When she is clean and feeling human again, she curls up with her iPhone on a big chair in the living room. She frowns at her phone. There are several missed calls. One from Chris, a guy she briefly dated. Chris is very nice, on a track to success, and a good, solid person. Someone Beatrice would like and Amy should like, but couldn't. She thinks of their awkward fumblings in bed that never quite worked for her and blushes. Chris said she'd get it with time...she swallows. In the end she'd just made herself unavailable. He deserves someone better.

She scrolls down and sees her vet-wannabe friend Andrea called. Andrea will be sympathetic and probably make her laugh. Andrea will probably press her to see a shrink...but after she's done with that they can talk about their Equine Theriogenology course and everything will be good. Suddenly possessed not just with the desire, but the need to call Andrea, Amy puts the phone to her ear. That's when Beatrice walks in.

"It's been awfully quiet today," says Beatrice, sitting down on the sofa.

Putting down her phone, Amy looks up at her grandmother.

Reading the unformed question on her lips, Beatrice says, "I guess I just expected that the police would call. Or maybe the press..."

Amy blinks. "Please don't call the press, Grandma." The

last thing Amy wants right now is flash bulbs and interviews.

Beatrice snorts, and Amy smiles. Good, strong, private, Ukrainian Beatrice wouldn't want that.

"I don't think I'd worry," Amy says. "The police have my contact info. And they kept Thor and me for a really long time. They let us both go — the evidence was pretty..." Amy trails off.

"Oh, my!" says Beatrice. "I forgot. I have to go buy a new ham for my church group. Do you think you'll be okay if I go out?"

"Sure, Grandma," says Amy. She's actually looking forward to calling her friend Andrea. She might tell her some of the details she didn't tell Beatrice.

Beatrice gets up a little stiffly and heads towards the front door. A few minutes later, Amy hears the door slam and picks up her phone. She's just about to dial the number when there is a knock at the back kitchen door. Fenrir dashes towards it, and Amy scowls but gets up and follows.

Thor is standing right outside on the stoop.

Amy remembers her conversation with Beatrice earlier when she questioned Thor's trustworthiness. For a moment she hesitates, but then Fenrir does her happy dance, wagging her whole body and hopping on her feet. Fenrir doesn't like anyone, except maybe Beatrice and Amy. The whole reason Fenrir's name is Fenrir is because man-hating-bitch-from-Hell is too much of a mouthful, and you can't say it in polite company.

Amy tilts her head and looks at her ecstatic little dog. Pursing her lips, she opens the door.

"Amy," Thor says as Fenrir twines around his feet. He's wearing clothing that looks more decade appropriate, and she wonders how he got it. "I need your help."

Amy's brow furrows, waiting for him to explain. He lifts his hand to push back his hair, and she notices his hand is bleeding.

"Oh, wow! Your hand," she says. "Come in. I'll get the first aid kit."

He looks down at his hand as though puzzled but doesn't protest, just steps into the kitchen.

"Better wash it out in the sink," she says going to the cabinet for the first aid kit. "How did you do that?"

"Rusty gate," he responds.

Looking over her shoulder as she pulls down the kit she says, "I hope you have a tetanus shot."

He blinks as he puts his hand under the sink. "Tetanus?"

Raising an eyebrow, she says, "Tetanus, it's a disease caused by bacteria; it's also called lockjaw. A very bad way to die."

"Oh, a bacteria...I am safe from that." He lifts his hand up and stares at it. There is a huge gash running down the middle of his palm. "It's really not as bad as it looks," he says.

Shaking her head, Amy takes his hand. He doesn't resist.

"It's not going to heal very well. Every time you bend your hand it's going to open again," she says, staring down at the cut. "I have some Nu-Skin; it's a liquid adhesive bandage. It's probably your best bet."

"It's not necessary," he says.

"It is necessary..." Amy stops. The cut is melding itself back together before her eyes.

She gasps. "How?"

"Just a little concentration," he says. "I can heal myself quite well. Unfortunately, I can't do it for others."

Amy is suddenly aware that they are standing very close, and that she barely knows him. She should back away, but instead she pulls the hand closer to her, fascinated. The skin on his hand is fresh, new, and unmarred. She lifts her eyes to his face.

He smirks. When he speaks his voice oozes bitterness. "There's something in my nature, maybe it's a manifestation of my selfishness, my self-centeredness...but I can't heal anyone else, no matter how I might wish to. Even Thor, though he detests magic, has exceedingly good healing skills."

"What are you talking about?" Amy says quietly.

"Come on, Miss Lewis," he says. He's so close she can feel his breath against her hair when he speaks. "You already have discovered who I really am. And I've given you ample proof."

"You're crazy," she says, finally dropping his hand and backing up. "Or I'm crazy."

He takes a step forward. "No, you're not crazy. The wolf, the armor..." he smirks again. "The lovely lady you found yourself talking to last night. All real...or perfectly serviceable illusions."

Amy feels her back hit the wall. "No."

He grimaces. "And the picture folio catching fire and the candles last night were probably me, too — but I didn't mean for those to happen."

"Stop it," Amy says, moving sideways to the kitchen door. "Just stop it."

"No," he says, moving forward and catching her wrist. The clothing he is wearing seems to shimmer, like heat waves above a road on a hot day, and there he is in his armor again. "I need your help," he says, his face very close to hers, and Amy can see his blue eyes are so pale they're almost white.

"And you owe me."

"I don't owe you anything! Let me go!" Amy says, trying to twist her hand from his grasp. When that doesn't work she tries stomping on his feet...but he's not there.

From behind her his voice comes again. "Your life is worth more than a bed, some ham, and stuffed cabbages, Girl. You do owe me, and you will pay up."

Amy spins around. He's blocking the door from the kitchen to the living room.

She spins around again to run out the back door but he's already standing there, his head canted forward, a scowl between his brow. "I really do not want to hurt you. I need your cooperation, my sons' lives — "

"I won't!" Closing her eyes, she shouts, "Fenrir!"

From the floor comes a happy yip. She scowls down at the dog. When did her brave mutt become so unreliable?

"Just hear me out," he says through gritted teeth.

"No!" Amy says. "You. Are. Crazy."

"What do you want...Loki?"

Amy turns her head. Beatrice is standing in the doorway, purse in her hands; she is trembling slightly.

"Grandma?" says Amy. "I thought you were going to get a ham..."

Not taking her eyes off Thor...or Loki, or whoever it is, Beatrice says. "I forgot my wallet. What do you want, Loki?"

Straightening, mystery weird guy says, "A car ride."

Beatrice swallows but then juts out her chin like she does when she's about to complain to a store clerk. "You could have just asked."

"To Alfheim," he says.

"Oh..." says Beatrice. "Land of the Elves. Oh, my."

Amy runs to her grandmother and grabs her shoulders. "Come on, Grandma, let's go."

"No," says Beatrice, her eyes still on whoever it is. "You are worth more than a few cabbage rolls, Dear."

"Grandma," says Amy. "This is crazy, he isn't..."

"Amy," Beatrice says, meeting Amy's eyes. "He just changed his clothing into armor, and I saw him shape shift last night. We don't want to be in his debt."

"Good point, Beatrice."

Amy turns her head. Loki, Thor, or crazy fundamentalist home schooling escapee is walking towards them.

Shrugging, he says, "I'm sorry to be so insistent. Really, I've had a lovely time with the two of you. But I've recovered, and I can't dally anymore."

"Will you bring me back?" says Beatrice.

"Grandma!" shouts Amy, shaking her head. Beatrice brings one hand up to her shoulder and squeezes Amy's hand.

Bowing, he says, "Of course."

Beatrice narrows her eyes. "Do I have your oath?"

Whoever it is stops. He stands up straight. For a moment he says nothing. And then, tilting his head he says, "That is too broad a promise. You have my oath that I will do everything in my power to bring you back safely. More than that — " He lifts his hands and lowers his head, eyes locked on Beatrice.

"Grandma, you don't drive!" says Amy. The only reason Beatrice has a car is because the ten-year old Subaru in the garage belongs to Amy's grandfather and Beatrice doesn't have the heart to part with it.

"But I can," says Beatrice. Turning, she nods at the crazy man. "I will do it, Loki."

Crazy man beams. "It actually might be good fun for you. The Light Elves have nothing against humans."

Shivering a little, Beatrice smiles. "Might be worth it to see Alfheim, before I die."

"There's no such thing as elves!" Amy says.

"On Earth," says Crazy Guy. Bowing in her grandmother's direction, he says, "Beatrice, you are a true lady. If you were a few hundred years older — "

Beatrice's smile drops. "Stow it, Silvertongue. How long will this take?"

"This is crazy, Grandma!" says Amy, dropping her hands. Her grandmother doesn't even meet her eyes.

"About a day," he says, face going serious.

"Take what you think we'll need from the refrigerator. I'm going to get ready," says Beatrice. She turns around and starts walking towards the stairs.

Amy glares at Crazy Guy. "I'm not letting her go alone anywhere with you!"

"You're more than welcome to join us," he says, going to the fridge.

"You fucking jerk!" Amy hisses. "Taking advantage of an old woman like that!"

Loki-Thor-Crazy Person scowls over his shoulder at her. A rag on the counter bursts into flames. Amy's eyes widen. She looks at Crazy Guy. He is staring at the fire with eyes wide as hers. Turning to her quickly, he says nervously, "I didn't do that!"

Frantically pushing the burning rag into the sink with a stray fork, Amy douses it with the faucet. "Of course you didn't. That would be impossible," she whispers.

She's got to convince Beatrice not to go with this guy. As

soon as the flames are out, she runs up the stairs and finds Beatrice packing a small overnight bag in her bedroom.

...and she gets nowhere with her cajoling, arguments or pleas.

"I said I will drive him and I am going to drive him," her grandmother says.

"But it's crazy! You can't drive to Alfheim! Alfheim doesn't exist!"

"Then maybe we'll drive a bit and come home," says Beatrice.

"He's a lunatic!"

Putting a toothbrush and a tube of toothpaste in an overnight bag, Beatrice smiles. "A charming lunatic."

"So was Ted Bundy!"

Zipping up her bag, Beatrice blinks at Amy. "Who was he?"

"A serial killer!"

Beatrice's eyes go hard. "Do you really think Loki is a serial killer? Really?"

Amy remembers the picture in the van going up in flames, and Thor...Loki...nearly stammering, I'm sorry...I didn't mean...

Shaking her head, Amy closes her eyes. "No, but that is not the point."

Putting her bag on the floor and wheeling it out into the hallway, Beatrice says, "Well, then what is your point?"

"This is madness."

"I said I would drive him," says Beatrice, beginning her agonizingly slow descent of the stairs.

Strong, independent, stubborn, Ukrainian. She hasn't driven in years — Beatrice behind the wheel is probably more dangerous than Thor-Loki-whoever.

Swallowing, Amy shouts, "I'm driving!"

CHAPTER 7

A few minutes later they are standing in the garage in front of the Subaru. Fenrir is dancing happily next to them. It is not a great city car, but Amy's grandfather liked fishing and escaping the city on weekends. Thor-Loki-Whoever-It-Is is carrying a cooler. He is back in a tee shirt and jeans, a black messenger bag over one shoulder. He is looking at the late afternoon sky. "We'll have a few hours of daylight left."

Amy rolls her eyes. "This is crazy," she mumbles, hitting the unlock button on the Subaru's remote.

The SUV beeps, and Whoever-It-Is jumps. "Will it accept me since I am with you?"

Amy looks at Beatrice. Beatrice looks at Amy. Fenrir cocks her head at the man who may or may not be Thor.

"Yes," says Amy. "It was just saying hello."

"Hello, Car," says Thor, leaning tentatively forward.

Amy's eyes go wide, but she says nothing as she slips into

the driver's seat and hits the back door release. Thor puts the cooler and Beatrice's bag in the rear, closes the back door, and helps Beatrice into the back seat. All very chivalrous. He also closes the garage door after Amy pulls forward. For a moment Amy considers hitting the accelerator and leaving him there in the alley, but she doesn't. She'll just play along, this will come to nothing, and maybe on the way home she can drop Thor off at a hospital where he can get professional help.

As Thor slips into the front seat, her foot goes to the non-existent clutch and her hand goes to the non-existent stick, but of course it's an automatic. For a moment they go nowhere.

Thor shakes his head. "This new advanced transmission system seems more trouble than it's worth."

Amy decides to say nothing. She just puts her foot on the gas and heads to the gas station to fill up the tank — because Thor insists the journey is about 200 miles. And then she heads towards Peoria and Randolf streets, just a mile and a half away. It's an area known for overpriced restaurants, not elves.

The building Thor directs her to is not a restaurant. It's one of the ancient warehouse buildings just south of Restaurant Row. There is an old iron gate that is thrown open, and a dark dirty alley leading to a neglected looking courtyard.

"Go in here," says Thor, pointing to the alley.

"Are we allowed to do this?" says Amy. It doesn't look like a regular alley. There is an archway above the entrance. "I don't think we should go in there. It looks like private property."

"For Heaven's sake, you can say you're just turning around," says Beatrice.

"Grandma?" says Amy.

"Go," says Beatrice.

Amy pulls into the alley, just up to the iron gate, and Thor says. "Stop here!"

Opening the door, he turns to them. "In a moment, I'm going to get back in the car. As soon as I do, pull forward. It's very difficult to keep the gate open."

Thor gets out and goes a few feet more into the alley. For a moment he bows his head and stands motionless. Then he flings out his hands as though pulling back a curtain. He moves quickly to either side, raising his hand, as though pulling the imaginary curtain back a little further.

Behind her, Beatrice is leaning forward. "Maybe this is crazy, Amy, but it can't hurt to indulge him, can it?"

Amy sighs and rubs her eyes. For the first time since this episode began, she feels genuinely sad for him. He did save her life. He's obviously mentally ill, probably schizophrenic, and he can't help that.

She takes a breath. She needs to get him to a doctor. They have treatments for schizophrenia now that are much better than in the past. He saved her life and she does owe him.

She blinks. She saw his armor, and the wolf, and the fire... maybe she needs drugs, too?

Ahead of her, Thor turns around quickly and runs back to the car. Opening the door he jumps into his seat. "Go now!" he shouts, shutting the door.

Amy sighs. "Here goes nothing," she says pulling forward. She hits the gas gently and drives forward...and the front of the car disappears.

"What!" screams Amy, putting her foot on the brake. "Oh!" says Beatrice.

"Just go!" yells Thor.

And Amy isn't sure why, but she hits the accelerator. Maybe it is her disbelief that propels her, because she certainly wouldn't have driven forward if she actually believed her car had dematerialized in front of her.

As the car goes forward, the dashboard, and then the steering wheel, disappear under her hands, and Amy is alone, surrounded by all the colors of the rainbow for the briefest of moments, her foot on the pedal of what would be the gas pedal if...

...and then her foot is on the gas pedal, behind her Beatrice is screaming, and next to her the man who still might be crazy is bracing his hands on the dash. "Stop!" he shouts.

Amy hits the brake.

Thor-Loki-Whoever, Beatrice, and Amy all take a deep breath. Fenrir whimpers.

"Have you recovered from your shock?" says Whoever-It-Is.

She had let the wheel go a little bit, and they might have run off the road. Amy turns her head to him. He's wearing armor again.

Her hands are shaking. "No," Amy says. "I really don't think so." Her eyes go to the window. Outside is a road, only a little wider than the alley — definitely not made for two way traffic. For some reason she isn't surprised it is yellow brick. On either side of the road is a dense forest. But...she peers either way. On one side it is dense and foreboding. On the other side it is open and light, and she has the urge to crack open the cooler and declare it time for a picnic right away.

He takes a long breath and rubs his face. "How can I help you recover?"

Amy looks around. "Can I get out?"

Thor-Loki-Whoever looks at the sun. "I would say yes, but

it would be best if we reach our destination before sunset."

Amy looks towards the dark wood and then looks back to her grandmother. She is looking in the same direction.

"That side doesn't look friendly, Loki," says Beatrice.

"Exactly," says Thor-Loki-Whoever-It-Is, his voice grim.

Amy puts her foot gently on the gas. "Loki," she says. He really might be Loki.

"Exactly," says the man sitting next to her, and this time she can hear the smirk in his voice.

Amy wills herself to breathe and keep her eyes on the road. Which is hard. She wants to stop and look. The trunks of the trees look lavender on the light side, the leaves almost blue. On the dark side, the tree trunks look so purple they are nearly black.

"There was color when we...crossed," says Beatrice. "Like a rainbow — "

"Yes," says the man who actually might be Loki. "Time acts like a prism at the edge of the World Gates."

"The rainbow bridge," says Beatrice quietly.

Loki tilts his head. "I believe that humans did call it that once."

"The light," says Amy. "The light here is different." Everything seems a little bit blue.

"The star that is this planet's sun is much older. I believe you would call it a white dwarf," says Loki.

"Oh," says Amy. She blinks. "We're on another planet."

"Yes. In a whole other solar system," says Loki.

"My, my," says Beatrice. Amy looks in the rear-view mirror and sees her patting Fenrir on her lap. "My, my."

For a few minutes, Amy drives in silence, too overwhelmed to speak. Beatrice must feel the same because she says nothing. After a while, Amy hazards a glance over at... Loki. His mouth is set in a firm line, his eyes focused far ahead. He looks handsome, noble even.

"Can you drive faster?" he says. The question sounds genuine, not like he's second guessing her driving skill.

Amy looks down at the speedometer. She's going all of 20 miles per hour. "Can I expect any oncoming traffic?" The road is narrow and straight, and there are a few rolling hills that could be dangerous.

He closes his eyes. "There is none for at least 30 miles."

Amy glances sideways at him. "How do you know?"

He tilts his head and then blinks. When he speaks he sounds slightly awed. "Astral projection. The concept has entered your vocabulary in the last sixty years. Even though you're incapable of it."

She's on another planet, on a yellow brick road; astral projection doesn't seem like that much of a stretch of the imagination. "Good enough," she says and hits the accelerator.

For a few minutes, no one says anything. She glances and sees Loki's eyes focused on the road, his mouth a thin line. She focuses directly ahead, her brain churning.

"Why so solemn?" says Loki suddenly with joviality that sounds a little forced. "From you, Amy, I would expect it, but from you, Beatrice — "

He turns towards the back seat and then says softly. "She appears to be asleep."

Amy peeks in rear view mirror. Beatrice is slumped slightly to the side, her head bent, her eyes closed. Amy looks at the clock in the car. "Yes," she says. "She normally takes a nap this time of evening."

"This isn't exciting to her?" says Loki.

Amy tilts her head. "It is exciting, maybe so exciting she needs a mental break...and..." Amy bites her lip. "People tend to nap a little bit more as they get older, and then not sleep so well at night. That doesn't happen to...your people?"

"We don't get old," says Loki.

"Oh," says Amy. She tilts her head. "Lucky." She goes back to focusing on the road. Another planet...and Loki said something about time bending at the edges of the World Gate so —

Loki sighs loudly. "Come now, there will be plenty of time for silence when you're dead, and I'm..." He waves a hand dramatically, "Gagged with wire or stuck in a cave. Surely you have questions for me?"

Amy's eyes widen. "Sorry, I'm just over here quietly revising everything I thought I knew about the universe."

He chuckles. "What a novel way of expressing it."

And then Amy has a thought. "Astral projection isn't one of your powers in the myths, but it is in the movies and comic books."

"I'm not sure I'm clear on how comic books and movies differ from myths," says Loki. "Except in the medium."

"Well, myths exist for the purpose of explaining the universe and imparting moral values," says Amy.

"Don't leave out entertainment," says Loki.

"Okay, and entertainment," says Amy. "And comic books and movies, well, the type of movie and comic book we're discussing, are for entertainment."

Out of the corner of her eye she can see Loki turning towards her, puzzlement on his face. "They don't impart moral values or attempt to explain the universe?"

Amy is about to say no, but then she blinks. "Actually...I

guess they do. But in a more round-a-bout way."

"Myths aren't exactly straightforward," says Loki.

"Touché," says Amy, scowling at the road in front of her.

"...or completely accurate," he mutters.

Amy smiles. "Yeah...no shape shifting. Right. Are you Thor's brother? In the comic books you are."

There is a snort. "No."

Amy grips the steering wheel and narrows her eyes. "What about Sif's hair." It's probably the most famous Loki myth. Sif was Thor's wife. Loki cut off her hair as a prank and paid dearly for it, if she remembers right.

She can hear the grin in his voice when he says, "Snip! Snip!"

"Really?" Amy says, twisting her hands on the steering wheel. "Why?" It sounds positively childish.

"To prove that she was a lying, cheating whore."

"How does cutting someone's hair prove they're a whore?" says Amy, gripping the wheel more tightly.

"It is the traditional punishment for female adulterers."

Remembering the story as her grandfather used to read it to her, Amy scowls. "So you sneak up on her in a glade and cut off her hair and that is supposed to prove she is a ho?"

There is a moment where the only sound is the hum of the engine. And then Loki erupts into what can only be described as cackles. "I didn't sneak up to her in a glade. I facked her!"

Amy's eyes go wide. "Facked?"

"Am I getting the verb right? Fac, from the Latin, 'to do'. Oh, wait, no that isn't right. I fuck — "

"I understood!" says Amy. She glances at him, her mouth agape.

He is blinking at her, smiling, looking very pleased. "It

was really very selfless of me. No one really appreciates that. Everyone knew she was a whore, but no one else was brave enough to bring it to Thor's attention. Well, except Odin, but he went about it in this convoluted way where he disguised himself as an old man..." There is a snort. "...like that was difficult. And told Thor to his face, but as a stranger. I delivered proof."

She thought he was handsome? She thought he looked noble? Amy's lips curl up in disgust. "Wasn't Thor, like, your best friend?"

There is silence again. Amy glances over and immediately looks back at the road. She swears his eyes are glowing. "No," says Loki, and the air seems to ripple with his voice. "No, not then. Not at all."

Loki is close to 50 earth years old. He and Thor, not much younger, are waving goodbye to a group of happy human peasants who are jumping up and down and waving at them. The humans haven't changed since Loki's first visit here. They are small, dirty, smelly, and lacking many teeth. But their love is still palpable — which keeps Loki from sneering at them, or picking disdainfully at the troll guts sticking to his armor.

Said troll lies dead behind Thor and Loki. It was a particularly large creature, nearly as big as an Earth Asian elephant — they had a few in the gardens of Asgard when Indian clothing and architecture were in vogue.

"Heimdall! Bring us home!" Thor shouts to the sky.

There is a flash of light, a blur of color, and then Loki and Thor are facing Heimdall in the great circle of Midgard's World

Gate on Asgard.

"Four times!" roars Thor with a smile on his face. "Four times I've been to Midgard troll hunting and not once did I find a troll. The one time I bring Loki, this beast — " he gestures with his hand towards the felled troll. "— this beast sets upon us immediately."

"It is a fine trophy, my Lord," says Heimdall, and his voice holds only reverence. Since Thor's return to court, Odin's bastard son has done nothing but make friends. Mostly because Baldur the beautiful, crown prince, son of Odin and Frigga, has taken a shine to his "big brother" and declared Thor "fitting to be in a court among Gods." Baldur possesses a type of magical glamour that not only makes him beautiful, but allows none to gainsay anything he says. Even Frigga has decided she likes Thor now.

Before Loki knows what is happening, Thor swats Loki's back with his hand. Stumbling forward, Loki barely manages to keep his feet. "From now on you come with me on every troll hunting expedition, Loki!"

"Lovely," says Loki, scowling down at the troll innards on his armor. Not that he doubted it would be otherwise. Just before this trip Odin informed Loki that his job as retainer now was to accompany Thor on all his quests.

"We should tell Baldur!" Thor declares, pulling Loki by the arm away from the World Gate. "We'll invite him to come with us on our next adventure."

Loki's stomach twists and he scowls. He detests Baldur. He detests that everyone thinks Baldur is beautiful, brave and wise. He detests that they think Baldur is good. And he detests that Mimir has suggested that the reason for this seething dislike is jealousy...and that there may be some truth to that.

Loki would never be accused of being ugly, but his 'fair

countenance' is almost an insult in itself. He doesn't look as roughly hewn or as square in the jaw as a typical Aesir, or even Jotunn. He's only of average height, and he's too thin, despite the fact that only Thor's appetite is a match for his.

And Loki's not considered brave. He's simply not much good at feigning battle lust or interest in killing trolls. If he wasn't ordered by Odin to watch after Thor, he would have spent the last few days in the library — he'd really like to master astral projection.

Finally, absolutely no one would consider Loki wise. He has too much fun with his magic. Loki knows he shouldn't take such delight in making himself appear like a Valkyrie upon occasion, or pulling the occasional flower from Odin's nose, but he just can't help himself.

Looking for any way to avoid a run in with Baldur, Loki says, "Shouldn't you go home to see your wife Sif first?"

"No, no, no," says Thor, walking briskly towards the palace, now under the illusion of Roman Golden Age architecture. "She'll understand. She is a fine wife, Loki, and doesn't begrudge me a bit my adventures and traveling — this is just a bit more of the journey."

Loki raises an eyebrow. She doesn't begrudge it probably because it leaves more time for her whoring. Sif is so easy with her affections, even Loki is uninterested in her.

Thor smiles and looks sideways at Loki. "But perhaps you'd just like to see your Lady Sigyn?"

"She is not my lady," says Loki , feeling heat rise to his face. Are his affections so obvious? Sigyn left the court for a few decades to live in the realm of Alfheim — the stay has given her an interesting perspective on a foreign culture and on Asgard's own. She is a rather fascinating companion for conversation. And she still *seems to fancy Loki, maybe because Loki occasionally protected her with his magic when they were children, or maybe because she hasn't been steeped in court gossip — Loki does have a bit of a reputation. It is pathetic, but her genuine warmth towards him makes Loki go absolutely soft inside. And although he protests her decline of his physical advances he actually rather respects her for it. How many times after a physical conquest has he decided the prize was too dull to be worth keeping? Even Freyja for all her beauty and charm was rather a bore after a while.*

Loki blinks. Perhaps Sigyn does know his reputation.

"She hasn't hooked you yet then!" yells Thor, slapping Loki's back again jovially. Loki tries not to wince; it takes effort. "But she will!"

Loki keeps his eyes forward. The idea of being hooked by Sigyn is strangely not as unsettling as it should be.

They veer away from the palace proper to Briedablick, Baldur's hall. As Briedablick comes into view, Loki scowls again. He's heard the place is quite beautiful to others' eyes; everyone tells Loki it glows. All Loki can see is the dark swirl of Baldur's magic around the massive gray stone structure as they approach. As usual, when he is around Baldur, he feels the hairs on the back of his neck rise.

A few minutes later they are ushered into the foyer by a servant who bows and says, "I will go inform my master you are here, Thor." Tipping his head first to Thor and then Loki, he leaves.

From down the hall in the opposite direction of the servant's departure comes a feminine squeak and a rough male gasp.

Thor's eyes go wide. "The servant went the wrong way!" he says delightedly.

Rolling his eyes at Thor's childishness, Loki says, "So it would seem." *Tipping his head in the direction of the exit, he says,* "We should go."

Another male grunt echoes in the foyer.

Snickering like a little boy, Thor doesn't move. "Who do you think is sampling Baldur's beauty right now?"

Loki's jaw tenses and he stares at the large man before him. Despite the fact that Baldur likes Thor, Loki doesn't hate him. Thor is loud, gregarious, and far too trusting. But he actually complimented Loki on an illusion he cast to confuse the troll they killed — it is nice to have his abilities are appreciated for once.

And Thor isn't stupid, no matter how he tries to hide his brain on occasion. They had a decent conversation about Troll nesting habits as they started out on their quest. Loki thinks he could actually like Thor, if he were to let himself. Even Mimir has said that Thor has the potential to be Loki's ally and true friend... and Loki can see that happening, if he just plays along and is nice.

But he can't quite do it. Smirking, Loki says, "Well, I think we can safely assume it isn't his mother."

Thor tilts his head, his childish grin fading.

Lifting an eyebrow, Loki crosses his arms over his chest and leans against the wall. "But other than that...really it could be anyone."

"I think you insult Baldur and a great many virtuous women," *says Thor, a furrow settling in his brow.*

Loki should stop, should apologize. Instead, he lets the truth slip from his lips. "Oh, I suppose the old men are probably safe, and probably the livestock, too." *His lips quirk.* "Maybe."

Thor steps forward, his face going a little red. "End this jest now, Trickster."

And Loki should, because Thor, like everyone but Loki, is blind to Baldur's shortcomings. Thor doesn't see how Baldur's charms, illusory though they are, are irresistible to all of Asgard. Thor doesn't see how Baldur abuses them.

Loki shouldn't test Thor this way, shouldn't set himself up to lose a potential comrade. There is a loud grunt from down the hall. Thor turns his head, momentarily distracted.

Loki should apologize. But he can't.

There is the sound of a door creaking. And then there is the sound of soft feminine footfalls. Thor, looking in the direction of the footsteps, smiles. It isn't a friendly smile.

Curious despite himself, Loki lets his gaze go down the hall... and sees a rumpled Sigyn emerging.

Loki's mouth drops. He feels like he may throw up.

Thor pulls away from Loki to let Sigyn pass. Her eyes go up to Thor's and her face reddens. And then her eyes meet Loki's.

Her face crumples into a look of confusion and sadness. "Loki... I..."

Loki's mouth goes to a hard line, and he looks away from her.

From the corner of his eye, he sees her bow her head. Turning, she runs out the door.

Thor laughs lowly. "You should see your face."

Loki hears a grinding noise...it's his own teeth. He is suddenly angrier at Thor than he is angry at Sigyn or even Baldur. Sigyn was obviously charmed by Baldur's glamour, like everyone else. Baldur was just an ass, like always, and Loki expected no better from him — nor can Loki retaliate against the crown prince.

But Thor...Loki had hoped better of Thor. He had hoped for the bastard's friendship — some loyalty, some understanding. Loki uncrosses his arms and steps away from the wall towards the larger man. The air between them seems to shimmer. Thor narrows his eyes and his hands ball into fists.

At that moment Baldur comes down the hall. "Oh, brother!

Loki!" Baldur says, and both Thor and Loki turn. Baldur is
adjusting his shirt. Loki has seen paintings of Baldur, he knows
what other people see, a crown of golden curls, tanned golden
skin, blue eyes on a face chiseled like a roman sculpture, broad
shoulders and height nearly as tall as Thor's. Loki sees a tangle
of light brown hair, a slightly pudgy face with narrow hazel eyes
and a soft body only as tall as his own.

"Loki," says Baldur, smirking slightly, though Loki has no
doubt he appears to be smiling benevolently to Thor. "I think you
know Lady Sigyn?"

"No," says Loki. "Not well."

He shoots a sidelong gaze toward Thor, daring him to con-
tradict him.

Thor says nothing. But he smiles, a knowing, cruel smile.

That smile changes everything.

Later that night at the banquet, Loki stands behind Odin
at the table, behaving like a truly proper retainer — albeit a
slightly drunk one. Thor is boasting of his exploits to a crowd of
happy admirers. In a far corner, Sif has her own admirers. Sigyn
is nowhere to be seen.

Odin, deep into his cups, slams his goblet down on the table.
The clang is drowned out by the sound of Thor's laughter further
down the table. Glaring in the direction of Sif, Odin snarls. "I
have warned him about her. He is becoming a laughingstock!"

Pushing back from the table, Odin growls and stands from
his chair. "I can't watch this."

Pursing his lips, Loki says, "If you permit me, sire, I'll take
care of it."

Snorting, Odin says, "Good luck." And then the giant man
turns and storms from the hall.

As soon as Odin has left, Loki walks over to Sif.

"Here to grace me with your silver tongue, Trickster?" the lady asks.

A reputation can be a helpful thing. Loki smiles. Very shortly afterwards he is in Sif's bedchamber.

After the "lady" falls asleep, Loki trims her golden locks. Gathering them in his hands, he ties them in one of her own ribbons. When Thor returns home Loki is waiting for him at the front door.

As he throws the shorn locks, the traditional symbol of an unfaithful wife, at Thor's feet, Loki smiles as sweetly as he can. "You should see your face," he says.

He completely expects the beating that comes next.

What he doesn't expect is for Hoenir and Mimir to be so unsympathetic when he comes crawling to the hut for help.

"You did what!" Mimir screeches. Loki winces from where he lays atop Hoenir's workbench, the self-satisfied smile slipping from his lips.

Hoenir slaps a hand down hard on a rib he is repairing. Loki's eyes go wide. Hoenir is actually scowling at him. Hoenir never scowls at him.

"I gave Thor proof of his wife's infidelity," says Loki, and Hoenir's hand comes down hard on another rib.

"You're supposed to be helping me fix that," says Loki lifting his head.

Hoenir just raises an eyebrow.

"You're lucky to be alive," says Mimir. "Do you know what you would do if someone slept with your wife?"

Raising an eyebrow, Loki drops his head on the bench. "As I don't have a wife and am unlikely to acquire one — "

"I'll tell you what you'd do!" Mimir says, voice trembling. "You'd cut him up into little pieces, that's what you'd do."

Loki blinks...there is something in that, something he can't quite place. He raises his head.

Mimir's face is livid. "And then you'd take all those pieces and flush them all down the —— "

"Mimir!" Odin's voice rings through the hut.

Loki's blood goes cold.

"Don't talk about that, Mimir," and Loki blinks because he almost thinks he hears worry in Odin's voice. But a few moments more and Odin is leaning over him. He doesn't look worried. Oddly, he doesn't look as angry as he did after Baldur's birth. He looks more...disgusted.

"You told me he was turning into a laughingstock," Loki says. "I told you I'd take care of it, and I have. I delivered proof that —— "

"Sif has told everyone you used your magic to sneak in on her while she slept," says Odin.

"And people believe that?" says Mimir. "From that trollop?"

Odin's eyes don't leave Loki's. "What matters is what Thor thinks. He believes his wife. Which is lucky —— otherwise you could be tried for treason."

Loki swallows, his brow furrowing. He was only obeying orders. The fickleness and duplicity of royalty.

"—— but he is only requesting your banishment," says Odin, his eyes narrowing.

The breath catches in Loki's throat. Odin doesn't mean banishment to Alfheim, Jotunheim, Vaneheim or any of the other civilized worlds. He can only mean Midgard. There is a very small part of him that wants to accept that fate, sees it almost as an open door from a cage, but his rational mind tells him what he would be accepting is a short, painful life, and death by plague —— or in his case, more likely hunger.

Odin's lip curls up. "Fix this, Loki." He stares down at Loki for a few moments more, and Loki feels himself shrinking. And then Odin turns and strides from the room.

Loki looks at Hoenir. He doesn't meet his eyes. He looks to Mimir, and the head winces. "You owe Sif, Thor and Odin a very big apology."

Staring at Amy, Loki feels the heat of Thor's first betrayal, that first cruel laugh, itching beneath his skin. How could he have trusted Thor after that?

Beatrice's voice startles Loki out of his dark reverie. "So did you get Thor his hammer, Sif the golden wig, Odin Daupnir and Gungnir — and the boat for Frey?"

"Daupnir, Gungnir, boat?" says Amy.

Loki smiles a brittle smile. "Daupnir is a lovely little ring. The boat is called Skidbladnir. It has a clever way of folding into time so that all of it that remains in real-time can fit in the palm of your hand."

Amy's face lights up, "It sounds kind of like the TARDIS!"

"Tardis?" says Loki, somewhat amazed that she seems to have grasped the concept at all. Humans usually didn't.

"It's a phone booth," says Beatrice.

"Bigger on the inside than outside," says Amy. "And it can travel through space and time too. Can Skidbladnir do that?"

Loki blinks. "Humans have such a vessel?"

"No, no, no," says Amy. "It's just a story." She frowns a little. "Just the way you described Skidbladnir, I thought it could be true."

Slightly disappointed, Loki says, "Other than its

compactibility, Skidbladnir is just a boat. We used it for camping trips. Until Odin gave it to Frey, chief of the Vanir."

"What about Gungnir, the spear that can hit any mark?" says Beatrice.

Tapping his chin, Loki says, "I did give that to Odin, but that was a different...adventure." Another one of his under-appreciated acts of self-sacrifice. Really, Odin should have appreciated what Loki did for Thor. It's not like sleeping with Sif was any great prize.

"Did the dwarf sew up your lips?" says Beatrice.

"Grandma!" says Amy, sounding absolutely scandalized. The gifts to Odin, Thor and Sif were made by two rival clans of dwarfs in a contest. The prize was Loki's head. At the last minute Loki convinced the winner that since only his head had been promised, it couldn't be detached at the neck. Said dwarf chose to sew up Loki's mouth in lieu of decapitation.

He's not sure exactly why Amy sounds so disapproving, but he senses an opportunity for comedy, or at least shock value.

With just the barest bit of concentration, he creates an illusion of wire stitches over his lips. Turning to Amy, and Beatrice he says, "Mmmphhhff!"

Beatrice sits back in her seat, hand over her mouth.

Amy gasps. "How can you even joke about that?!"

Loki tilts his head. The serious answer, the truthful answer, is how can he not? Joking about pain is the only weapon he has. It is the way he thumbs his nose up at the universe. The way he proves he is unbroken, and if not the god of mischief, then at least mischief's master.

But that isn't the funny answer.

He creates an illusion of himself in the backseat next to

Beatrice and lets that projection say, "Don't worry, m'lady. I am not offended by my joke."

"Ahh!" says Beatrice looking frantically back and forth between the illusion of Loki and Loki's real self.

The car almost swerves off the road. "Don't do that without warning me!" says Amy.

"Mmmphhhff," says Loki's real self, still feigning the stitches.

"Don't you people believe in proportional punishment?" Amy shoots him a glance that looks angry, hurt and scandalized all at once.

Loki tilts his head. In the scheme of things, that physical agony was small. He had done a wrong. He paid a price. It was logical. There were other pains, other slights that were random and unjust. They hurt more. But he cannot think of them, much less speak of them. Instead, he lets his astrally-projected self lean forward and whisper near her ear. "But if I hadn't had my lips sewn shut I wouldn't have learned the art of astral projection — out of sheer desperation to wag my tongue."

Beatrice snorts.

Loki lets the illusion of himself and the stitches fade. "And if Thor hadn't had the opportunity to hold me down while the stitches were put in, he might not have felt that he'd recovered his honor and we might never have become friends."

Amy shoots him a look that communicates both revulsion and disbelief.

But Thor and Loki had been friends, hadn't they? They'd both risked their lives for one another. And for a long time Thor's friendship had surely helped ease Valli and Nari's dealings with other Asgardians. They had been known more for Thor's patronage, and less as Loki's sons.

In the end what good had it done them, though? Even, brave, noble, supposedly honest, Thor had caved to Odin.

Loki clenches his fists. He cannot believe that Valli and Nari have met their ends. They are somewhere, alive, if not well, and wherever they are he will find them. Loki is very good at finding lost things, and the more impossible the task, the more likely it is he will succeed. Even Odin gives him that.

"So..." says Amy, eyes focused on the road ahead. "Can you tell us what we're going to do when we find gala drill?"

"Gala drill?" says Loki. A party and a drill? He scratches his ear... Did he hear right, or lose the thread of magic? Something tickles in the back of his mind

"You know, elf queen, in the books?" says Amy.

"And movies!" Beatrice pipes in.

"Ahhh...a name from a new myth," says Loki, the tickle becoming an itch. There is something about the name that feels almost, but not quite right.

Amy blinks. "I guess, maybe."

Shaking his head, Loki says, "No king or queen of the elves would reveal their true name. It would mean sacrificing too much of their power." Lifting his eyebrows, he tilts his head. "And believe me, power isn't something elven monarchs are keen on relinquishing."

Amy leans forward in her seat. She isn't wearing the figure-flattering shirt she wore the other day. What she is wearing now is baggy, and goes too far up her chest. Loki has no idea why someone with such astonishing breasts would want to hide them.

"Uh....is she going to be unhappy to see us here?" Amy says, looking nervously out the window.

"You and Beatrice? Oh, no, you are fine. The elves resented

Odin's orders to withdraw from your realm. They saw it their duty to play an active role in shaping human culture. They'll be delighted to see you. Me, on the other hand…" He puts a hand to his chin, and taps contemplatively. "I will need a disguise."

"The elf queen can't read hearts?" whispers Amy quietly.

Startled by the question, Loki turns to her. "Actually, the elf queen can read hearts, or minds rather. I'm sure that she'll see through the disguise, but it will confuse her court, and give her plausible deniability should Odin pay her a visit."

"You're on the outs with Odin already?" says Beatrice.

Choosing to ignore that question, Loki says, "As for what I want with the elf queen…I want a simple exchange of information."

He sees Amy's eyes lift to the rear view mirror and realizes she and Beatrice are exchanging a glance.

Let them wonder. He has been more than accommodating.

Amy squeezes Car's steering wheel. "What sort of disguise?"

Loki tilts his head. "The best disguise is like the best lie. As close to the truth as possible." He concentrates. His armor with its magical camouflage is too fine to belong to just any ordinary soldier. He dulls it to steel, painted dark gray. His hair he changes to brown, his chin and nose he broadens, and he increases his height and the width of his shoulders.

"Whoa," says Amy, "you were big enough already."

Unable to resist a chance to jest, Loki smirks. "Yes, yes, I was," he says in a deep, husky voice.

Amy tilts her head. "What does that mean?"

Before Loki even has a chance to purse his lips at her disappointing inability to grasp that little bit of sly innuendo,

Beatrice hits him on the back of the head.

That's more like it!

"Argh!" Loki screams, feigning pain. He turns and smiles at Beatrice. She scowls at him.

"Oh, my God," says Amy.

Loki smirks at her. "I'm not really a god, but I'll pretend to be one for you."

Beatrice hits him again. "Argh!" Loki cries, but he is unable to suppress a wide grin. There's nothing like a bit of comedy to take one's mind off a daunting quest.

"Was that an allusion to penis size?" Amy says, hands tightening on the steering wheel so hard her knuckles turn white.

Loki's smile drops. Cringing in genuine distaste he says, "Must you be so anatomical?"

Amy is silent for a moment. Dipping her chin and scowling, she begins to chant. "Penis, penis, penis."

Beatrice whacks him over the head again.

"...penis, penis, penis..."

"Hit her, not me!" Loki cries.

"...penis, penis, penis," says Amy, looking angrier and angrier.

"You started it," the old woman replies.

Huffing, Loki says, "To return to the previous topic — "

Amy stops her chant.

"Thank you," says Beatrice.

"I will not try to disguise my Frost Giant nature, but I will go by the name of Fjölnir Thorsbruter. It's a common name among Frost Giants in Thor's legion, and won't raise suspicion."

"You look like a Frost Giant now?" says Amy, looking him

up and down.

"Of course," says Loki, slightly vexed.

"You're not blue. In the movies Frost Giants are blue."

Loki stares at her, completely at a loss for what she could be talking about.

From the backseat comes Beatrice's voice. "Oh, my, how lovely."

Amy's eyes go back to the road. They have just come over a gentle rise, and now in the distance beyond cultivated fields, orchards, pasture lands, and a wide river, Alfheim's only city in the domain of the light elves is on full display.

"It's beautiful," Amy says.

Loki gazes at the city in the distance. Set into the side of a mountain, it sits beside the border road. The city's architecture is reminiscent of human European architecture from the 12th century. The entire city is made from white stone. Thick walls and ramparts with small slitted windows encircle more buildings with the same small slitted windows. There are peaked tile roofs, all in green. At the center of the city, rising up above the other buildings, is the castle proper. Dark green ivy climbs along walls; trees with lavender leaves lift their crowns alongside the buildings.

Loki hasn't been here in over a hundred years. Squinting, he looks hard for any changes in the scenery, but even the ivy and trees within the city gates remain exactly as he remembers them. Absolutely nothing has changed.

"I suppose it's quaint," he says. He's not sure how the humans can be impressed. Chicago, with its riot of styles from only the last century or so, displays more variety of architecture in a single block than the whole city of Alfheim. And Alfheim's city is so small. It is only a few miles wide and the tallest tower can't be over ten stories.

"Like a fairy castle," says Beatrice, her voice awed.

Loki snorts. "Well, technically — "

"Are those dinosaurs?" Amy says, looking out at the fields.

Loki follows her gaze. A few hadrosaurs dot the pastures, and two are being ridden in neat formation along the city's main wall. From afar they look a lot like the velociraptors Loki hatched so long ago. They have powerful hind legs and smaller forelimbs. They do not walk on their hind limbs exclusively though, and their mouths are beak-like. They also get much larger than velociraptors — up to the size of a bus.

"Yes," says Loki.

He blinks. He's a bit surprised English has a word for dinosaur. Loki doesn't know English particularly well. He uses magic to translate languages. On Asgard they call it "The Gift of Tongues." Humans might call it a "spell," but it's more a state of mind. Loki doesn't fight the magic that flows through Amy and Beatrice that wants to interact with the appropriate neurons in his brain's speech centers.

The trick has its limitations: if there is no corresponding word between languages, translations become difficult. But now there is a common English word for dinosaurs! Fascinating. Staring at the creatures, he realizes there is even an English word for specific dinosaur species. "Specifically, hadrosaurs, harmless herbivores," he adds. Harmless unless they step on you, of course.

Tensing at the wheel, Amy looks nervously to the dark forest still on their left. "I don't have to worry about T-rexes or velociraptors, do I?"

Loki's mouth drops open. "You know what a velociraptor is?"

"I've seen Jurassic Park," says Amy. Voice rising tremulously she says, "Are there velociraptors here?"

"No," says Loki. "No....nasty creatures though, I'll give you that."

Amy turns her face quickly to him. She doesn't look relieved for some reason.

Puzzling over that, Loki looks out at the road and his eyes go wide. "Look out for the hadrosaur dung!"

Amy hits the brakes and they screech to a halt just in time.

"It's the size of a dog!" says Beatrice.

"It looks like bird poop," says Amy. "White...but really lumpy. I wonder if I could get a sample and take it back to school? We have a thermos, don't we? I have a friend from undergrad in the micro lab at UIC. We could compare the genome of the hadrosaur dung bacteria to the bacteria in bird guano. If elves were on Earth at one time, there is a possibility that the bacteria might share a common ancestor!"

Loki blinks.

"We probably don't have time for that, Dear. Right Loki?" says Beatrice.

Loki stifles a laugh at Beatrice's conspiratorial prompting, but he's more impressed than repulsed. It's something Hoenir would do — at this point Loki is quite inured to dung collection. Pursing his lips he says, "Maybe later. For now, perhaps you should drive more slowly? We are close enough to the castle for it to be safe after dark."

"Right," says Amy, steering the vehicle so it straddles the dung.

Loki hopes none gets on the axles; it is quite foul smelling. He sighs. Elves. No appreciation for any type of evolution.

CHAPTER 8

Amy is glad for the chance to slow down. It gives her a chance to look around. As they cross the neat fields of what looks like wheat, she can see little thatched cottages. She catches sight of goats, sheep, small shaggy horses, chickens — and sometimes hadrosaurs. From afar their scales are reminiscent of tropical birds, deep, almost iridescent green, with spots of red and yellow.

As they drive along, people — well, they look like people — come out of their little homes, take one look at them, and rush back inside. If they didn't seemed so terrified Amy would probably stop the car and get out — no matter how much Loki might protest.

They are just a few miles from the city proper, when two knights come riding up the road towards them. She thinks they are knights anyway. They are wearing armor like the kind she is accustomed to from the Art Institute, are seated on shaggy little white horses, and are carrying lances. Their faces and ears are covered, so despite their proximity she can't see if they're Elves.

"Um…" says Amy.

Loki, now looking like a very pale Conan the Barbarian, looks at the door. "Where is the window crank? I'd like to address them."

"The button," says Amy.

"What button?" says Loki.

"Switch," says Beatrice.

"Ahhhhh…." says Loki.

"Wait, I have a better idea," says Amy. Pressing a button on the side of the door, she opens the skylight.

"Perfect!" says Loki smiling broadly. "I love this machine." He looks at Amy, an expression of deep earnestness on his now broad barbarian face. "Do you think it could ever love me?"

Unsure if this is another one of his jokes, Amy just stares at him.

From the backseat, Beatrice says, "Loki dear, they're jostling their sticks."

Loki looks out at the knights who are raising their lances. "Just give me a minute," he says, and then he stands up next to Amy. It puts his hips rather too close to her face. Her cheeks go hot and she's on guard instantly. She's really glad he's busy talking to the knights; otherwise she's pretty sure he'd have a bit of innuendo to throw her way just now.

A knight gives a yell, and Amy blinks and straightens. The knight is pointing at her car with his lance.

The words coming out of Loki's mouth seem smooth, almost musical. But the knights raise their lances and then both of them are yelling at Loki. Amy starts gauging the feasibility of a three point turn. The sun is slipping down on the horizon, and Loki has warned against the wisdom of traveling the road at night, but...

From the direction of the castle eight more knights come riding out on horses, followed by knights on hadrosaurs at the rear. The giant creatures move relatively slowly, but they are intimidating. Loki is still talking, and the knights are still waving their lances.

Hand going to the gears, Amy gets ready to switch into reverse. "Loki! Should I turn around?"

Pulling himself back into the car, Loki smiles broadly at her. It's even more disconcerting than it should be since he's changed his appearance to be more Conan the Barbarian-esque. Her brain is having a little difficulty wrapping itself around the concept that it is still the wiry guy with red hair in there. She wants to pinch his cheek or something, to verify everything is real, but the timing is a little inconvenient. And he'd probably misconstrue it as flirting. He's still in the middle of the front seat and way too close to her.

"No, no, we're fine!" he says, his voice still his own. Amy's not sure if it makes the Conan thing better or worse.

"Nothing to worry about," he says. "They're just giving us an escort."

As he says that, the first two knights run around their car, turn around and turn their lances on them again. In front of them the other knights bring their mounts around so their steeds and their lances are perpendicular to the road.

"See," says Conan-esque Loki. "Nothing to worry about."

"Oh, dear," says Beatrice, summing up Amy's feelings exactly.

Falling back into his own seat, Loki-Conan waves a hand

forward. "Go ahead!"

Amy checks the rear view mirror. Going backwards doesn't seem much of an option. She puts her foot gently on the gas and drives through the gauntlet. There is a bridge just ahead of them, and a river as wide as an eight-lane highway beneath. Amy notices on the side of the river near the castle the water reflects the sky. On the side of the bridge where the water drains into the dark forest, the river is a muddy snake of churning brown and black. She follows the river's path into the dark forest with her eyes to where it seems to split into tributaries.

"The Delta of Sorrows," says Loki softly. She looks over at him and he's shaking his head, one side of his mouth curled up in a crooked smile. "Luddites and hypocrites," he mutters.

Amy blinks and focuses her attention ahead. The knights are falling into formation behind them.

"The first fork in the road past the river, take a right turn toward the castle," says Loki.

Amy swallows and nods. As they get closer to the castle, Beatrice says, "Oh, my, it's even lovelier up close."

And it is. It's hard for Amy to keep her eyes on the road. The tremendous white wall on her left is covered with dark green ivy. Blue flowers are interspersed with the leaves.

"Yes," says Loki. "You have to hand it to the elves, they can make even man-eating plants picturesque."

"Man-eating?" says Beatrice.

"Let's say you wouldn't want to try and scale the wall by climbing the ivy," says Loki.

"Oh," says Beatrice. "It is so pretty, though...I wonder if it would keep the squirrels away from the bird feeder outside our kitchen window?"

"Grandma!" says Amy.

"It's difficult to get clippings of the stuff," says Loki. "It bites."

"A shame," says Beatrice.

Before Amy can say anything, Beatrice lets out a gasp. They're closing in on the main gates of the city, and for the first time can see within. More knights are riding out, but others are holding back a crowd.

Amy pulls the car through the gates, into what seems to be a market square with brightly colored tents for stalls interspersed with lavender-leafed trees with white bark. Great buildings of white stone look over the square. They are able to see the people of the realm up close for the first time. They are slender, and not terribly tall. Most appear pale, but Amy sees every shade of skin tone. They seem to all be blessed with delicate, doll like features, and there is no mistaking the pointed ears.

"Elves..." breathes Amy.

Conan-Loki snorts. "You expected trolls?"

Neither Amy nor Beatrice bother to respond. A moment later the sun slips completely from the sky, and all around them great orbs of green light rise into the air until they reach a height just above the great wall around the city. The car's headlights become brighter.

From the crowd there is a collective, "Oooooh."

"Clever car," says Loki, patting the dash.

The elves in the market push against the knights holding them back and begin to smile and wave at Amy, Beatrice and Loki. Amy hears shouts rising up in the crowd. In the corner of her eye she swears she sees an elf raising his fist at the knights.

Amy cranes her neck for a better view, but Loki says, "Keep driving. The hadrosaurs can tip us over." He looks over his shoulder. "Or step on us."

That does wonders to focus Amy's attention.

They follow a knight through the market, and between buildings that are a few stories tall, the knights on hadrosaurs close behind them. In the glow of the orbs the white stone looks green. Some of the buildings have wide windows. Behind her Amy hears Beatrice say, "Oh, that looks like a dress shop, and that looks like toys maybe...Oh, my, the people are just darling."

Amy wishes she could look, but trains her eyes on the knight leading them. She tries to keep track of the way they're going. It's dark, and a little difficult to tell for sure, but it seems to be one main road that switches back on itself as it makes its way up the mountain.

They make a few more switchback turns and come to a street that has walls on both sides. On one side the wall is covered with the ivy and flowers.

"Oh, the shops are gone," says Beatrice.

"We're nearly on the palace grounds," says Loki.

The knight in front of them holds up a hand. Abruptly, the ivy on the wall slithers away like a mass of snakes and a metal gate is revealed. Beatrice gives a startled cry, and Amy swallows.

The gates swing open with a loud, metallic clang, the knight shouts, and Loki says, "Drive in."

Amy's foot is already on the gas. She eases through the gates. Up until this point they've been driving on a steady incline up the mountainside, but before her the ground plateaus. There are trees, bushes, and masses of tall flowering plants. The road leads to what can only be described as a palace — it rises up at least ten stories. Its delicate towers and walls crawl with more ivy. Above the road hover the green orbs. All along the road are elves standing at attention, wearing what looks like chain mail. From the palace more elves are coming. Even at a distance, Amy can see they are not wearing armor of any kind. Male and female, they wear clothing that looks medieval, but Amy's pretty sure that human medieval clothing did not glow.

The knight in front of them barks an order. "Time to get out," says Loki.

He turns to them, his features sharp. "Remember, I am Fjölnir Thorsbrutter." He tips his head. "If Odin finds out I am here, it will be difficult for me to return you to your realm."

Amy hears the back door open. "I don't know if I'd mind staying," says Beatrice as the retinue of elves in glowing gowns draws to a halt in front of them. "My, my." With that she climbs out of the car.

Loki looks at Amy, his eyes wide.

"Don't worry, Amy says. "I don't want to stay anywhere that doesn't have antibiotics." Or a good laboratory. What fun was dung if she couldn't analyze it?

Mouth grim, jaw hard, Conan-Loki says, "Smart girl."

An instant later he is standing outside on the golden road, smiling broadly.

Amy slips the key from the ignition and watches him. He's like a chameleon, and not just in the way he changes his physical appearance.

Stepping from the car, she takes a breath and pockets her keys and attached pepper spray. The air is cool, clear and untainted by the car's air freshener or vents. The sun may be gone, but everything still smells like sunlight and grass, and floral smells she can't quite place. She looks up past the orbs. The stars are bright, but the Big Dipper is nowhere to be seen. Her mouth drops open, and then she smiles at the wonder of it. She is on another world.

Smile still in place, she walks around to where Conan-Loki and Beatrice stand. One elf, a man dressed in subdued black who looks no older than Amy, is talking to Loki. The other elves are thronged around Beatrice.

"You human!" says a young man in a sing-song voice to Beatrice. His hair is golden and long. He is wearing long robes of dark blue velvet with embroidered stars that literally sparkle. He turns to Amy. "You, too! Come to feast!"

"First, clothes!" says a woman. Amy blinks. At her side is an elf woman with skin dark as ebony. She wears a dress of emerald green, cinched tightly at the waist, low cut on the front, with gold brocade along the neckline that seems to project its own light.

Small hands go to Amy's arms and pull her forward, but then a heavier arm drapes over her shoulder. Conan-Loki's voice whispers in her ear. "I told them I was accidentally drawn into your realm, and that I rescued you, and this is how you are repaying me. The only detail I've changed is my name. Fjölnir. Thorsbrutter. Don't forget."

Before Amy can even respond, Loki's arm is gone, and he's stepping around the crowd to the elf in black.

As the lady in emerald scoots up to Amy, Amy turns her head to see the man in blue, arm-in-arm with Beatrice.

Touching Beatrice's hair lightly, he speaks with an oddly lilting accent Amy can't place. "You like most beautiful gnome

I have ever seen."

Amy's eyes bug out, but Beatrice just giggles and smiles.

"My name Belladal," says the woman next to Amy in the same lilting tones as the man.

"Amy," says Amy, trying to keep her eyes on Conan-Loki, walking ahead of the throng, towering next to the elf in black.

"Aaay Meeee," says Belladal.

"Aaay Meeee," say the other elves in unison.

Amy turns her eyes to them for an instant. Beatrice and Amy are positively thronged now. She smiles and they gasp. "You many teeth for human!" says Belladal. Confused, Amy blinks. Turning her head she tries to find Loki, but he and the elf in black are nowhere to be seen. Before she even has a chance to process that thought or be afraid, great wooden doors ahead of them open and light spills out of the palace.

She hears the elf man next to Beatrice exclaim. "No, no, no! You not 85! Humans not live that long!" She can't hear Beatrice's response. Her eyes are nearly blinded by the golden light in the palace, and elves in much simpler attire are running out of the doors singing or maybe talking in musical tones.

"Dresses! You get dresses!" says Belladal. "Elves like humans. Not see so long! You like dresses! Music! Feast! Happy! Happy! Happy!"

"Happp—eeeee!" sing the elves.

And Amy isn't sure if it is magic, or just that everything is magical, but she begins to feel her heart lift, and her lips pull into a wide grin.

Beatrice slips her arm into Amy's as Belladal glides into the palace ahead of them, her dark skin warm and glowing in the light. Following the elven woman with her eyes, Beatrice shakes her head and whispers to Amy, "the elves have Negroes, too. I never would have expected that."

Amy squeezes her eyes shut and resists the desire to face-palm. Beside her Beatrice doesn't seem to even notice. She's chattering away with the elven man.

Amy sighs and opens her eyes. At least Beatrice didn't say anything about Belladal getting a position of lady or princess elf through affirmative action. She smiles ruefully; some of the magic of the place must be rubbing off after all.

An hour or so and a magically altered dress later, Amy's standing in a great hall. Lining the wall are tapestries that glitter, glow and almost seem to move. A giant orb of gold is suspended in the air. The floor beneath her feet is white polished stone. To one side of the room are large ornately carved doors that lead, she's told, to "big feast...little wait only." Music that sounds like harps and flutes is floating through the air, but she can't see any musicians. She looks around the room a little anxiously. She hasn't seen Loki since they entered the palace.

Fenrir isn't here either. During the dressmaking session an elf woman had taken the dog away — Belladal said it was "so small beast no smell like dead things." Amy would have protested more, but it was true, her little beast still stunk. Fenrir's supposed to be back in time for the feast, though. Looking around again, Amy pats her skirts and feels the comforting lumps of her key chain and pepper spray beneath the fabric.

At the other end of the hall Beatrice is sitting down on an elaborately carved wooden chair, a throng of elves around her. Grinning ear-to-ear, she looks beautiful. Her dress is palest rose with an elegant princess neckline. Her white hair is lifted up in a bun that is crowned with pale pink flowers. It occurs to Amy that Beatrice must seem far more exotic to them than Amy herself does. No one in the hall looks older than 25.

Amy looks down at her own dress self-consciously. It's very pretty, creamy with emerald green trim. But the neckline is painfully low and wide. She's afraid if she bends forwards she might spill out. She tried to ask for something more discreet, but her protests were met with laughter. "Why hide best feature?" Belladal had said. And then Belladal's expression had contorted to one of genuine curiosity. "Are you wet-nurse?"

Remembering that comment did nothing to ease Amy's self-consciousness now. The elves, male and female, crowded around her speaking in their musical tones and staring at her breasts doesn't help either. Different ideas about propriety, obviously. None of them seem to speak English the way Belladal or the elf man in blue are able to, so commenting on her embarrassment doesn't help.

Figures clad in black and gray emerging from a small door at the side of the hall catches her attention. It's Loki at last — still looking like a pale version of Conan the Barbarian. The elf in black is next to him. Grateful for a chance to escape her ogling little throng, Amy casts a smile around her, looks apologetically in the direction of Loki, and then back at them. The throng seems to understand because a narrow path opens up before her. She bolts through it without a backwards glance.

Loki catches her eye, says something to the elf in black, and then tilts his head towards a hallway off to the side. A few moments later Amy is there beside him. His armor is still the dark gray he changed it to in the car, and he's donned no other finery. His face is uncharacteristically pensive.

"What's wrong?" she asks, and he blinks.

"Nothing," he says. "I will be granted an audience with the queen during the feast." Her brows furrow slightly. She thinks they are alone in the small hallway, the noise of revelry at their backs, but she's not quite sure. Lowering her voice to a whisper, she leans close to him. "Are you worried she'll know who you are?"

Smiling a little sadly, he says, "I'm certain that she will. That isn't what disturbs me."

"Well, what then?" says Amy, a hand almost unconsciously going to his arm.

Not meeting her eyes, his lips quirk slightly, his expression looks sad instead of happy.

"I find myself nervous about the answer to my question," he says.

"You never told us what the question is," Amy says.

His eyes narrow, though the quirk of his lips doesn't disappear. "I try, as much as possible, to push it from my mind. If I think of it I might go mad." He looks so distraught, Amy has the urge to give him a hug.

Stepping back, he takes her hand. "But where are my manners? You look lovely."

From the great hall there is the sound of horns.

"Nice breasts," says Loki, barely audible over the din.

Amy's jaw falls. Every time she feels the slightest bit of sympathy for him, he just has to go and ruin it. "Did you just say nice breasts?"

He quirks an eyebrow. Leaning in he says, "Actually, I said nice dress."

Amy blinks and reddens; how foolish of her. She's about

to apologize when still holding her hand, his eyes drift down and his mouth stretches into a leer. "But now that you mention it...."

Her hand connects with his cheek a moment later with a satisfying smack.

Rubbing his cheek, he just grins at her.

Amy points at her eyes and says, "Focus."

The grin vanishes. "You're right, I can't be seen to be fraternizing with the help." He smirks. "Who knows, the queen may want to take advantage of my silver tongue."

"Huh?" says Amy, not seeing any connection.

The smirk vanishes.

Amy blinks.

Patting her shoulder, Loki sighs. "If I ever need to capture a unicorn I'll be sure to let you know."

Conan-Loki's inappropriate leers are immediately forgiven. "I would love to see a unicorn!"

Putting a hand to her back, he guides her towards the hall. "And I'm sure one would love to see you." As they step into the great hall, Loki says, "Dinner has just been called. I will see you later."

The elf woman who had taken Fenrir away during the dressmaking session approaches, Fenrir at her feet, bathed, groomed and looking — well, almost like a dog. "This way," the elf woman says.

Eyes going wide, Amy says, "You speak English!"

The elf blinks at her, as though surprised to be understood. "Yes. But secret, please?"

Amy tilts her head, curious. But all she says is, "Of course." She turns to look at Loki but he's already gone.

As the rest of the guests are herded into the dining hall, Lionel, the steward, leads Loki to a small antechamber dimly lit by dancing fireflies. It's furnished only with a tapestry on one wall, and two chairs facing one another, a low table in the middle. It is exactly the sort of thing Loki would have expected.

Closing the door behind them, Lionel presses his ear to it as though listening for something.

Loki tilts his head. Lionel meets his gaze, nods, and then moves quickly to the room's only window and draws the curtains. Putting his finger to his lips, Lionel moves to the opposite wall and draws back the curtain. Pressing against a few of the white stones in rapid succession, Lionel backs up. The stones seem to dissolve, as though made of sand, revealing a dark narrow passage.

Lionel gestures with his hands for Loki to enter.

Loki does not move. "Where are you taking me?"

Lionel is small and thin even for an elf. He swallows. "The queen will speak a few words at the feast, and then she will retire to her chambers. She will meet you there."

Loki stares at him for a few uncomfortably long heartbeats. Not because he doesn't believe Lionel's words — Loki can't read hearts, but he has a sense for lies. It is the truth, but still unbelievable. Loki is nowhere near the queen's station, whether a member of Thor's personal legion or as Odin's retainer...*former* retainer. Having him in her chambers would be scandalous, but it would explain the secrecy; and a secret passage would make perfect sense.

"If you like, I will go first," says Lionel.

"I would like," says Loki. Lionel may not be lying, but he wouldn't put it past a monarch to leave a surprise without their retainer's knowledge.

Lionel bows his head. Reaching into his pocket, he pulls out a dull olive orb. As he lifts it, it lights from within, casting the same green glow as the orbs outside the palace. And then Lionel steps into the dark passageway, Loki following.

Loki hears the tapestry fall back into place, and a sound like pebbles sliding together. When he looks behind him there is a seemingly solid wall.

After a few paces, the passageway changes to a stairway. The steps are low and narrow. Loki touches the walls. They are dry and cool beneath his slightly warm damp fingers. He can feel his pulse quickening. This is it. Soon he will know where his sons and Sigyn are, whether they are alive or dead.

Taking a deep breath, he tries to calm himself as best he can.

They have gone a few flights when the scent of stone and dust gives way to the smell of green living things, pine and sage maybe. It's not unpleasant at all. Loki suddenly has an overpowering sense of deja vu. He blinks. Prophecy is completely beyond him. He is over 1,000 years old. He may never have been in this stairway, but he has been in ones like it. Surely.

And yet...the fragrance. He takes a long breath. He is just anxious.

In front of him Lionel draws to a stop. Loki can't see what he does with his hands but the wall falls away, and they step from behind another tapestry into a living area. The smell of pine and sage is stronger, and there is also the smell of meat and fresh bread. There is a chandelier above that looks like a mass of long silver leaves. There are no candles or orbs set in it: the whole thing glows, casting a glow like moonlight. Below it are two chairs, and a table laden with food. Nearby Loki can hear the sound of falling water.

"Her Majesty's chambers," says the steward. He gestures to a seat. "Please, sit and eat your fill."

Loki's mouth is watering, but he doesn't sit down. He tilts his head to the sound of water. In his mind he pictures a living wall of lichens, a small spout emerging from it, and a stream of water falling into a semi-circular pool set flush in the floor. Turning, he walks quickly from the little room, Lionel at his heels, saying, "Stop! Wait!"

He steps into the next room over and draws up short. There are the wall and fountain just as he imagined them.

"Sir," Lionel says, "you are to wait in the other room."

Loki doesn't move. And then he sees it, magic, the same color as moonlight, spilling from behind his back.

"Leave us, Lionel," says a feminine voice as smooth and sure as water over rocks.

Loki and Lionel both turn. The elf queen approaches them. She wears a simple circlet on her brow. Her ears peek out from straight black hair. Her eyes are almond shaped, almost like a human from the continent of Asia, but they are nearly as light as Loki's own. Her features are fine, delicate and almost painfully symmetrical, like all of the elf race. She is as slender and willowy as a reed — not precisely his type, but undeniably beautiful.

Loki has seen her several times before. He's always looked at her from a distance, or from over Odin's shoulder as a retainer. She's never met his eyes before. She does now. Loki has the peculiar sensation of coming in from the cold to find a warm and welcome fire.

For some reason he almost says "Gala" aloud, but holds it back. Strange to be affected so by a silly human myth.

He tilts his head. This feeling of belonging, is it a trick of her magic?

"Yes, my Queen," Lionel says, drawing Loki from his reverie. Bowing quickly the retainer leaves the room.

"Loki, son of wildfire and the green and peaceful isle," says the elf queen.

He hasn't heard his heritage described that way before, but he doesn't argue. Bowing, Loki lets his disguise drop and prepares to kneel.

"Please," says the elf queen holding out a pale hand. "Don't."

Loki straightens. There is something in her voice, fear or apprehension; he can't tell.

"Why are you here?" she says coming forward, magic swirling in the air so much it warms his skin. She cannot possibly be afraid of him, her magic is so much stronger.

"I mean you no harm, your highness. I come only for an exchange of information."

"What information do you wish to give me?"

Loki tilts his head. "A pathway, from your realm to Asgard."

"I know many of those," she says dropping her eyes and moving quietly as a shadow so they are no more than a foot apart. That closeness should strike him as odd — but it doesn't, and that is truly odd.

"Ah, but this is a very strategic one, your highness. Right from the heart of your realm to just behind the throne of Odin himself."

The elf queen's eyes shoot up to his and then she looks aside and walks away. "I already know of such a pathway," she says.

Loki feels the first prickle of worry. "But this, your highness, this one...." He licks his lips. "It is very near, but so small you would never find it unless — "

"The one inside our wine cellar," she says.

Loki's eyes go wide. He feels as though the wind has been knocked out of him. He brings a hand to the chest plate of his armor and feels the press of his book tucked inside there. The queen's eyes follow the movement, and for an instant he thinks he sees something cruel and predatory flash in them. But then the look is gone, and her features again are cool and distant.

"Someone already bartered that piece of information to me...long, long ago," she says, her eyes dropping to the small pool in the floor.

She looks sharply at him, and then comes forward again. Tilting her head she says, "But I would hear your question anyways."

It takes a moment for Loki to process her words. No barter? No exchange? When do gifts ever come freely?

"Tell me," she says. And again she is very close, too close for decorum, and again it is a fact that hovers at the edge of his consciousness, something that should strike him as uncomfortable and off, but the feeling of her proximity is completely different. It's like a warm fire.

He closes his eyes. He sees Valli and Nari as children, with Helen — who he also lost. He cannot think them lost, too — or Sigyn, gone like his Aggie. "My sons, my ex-wife, Sigyn, I want to know where they are, " he says softly. She draws back, just a bit. Maybe he isn't speaking softly, maybe it just sounds faint over the angry pounding of his own heart.

"I don't know," she says, her gaze firm on his. "I cannot see everything. I am sorry."

She's not lying...and yet...

His next breath is too hard and too loud. He wants to turn away, but doesn't think he can. Valli and Nari's faces and the blackness of space flash before him. His sons...his beautiful sons.

The elf queen takes his arm, and that act of comfort is scandalous, ridiculous, coming from a queen. Not that he hasn't gotten women far above his station to do things far more scandalous — but not without trying.

"Come sit down," she says pulling him towards the chairs in the other room.

"I should go," he says. He doesn't know where.

"Odin does not know you're here," she says.

That is pure truth.

He lets himself be led and sinks down into the chair. She doesn't move away. Rubbing a hand on his shoulder she says, "Loki, Loki, Loki," as though practicing the word. Her touch is oddly familiar.

Almost unconsciously he takes her hand in his and she comes around so that she stands just to the side of him, very close. She leans down so their eyes are level; locks of her black hair fall down over her shoulders. "If I cannot give you the knowledge you need, at least let me give you comfort," she says, her face close to his.

When Loki jested with the human girl earlier about the elf queen taking advantage of his silver tongue, it had been just that, a jest, and nothing more. The queen was not known to take lovers casually, if at all. Even Baldur had tried and failed.

And yet...Loki looks at the pale skin where her neck meets the junction of her shoulders. He has the feeling that if he ghosts his lips there he knows exactly what sound she'll make. He looks at her lips and thinks he knows exactly how they will taste.

He pulls her closer and she doesn't resist. When he kisses her it isn't like a first kiss, laced with excitement and uncertainty. It's like comfort and homecoming. He needs those things.

And she tastes exactly as he thought she would.

Afterwards, when he feels a brief bit of peace, it feels natural to fall asleep with his arms draped around the elf woman he hasn't called anything less formal than "your Majesty." He dreams of a younger Alfheim, with a brighter, yellower sun, of gazing out the window of the palace at a mortal peasant man come to visit. The human smiles at Loki and it's warm, good humored and yet it fills him with dread.

His eyes snap open. He hears fast footfalls, and then the sting of sharp cold metal at his throat.

He looks up. The elf queen is there, holding his own blade against his neck with one hand, his book in the other.

This is not good.

The dining room is as grand as the other halls of the palace. More tapestries, another glowing orb in the ceiling, and a great table still piled high with food — even though the diners are mostly done.

Amy sits back in her seat, pleasantly full. Near her feet

Fenrir whines. Amy glances around. All eyes in the hall are trained on Beatrice, who is recounting the story of her life. Taking advantage of their lack of attention, Amy slips a piece of cheese to Fenrir.

The queen came into the hall a few hours ago. From a raised dais at the end of the table she bid Amy and her grandmother greetings in English nearly as perfect as Loki's, before addressing her own people and then taking her leave.

Amy was asked a few questions during the meal by Belladal, but Beatrice very quickly became the star of the show. Now Beatrice is telling the story of her life, how she was born to a formerly wealthy clothing merchant in the Ukraine. She has described her parents, her family and her friends in greater detail than Amy has ever heard. Amy is as enraptured as the elves are to hear previously unheard stories of her family's history. The tale is interrupted frequently by the elf man in blue translating for the rest of the table.

Beatrice comes to the part of how her family and friends were persecuted after the communists took power, and the elves hiss before the translation even starts. Startled, Beatrice, a few seats down and across the table, meets Amy's eyes. Next to Amy, Belladal says, "We know of these communists. Killers of kings, queens, lords and ladies...but not only just! Kill common people, too."

"Yes," says Beatrice nodding gravely at Belladal. "They caused a great famine."

"This we know not!" says the elf man. The whole hall goes silent, as though they are hanging breathlessly on Beatrice's words. When she finishes describing the Holodomor, the famine induced by Stalin that killed nearly 2.7 million people, the elf in blue begins to translate again. Amy notices he doesn't just address the people at the table, he also addresses the servants in the background.

For some reason it makes her stomach feel heavy.

At one point Belladal leans to Amy and whispers. "Your grandmother. So brave. Journey to lawless land no king. No queen. Much danger!"

Amy puts the crystal goblet in her hands down on the table. There is a sweet liquid within it — she's pretty sure it's alcoholic and wishes she could just drink some water. She is the designated driver after all. "We do all right," she says to the elf woman.

Belladal's eyes go wide. "If you not saved by Frost Giant..." She shakes her head. "No king. No queen. Is...is...discord.... chaos."

Amy scowls a little. "Well, no..." But Beatrice has begun to speak again and Belladal's head turns away. At Amy's feet Fenrir whimpers.

"I have to take her out," Amy whispers to Belladal.

Belladal looks like she is about to get up, but the servant elf Amy had spoken to briefly is by Amy's side at that instant. "Don't worry," says Amy. "I'll go with her."

Belladal nods and returns her gaze to Beatrice who has just begun her story of her voyage to America. Amy wishes she could stay for it, but part of her also wants to flee the hall as soon as possible.

The servant leads Amy and Fenrir out of the dining hall and Amy finds herself close to a place she remembers from earlier — the restroom. There is a group of elves in drab garb with an orb like the ones that line the ceilings and hover in the sky. But this one is brown and murky. As Amy watches, they take the orb into the restroom.

Drawing to a stop, Amy tilts her head. "What are they doing?"

The elf woman next to her bites her lip. "The orb magic water...used up. They empty. They refill new magic water."

Amy's eyes widen. "Are they flushing it down the toilet?" Despite the quaintness of the elf architecture, they do have flush toilets, thankfully.

The elf woman bites her lip again. "Yes. But don't worry. Dark water goes down to delta. We get drinking water and fish up river."

Fenrir begins tugging at the leash, and the elf woman pulls Amy down the passageway. Amy follows obediently, but the image of the river churning brown and black towards the dark lands is heavy in her mind.

A few paces later, they are stepping out into the cool night air onto a path of worn stones. The green orbs hover in the air, and light blue fireflies dance around them.

"What is your name?" Amy asks.

"Dolinar," says the elf woman.

"Dolinar," says Amy. "Do elves live down river?"

For a moment there is just the sound of Fenrir's leash in the grass, and Dolinar's and Amy's footfalls. And then Dolinar says quietly, "Yes. But only thieves, murderers, traitors...and those who will not obey the life price."

The night air suddenly feels very chill. Clutching her arms to her chest, Amy says, "That's wrong. Even if it's criminals down river, poisoning them is still wrong."

Dolinar looks quickly to the palace, and then back to Amy. Pointed ears trembling, she whispers, "Yes, I think so, too."

They stare at one another a moment. It occurs to Amy that

even dressed in plain servants' garb, Dolinar looks more noble than Amy ever will. Dolinar's hair is a deep walnut brown. Her eyes are hazel, and Amy is sure she sees light flickering in them. Her facial features are so delicate, and so perfect; her body is as small and poised as a ballet dancer.

Dolinar looks away from the palace and into the darkness. "My life mate works in stables. You say you are studying to be animal doctor. Want to see animals?"

Amy's eyes widen, and she starts walking into the darkness and direction of Dolinar's gaze. "Let's go!"

A few minutes later they are approaching a building that is at least four stories tall. Through narrow windows Amy sees the glow of green orbs. There is an enormous door at the front, but Dolinar leads her around to a small door in the back.

As soon as they enter the stables, Dolinar runs forward. Out of the shadows an elf man in drab pants and a simple shirt comes forward. His hair is long and blonde, his eyes are brown. He takes Dolinar in his arms and they begin speaking quickly in their own tongue.

It's touching, but Amy's eyes almost immediately go down the row of stalls. Her mouth opens. On one side of the stable are horses. On the other are hadrosaurs. The dinosaurs sit on their powerful hind limbs, their front limbs pulled up, and their beak-like snouts turned on their long necks and tucked against their bodies. They look like nothing so much as roosting birds.

Feet moving of their own accord, she approaches one of the sleeping dinosaur's enclosure. The creature untucks its neck, brings its large snout around and blinks yellow eyes. Between its eyes and its colorful, nearly iridescent scales, it looks like a giant parrot. A small gasp comes from Amy's lips.

"She gentle," comes a man's voice from behind her. He says something in elvish and then Dolinar says, "You may touch her, if you wish."

Amy doesn't have to be coaxed. She holds out a hand. The hadrosaur brings its snout forward and sniffs. Then walking forward on its large hind legs, it drops its snout and begins rubbing the side of its head against Amy's fingers. Up close, its scales are actually more like feathers, and they are soft as a chick's down. Amy bites back a laugh of pure wonderment. She doesn't doubt that the moment is real. She can smell the familiar smells of horses and straw, but there is also the smell of the hadrosaur, very akin to a bird. The animal is making soft huffing noises, and Amy catches the odor of its breath, warm and thick with the smell of half digested vegetation. It's wonderful. Magical.

Suddenly, everything that has happened — her horrible sickening run-in with a psychopath, her fear, the horrible sensation that her life was just a dream, the elves Amy is beginning to suspect are charming fascists, Loki frightening her in the kitchen, and his terrible come-ons, it is all worth it. Even if she can't breathe a word of this moment to anyone except Beatrice; she will know it happened. The universe seems to be grinding along with such beautiful perfection, and Amy's part may be insignificant, but it is still wonderful.

She rubs the hadrosaur's head and finds a small opening. She smiles; it is the animal's ear. She scratches just behind it and the hadrosaur lets loose a deep, pleasant, lowing noise.

"She like you," says Dolinar.

Amy doesn't say anything. Just continues rubbing a few minutes more, feeling the exquisite, alien and yet familiar softness of the creature's scales. She can feel her pulse racing just from the sheer joy of it. This perfect moment, it is all Loki's fault, and that thought almost makes her laugh.

The hadrosaur abruptly pulls itself further upright, shakes its head, and then tucks its snout against its body again.

"Now go back to sleep," says man.

Smiling, Amy turns to them. "Thank you so much..." She blinks at them standing arm in arm. Her brain disconnects from the moment she's just experienced. Tilting her head at the lovely couple she says, "How come you speak English?"

Squeezing the man's hand, Dolinar steps forward. "We do not speak English. We use magic to translate. My life mate, Liddel, and I study magic in secret."

Face very serious, Liddel draws closer to Dolinar. "We would like to learn more magic. We are both hard workers and we were wondering..."

"We have to leave," Dolinar says quickly. Amy's eyes widen and she steps back.

Dolinar swallows. "We haven't paid the life price. "

Overwhelmed and confused, Amy says in a small voice, "Life price?"

"I am pregnant," says Dolinar and Amy's eyes flash between the two elves. "But no one in family has died so it is not allowed. Balance of elves and other creatures will be disrupted...."

Charming fascists indeed! "They aren't going to kill your baby?" Amy gasps.

Dolinar and Liddel blink at her. "No," says Liddel. "They will take him away."

"Oh," says Amy. That is better — but not by much.

"Fjölnir," says Dolinar. "The Frost Giant you came with, we see his magic, he is very powerful...maybe more powerful than queen."

"Would he take us as apprentices?" says Liddel. "Just me for now, but later..."

From outside there come loud shouts and the sound of horns. Liddel's eyes widen. "It is the royal messengers. They may be angered if they know I've let you both into Queen's stables. Hide!"

Dolinar takes Amy's hand and pulls her and Fenrir towards a hadrosaur stall. She opens the latch with trembling hands as Liddel walks to the main door, shouting something. Amy, Fenrir and Dolinar swing into the stall next to an oblivious hadrosaur, and Dolinar shuts the stall door just as the main door of the stables swings open, and green orbs float in above.

There is much shouting and whinnying of horses. Amy scoops Fenrir up and wraps her hand around her dog's muzzle before she can bark. Wiggling in her arms, Fenrir makes muffled yipping noises anyway.

Outside the stall door, someone says something that sounds like a question. Amy hears Liddel responding. The stall door rattles.

Turning towards Fenrir, eyes wide, Dolinar points a finger at the dog's mouth just as her muzzle slips through Amy's fingers. Fenrir opens her mouth, the stall door rattles again, and Amy's heart misses a beat. Her dog's jaws open and shut, Amy can see her tiny lungs heave...but then no sound comes out. Amy looks at Dolinar...the elf woman's brow looks damp and she brings a finger to her lips.

Fenrir blinks and starts rubbing her muzzle.

The door of the stall shakes, and then someone says something, and Amy hears footsteps going away. Heart pounding in her ears, she lets out a breath and settles into the shadow of the hadrosaur, still sleeping peacefully.

Amy's not sure how long it is before the elves leave the stable; it feels like an eternity. She hears the sound of livery being readied, and hooves marching out into the night. At last, the stall door swings open, and Liddel's form appears. Looking perplexed, he says, "The messenger and an armed escort is going to the World Gate. It's strange so late in the evening."

"World Gate?" says Amy. "World Gate to where?"

The elves turn to her and look at her as though she has asked a silly question. "To Asgard."

Amy's heart leaps to her throat. "I have to get my grandmother...I have to get my car..." She runs forward and takes Dolinar's hands. "I don't know if Loki needs an apprentice, but I'm sure he'll let you come with us."

"Loki?" say Dolinar and Liddel in unison.

Amy puts her hand to her mouth. The one thing she wasn't supposed to do and she's done it!

The elves look at each other and whisper back and forth in their own language. Liddel puts a hand on Amy's shoulder. "We thank you for your kindness. Perhaps it would be better for you if you come with us to the Dark Lands."

Amy looks between them. Their eyes are wide and sincere.

"No, no, he's really not that bad," Amy says. "He saved my life...and he's kind, a little pervy, ...but..."

The elves exchange glances.

"Please don't tell!" Amy says. "Just please don't tell."

Liddel's eyes narrow. "We will tell no one."

Narrowing her own eyes, Dolinar smiles slightly...and it's not a kind smile. "Let the queen deal with the breaker of worlds."

Chapter 9

Loki pulls his neck back instinctively from the sharp bite of his blade. He just needs a moment's distraction. He glances around the room. Perhaps if he set the curtains on fire...

Hissing, the elf queen steps forward and he feels the point nip at his skin again. His eyes return to the shining piece of steel.

"You should not be awake," she says. That answers a question at the back of his mind. She'd enchanted him. He searches for something pithy to say, but before he can open his mouth, she shakes the book and shouts, "My lover's book. You have it! Why?"

The book is Lothur's journal. Hoenir gave it to Loki centuries ago. Shocked by the question, Loki just stares at her dumbly. She wears only a dressing gown tied loosely at the waist. Her eyes are narrow and too wet, her mouth open and slightly turned down. He tries to parse the emotions he is seeing: anger, sadness, disbelief.

"Can you read it!" she says, pricking the blade beneath his chin. He feels the warm ooze of a trickle of blood.

Loki scrambles backwards on his elbows, the sheet falling away from his bare chest. "Gala—," he starts to whisper.

"How do you know that name?" the elf queen shouts, sword shaking dangerously in her hands. "Only she knew that name!"

Loki blinks. How does he know it? Amy told him...but it's more than that. She lowers the blade a fraction. "Can you read the book?" she says her voice a low hiss.

Staring at the gleaming steel, he says, "Yes."

"Prove it!" she says, throwing the small, ancient volume towards him.

Loki's heart nearly stops as the book tumbles through the air and opens like a bird. Heedless of the blade, Loki throws up his hands and catches it as gently as he can. Glaring at her, he pulls it to his chest.

"Read," she says. Taking a step forward, she brings the blade to his neck again.

He blinks and looks down. The book has fallen open. It always opens to the same place; it's a passage Loki knows well. He makes a move to turn the page, but the elf queen says, "No, read that page. I know that page."

Loki looks up at her and then down at the book. He doesn't like reading this passage. There is something about it. It makes his heart fall and a lump form in his throat. He reads it anyway, maybe because of the sword in the queen's hand, or maybe because with it open in front of him, he can't turn away.

"And I have dreams of my love, who was not my love, but

was. Her father said words low against me, so low that it caused her heart to flame."

Swallowing, Loki tries to banish the imagery that dances in his mind. The passage is too real. Not like a story, more like a memory.

"Keep going," says the elf queen.

With a deep breath, Loki reads. *"And the flame of her heart spread to the utmost ends of her limbs. My love died in flames..."*

There is a loud clang. The vision of flames in Loki's eyes vanishes. He looks up to see the elf queen has dropped the blade on the ground. She stands before him, her shoulders slouched, her face empty. "Only my lover, and Lothur, could read that book," she says.

Loki looks down at the pages. There was an entry at the very beginning where Lothur said he'd enchanted the volume to be readable by no one but himself. But Loki could read it; he'd always assumed that Lothur was a touch mad.

Suddenly very curious, Loki says, "But my lady, you have the Gift of Tongues. You must be able to read it."

Shaking her head and not meeting his eyes, she says, "No. No, I cannot." Swallowing, she meets his gaze, her eyes red, her ears trembling slightly. Despite the rude awakening, Loki has an inexplicable desire to go to her and comfort her.

He resists on principle. Tilting his head, he says, "This book was a gift. I did not steal it from..." he lets his words drift off.

"Loka," she says. "Loka...she died over 2,500 years ago. I betrayed her to Odin."

That is long before Loki's time, but he feels a ripple of anger on Loka's behalf. Loki shuts the book sharply.

The queen meets his eyes. Her jaw goes hard. "I sent the

royal messengers to Asgard moments before you awoke." Turning quickly she says, "Gather your armor and meet me at the pool. We have only a little time to find your sons, and for you to make your escape."

Loki looks around the bedchamber at his blade lying on the floor and his armor strewn about like a jigsaw puzzle. Cursing, he rolls out of the bed, pulls on his breeches, and then yanks a sheet off the mattress. Spreading the sheet out, he tosses his armor onto it, then gathers it up by the corners, throws it over his back, and grabs his sword.

As he paces into the other room, he has half a mind to run the elf queen through with his blade. But she's standing over the pool. It's casting white light on her face, and the murderous thought is subverted by curiosity.

He goes to where she stands and looks into the water. Instead of their reflections he sees the front of Hoenir's hut, its door flung open to the night. Hoenir and Sigyn are standing there and Loki's eyes widen.

"This is a few days ago," says the queen.

There is a flash of light outside the hut, and there are Valli and Nari, falling to the ground and gasping for air. Loki squats to the floor in front of the pond and holds out his hand as though to touch them, his mouth falling open in hope and relief. In the pool, Hoenir and Sigyn run forward and pull Loki's boys into the hut. "They're alive," he says running a hand through his hair. "They're alive." He feels lighter. Like laughing aloud, like picking up the queen and spinning her around, faithless witch and betrayer though she may be.

The elf queen begins to chant. The scene begins to move too quickly, like a human film played too fast. Dawn glows on the horizon beyond the hut and Heimdall appears with armed guards. Valkyries swoop and land to encircle the small dwelling. Loki scowls as Odin walks onto the scene and stands just within the circle of guards, about ten paces from Hoenir's door. Loki can't hear the words, but he sees Odin's lips moving.

Heart beating too loud in his chest, Loki watches as Heimdall goes forward. He is accompanied by Skaddi, a Frost Giant like Loki and the self proclaimed "goddess of justice."

The Valkyries begin to raise their spears, lightning flashes on the scene, and all eyes turn. Thor appears. Guards fall back to let him pass. He goes and speaks quietly to Odin and Heimdall. Heimdall scowls and Thor walks forward, turns so his back is to the hut, and holds up his hammer.

Loki's mouth falls open. "He's protecting them. Thor is protecting them!"

The guards don't move, but Loki sees them scowl. Heimdall is saying something to Odin, and Loki can tell without hearing that the gatekeeper is shouting. Loki sees a few Valkyries pound their spears. He can see them shouting, too. Someone shoots a bolt of fire; it seems to go into the sky...

But then at the top of Hoenir's roof, there is a burst of flame. A swarm of butterfly snakes take to the air, birds with lizard heads take wing. New flames lick at the foundations; Loki doesn't know how they even got there.

Thor turns and tries to rush into the hut, but Heimdall and Odin hold him back.

Loki's eyes widen. "What is happening, what is happening!" Loki shouts. In the scene in the pool Thor holds up his arm, and Loki sees the sky darken. Thor's calling rain. Loki has never been so grateful he gave Thor the damned hammer.

The queen chants more quickly. The scene in the pool is

smoky and obscure, but Loki sees the flames leap, even as the rain begins to fall. The flames surround the hut like a curtain. He can't make out doors, windows or chimney. Odin pounds Gungnir into the earth in front of the hut and leaves it there upright.

The scene is moving incredibly fast. It's early morning there in the pool...and the curtain of flames is falling. He sees the downpour is now a drizzle

Gungnir is gone...and Hoenir's hut is not there. Where the hut stood there is only charred ground.

Loki stares at the pool, not really seeing it. He feels as though a weight was briefly lifted from his body and then hurled down upon him. He puts his hands to his head, runs his fingers through his hair, scraping his nails against his scalp with such force it hurts.

As though from a great distance he hears the crackle of fire, and screaming — his mind supplying the details of Valli, Nari, Hoenir, Mimir's and Sigyn's brutal ends?

And then another sound comes. Loud and insistent — the sound of a car calling for its master. Loki blinks...Amy and Beatrice...he has an oath to keep to them.

He wants to stay, he wants to fight Odin and his legions — not to win, to die. Helen, Aggie, now Valli, Nari, Sigyn, and even Mimir and Hoenir. He squeezes his eyes shut. It's because of him, somehow it is all because of him. Loki knows there is no afterlife, no Valhalla for the valiant, no Hel for the meek. And that is good, he wants the release of nothingness.

The car calls again — it sounds so close, and the way its call echoes through the palace it sounds almost as though it is inside. Taking a sharp breath he opens his eyes. He doesn't break oaths.

That thought is the thread of strength that makes him stand up. He looks around. To one side is the receiving room he entered by last night, to the other side is the elf queen's bedroom, now in flames. She stands in front of him, haloed by the fire, her face calm. "Once again you leave me for a mortal," she says.

Loki has no time for her games. Narrowing his eyes he says, "How long do I have?"

"I will give you five minutes to leave the palace grounds before I send the guards after you. After that you're on your own."

Loki tilts his head. In the receiving chambers he hears the crackle of more flames.

"I cannot afford to let Odin think I allowed you to escape," says the queen.

"Of course not," Loki hisses. For a moment the air between them shimmers. Loki wants to see her smooth beautiful body burst into flames. But another part...another part of him feels sorrow, pity and guilt that he cannot understand.

The queen's face is as unworried as a Greek statue, and that's a shame. Such a beautiful face would be more beautiful with emotion on it — even if the emotion were anger or hatred.

"You don't have time for this," the elf queen says. "Run."

Loki stares at her a heartbeat more. And then securing his makeshift pack over his shoulder, he backs away from her into the receiving room. The door to the secret passage is open, the covering tapestry nowhere in sight.

Loki runs.

CHAPTER 10

Maybe it won't be so bad if the elves alert Asgard, and presumably Odin, that Loki is in Alfheim. Maybe Odin will just take Loki, send Beatrice and Amy home, and be on his way.

Or maybe he'll leave Amy and Beatrice in Alfheim forever.

Amy swallows. The truth is, no matter what mercy Odin might grant to her and Beatrice, Amy's worried about Loki. Twisted and perverted as he may be, if it weren't for him she wouldn't be alive — or have ever seen a hadrosaur.

Hands shaking, Amy drives up the road to the elf palace. The sky has turned overcast. There is no starlight, just the light of the green orbs that seem to be the elven version of street lights. A light drizzle is in the air. At the top of a staircase of long low stairs, four elf guards stand in front of the wide front door. As she gets closer, they cross their spears. It will take a long time for Beatrice to get down those stairs... and Amy still has to find her.

Biting her lip, Amy stares at the guards. And then she is struck by inspiration.

Pressing a button on her keychain, she lets the car alarm shriek. The guards visibly jump.

From the door the elf in black who had spoken to Loki emerges. "What going on?" he says.

Turning off the alarm and switching into 4 wheel drive, Amy sticks her head out the window. "My car, he wants to come in — we hurt his feelings leaving him out all night and now he's worried about Fjölnir and Beatrice!" Hitting the gas, she edges to the stairs. Craning her head out the window, she adds, "Please, open the door! He'll be good if you just let him in and we find them."

The elf in black says something to the guards again. They eye the car warily but open the doors. The man in black runs inside.

Slipping back into the driver's seat, Amy puts her foot on the gas and bumps up the steps.

She hits the horn as soon as she gets into the foyer and then jumps out of the car. Pressing the alarm button again, she says, "Don't go near him! He might bite!" Then she runs around the car towards the dining hall and her mouth falls open.

The elf in black is leading four other elves who are carrying a large chair between them. On the chair slumped over asleep is Beatrice.

Looking visibly worried, the elf in black says, "She drink too much our mead. Beastly chariot not angry?"

Amy's mouth forms a small 'o'. "I think he'll be fine if we just put her inside and he can see she's alright."

Shaking his head, the elf in black says, "We not mean

insult. Not know chariot have feelings."

Trying to keep a straight face, Amy says, "It's okay, I'm sure he'll understand..." She looks at her grandmother snoring softly. Maybe it's for the best she won't be awake. She has a feeling this will be a rough ride.

Running down the steps of the secret passage, Loki has no idea how he'll manage to round-up Beatrice and Amy in time to escape the grounds in only a few minutes.

He bursts into the first private receiving chamber, still lit by fireflies. And then he hears it again. The car...it sounds so close. Could it be?

He runs through the door, down a passage, and around a corner, and his eyes go wide. The car is parked in the foyer of the palace. Some elves and Amy are securing Beatrice in the back seat.

"That's good," says Amy. "Get out, please. Don't make the car mad. He doesn't know you, thank you, that's good...now we need to find Fjölnir..."

She turns around and her eyes fall on him and go wide. "Lo — Fjölnir!" The car gives a happy little chirp. "Car is so happy to see you!"

Loki blinks for a moment. She's lying; he can feel it.

Raising her voice above the murmuring of the crowd that is rapidly forming, she says, "Car wants to go home, so we have to go. Now." She hops into the driver's side, and motions to Loki to get into the passenger's side. He hurries to comply, throwing his sack of armor and sword on the floor of the back seat in front of Fenrir and a gently snoring Beatrice.

Before he's even closed the door, Amy's sticking her head out the window saying,"Thanks for everything, everyone!" The car starts to move and she says, "Oh, sorry! Car is anxious! Long, lonely night for him! Got to go!" She pulls all the way into the car, turns it around, and heads towards the door and the stairs. The car gives a few more happy beeps.

Loki stares at her, stunned. It was all lies. Brilliant lies, on her part and possibly Car's. How did she know?

"They sent messengers to Asgard, Loki," Amy says, as they bump down the front steps of the palace. "I'm not sure...but I thought maybe we should leave."

"Good thought," he says. He owes this girl more respect than he's given her.

A look of confusion crosses her face. "Where is your armor? Why aren't you wearing a shirt?"

But in some ways...she is really so naive. Normally, he might make a joke, but he feels too empty. "Drive as fast as you can; we don't have much time."

Scowling at the wheel, she says, "Why? What happened? "

"Just drive," he says.

"Did you get your answers?" she asks.

"Just drive," he says. "Please!"

There must be something in his voice, because she hits the gas. It's still dark outside. There is the soft patter of rain on the car roof. Ahead, a long shadow is covering the gate of the palace. Loki's heart skips a beat. At his feet is the army knapsack. Reaching into it he pulls out a grenade.

"The gate!" Amy cries. "It's open but the vines are down. Can they hurt the car?"

Loki has no idea. Before he can say anything, the girl says, "Is that a grenade in your hand? Use it!"

The top window opens. Loki's not sure how, but he doesn't have to be told twice. "Stop Car!" he shouts.

The car screeches to a halt and he stands up in the rain. Blinking to clear his vision, he flings the grenade at the curtain of vines. Pulling back into the car, he pushes Amy down so they are both protected by the dash. There is a boom, the car shakes, but the window does not shatter. They both sit up to see a large hole in the curtain, but long tendrils are already snaking down to close it.

Hitting the gas without even being asked, Amy grumbles. "I don't want to be stuck here with these pointy-eared fascists!"

He looks at her for an instant. She is wearing clothing finer than she probably has ever worn or will ever wear again. Her hair is upswept, with crystal flowers woven into it. She looks radiant and beautiful, and if she stayed here the elves could help her remain so for a time...in her own realm she'll be doomed to fade and age so quickly. Yet she wants to leave. Part of him wants to smile at her, but he can't. His face feels frozen into a slight scowl and a frown. He has a lump in his throat that has nothing to do with her.

He hears a rumble of hooves and heavy feet behind them. "That will be the guards," he says. He looks up; the top window is already closed. He touches his wet face and looks at the pavement shining beneath the green orbs.

Amy's eyes go to the rear-view mirror. "What? Why are they following us? They seemed fine letting us go...maybe we should stop?"

Loki feels the car start to slow. "No, do not stop! It's a ruse — the queen cannot let Odin think she let us go too easily."

The girl speeds up a little but her eyes dart to the mirror

again. "They're closing in fast..." Turning her attention back
to the road, she swallows. "I can't go much faster than them
on the hairpin turns, especially since the road is wet."

"Go as fast as you can," Loki says, bracing himself as she
makes a sharp turn.

"I am, I am!" Amy says, a frantic note in her voice. Car's
wheels screech and Loki hears the shouts and hooves of the
rapidly approaching cavalry.

He scowls. He needs to put on his armor, but their pursuers are catching up to them too fast. Reaching up, he taps the
overhead window that now is closed. "Car, open up."

Amy looks at him, eyes wide. The window slides open,
and Loki stands up.

"What are you doing?" Amy shouts, her voice just audible
over the sound of the rain, the hoof beats of the elves' horses,
and the lowing of the hadrosaurs.

Not responding, Loki turns to face their pursuers.

"Halt now!" one cries in the elf tongue. "By order of the
All Father!"

They don't shoot at him, though some carry bows. Odin
must want him alive — he won't let that happen again.

Loki thinks of the brief flare of hope he had when he saw
Valli and Nari in the pool disappearing into the hut, and
then the cold realization just moments later when he saw the
flames. Let the elves feel the hollow cold of his heart.

Car makes another sharp turn, and Loki is nearly thrown
out. Righting himself, he focuses on the rain falling on his
pursuers, and the water rivulets running down the cobble-
stone street. He sees the magic between the water and himself
and he pulls on it, tugs at it, imagines the magic stilling the
water, calming it, deep at the molecular level — so the water's

spinning hydrogen atoms lock together and crystals form on the ground and in the sky.

Horses scream and the hadrosaurs bellow in terror as the rain turns to snow, and the road behind Car turns to ice.

"What's going on?" says Amy.

Loki falls panting back through the open window.

"Ice...you turned the road to ice..." Amy says, eyes in the mirror.

Turning his head, Loki looks back. Where there had been at least a dozen elves on horseback before, and two hadrosaurs, now there are no dinosaur mounts, and only four horsemen are left — but they are pulling out lances and looking very determined.

Rain is streaking in through the open roof.

Amy glances at him, eyes wide. "You probably broke the horses' legs."

"Not enough of them," Loki says, lip curling upward.

"You can't do that!" Amy says. "It's not the horses' faults!" She twists the wheel as they take another sharp turn.

He stares at her a moment in disbelief. And then his disbelief turns to rage, red and hot beneath his skin. "Fine," he says. "I won't use ice this time." He stands up again.

"What — "

He can't hear the rest of what she says. He looks back at the horsemen in the rain. "Stop now, Loki!" one calls. "You'll never get through the main gate!"

Loki lets his rage loose in a scream. What he expects to happen, happens. Magic rips the water molecules apart into oxygen and hydrogen, and excites the hydrogen atoms to the point where they burst into flame. But it should have just been a little spark in the air before the horses' eyes. Instead a wall of flame forms between Car and the riders, as thick and as high as the flames that overcame Hoenir's hut.

Loki falls back into the car, his eyes wide. Amy is silent, but he sees her hands shaking.

He hardly feels as though he's exerted any energy at all. He looks over his shoulder. The flames still burn — he can't see beyond them. Something is wrong. He's not that strong. "Gala..." he murmurs to himself. "It must have been the queen's doing."

"What?" says Amy.

"She wants to let me escape," Loki says almost to himself. "But needs it to look like an accident..."

The flames behind them make the window in front of them reflective for a brief moment. Loki catches sight of his face, slightly blue in the strange light. For an instant he is looking at his daughter Helen's face, or half her face. He shakes his head. Is he going mad with grief?

Car's wheels screech, and Loki's body bangs into the door as they make another sharp turn. And then they're at the marketplace. Car's horn lets out a loud alarm. Some elves part and run in front of them.

"Ummm..." says Amy. "If she wants us to escape, why'd she lock the front door?"

Looking at the closed doors of the heavy metal gate, Loki's heart falls. He doesn't know any trick to open it — he can move small things with his mind, but this is too large, too heavy, and too fireproof. He looks down at the bag at his feet. There is one more grenade, but it won't be strong enough...his jaw tightens. He reaches into the bag, and says, "Car, open your top window again!" Loki doesn't remember when it even closed.

Hitting the brakes, Amy gives him a funny look. But the window opens. Standing up, Loki pulls the pin and hurls the last grenade. He pulls back into the car. Amy's already ducking. Loki presses himself down as far as he can, his chest pressing against Amy's back.

The blast goes off, and the car rattles. Loki and Amy both lift themselves up. The gate is closed.

"Oh," says Amy, her shoulders sagging.

Loki closes his eyes. "I won't be taken alive," he says. "Not this time. I'll fight to the death."

There is a loud creak.

He opens his eyes and blinks. There is a shimmer of magic the color of moonlight, and then the gate creaks again and swings open. In the open way stands the elf queen, or more likely an astral projection of her, considering she floats above the ground.

In her own language she says, "Be gone from my realm, and set no more of my people aflame — or not only Odin will hunt you!"

Loki blinks. He didn't create that inferno...did he?

"What did she say?" Amy says, hunching over the wheel.

In front of them, the projection disappears. "She wishes us well and bids us be on our way," says Loki.

Amy puts her foot on the gas. "It sounded more like she was angry."

"Mmmm..." says Loki settling back into his seat. "Go quickly as you can. The armies of Asgard will be upon us quickly."

"Armies?" squeaks Amy, turning out onto the lane that will take them to the Border Road.

"Don't worry," Loki says. "I'm sure you'll be able to

convince Odin that you were deceived by the God of Lies and he'll spare your lives."

Car's lights become even brighter and Amy speeds up. Her voice shaking, she says, "I would rather you not die either."

Loki looks over at her, his mouth still frozen in a frown, his brows still knit together. He brings destruction to everything he touches, and everyone he loves. He wants to die.

Amy casts a worried glance in his direction.

He cannot die now. He has an oath to keep.

Without a word he turns in his seat and begins to rummage through the makeshift sack for his armor. Beatrice is still asleep, but Fenrir eyes him curiously.

He's got his shirt on and is awkwardly attaching his breast plate when Amy turns onto the border road. She steps on the gas and they surge forward at what feels like dizzying speed. They're still in a relatively populous region; farmlands line the road on their left. They don't have to worry about dark elves just yet.

He tilts his head. Over the elf queen's lands, the sky is just starting to lighten.

He's sure it must be taking all of Amy's concentration to remain on the road, but then she begins to speak. "You were blue for a few moments when the fire started. Is that your natural color? I thought Frost Giants only turned blue when they were cold."

He freezes, his hands on the buckle of an arm guard. "I don't turn blue." He isn't Helen.

"You looked blue," says Amy.

"That was a trick of the light," Loki says, his voice coming out nearly a hiss. He doesn't have time for this inane chatter.

"You looked good blue. Not like in the movies with pointy

teeth and a giant horny head," she says her words running together as though she's just speaking to hear herself speak. "More like — "

"Be quiet," he snaps.

"I thought you weren't sensitive about your Frost Giant nature?"

"Frost Giants are not blue!" he says. "I should know. I've been one for more than 1,000 years!"

"Huh," says Amy.

"The forest is approaching," says Loki, turning his attention to the mail links that cover his right elbow. "If you hit anything or anyone just keep going."

"Just because the queen thinks the elves over there are bad doesn't mean they are!" says Amy, slowing down as they slip into the forest.

Looking up, Loki blinks at her, surprised how much of Alfheim politics she's managed to divine in such a short time. Ordering her isn't going to work. He sighs inwardly.

"No, they're not," he says quietly. "I've had dealings with Dark Elves before. But trust me, any Dark Elf that would choose to attack Car merely for transversing the border road isn't one you should stop for. Under any circumstances."

Amy swallows and her hands shake even more violently.

Loki turns back to his armor and curses. The plate that covers his upper left arm is completely missing. He grabs the piece for his forearm and attaches it best he can, without the anchor of the upper section.

It's only a few minutes later when a shadow seems to fall on the land in the East, and the wind and rain outside them pick up.

"Ummm..." says Amy.

"Thor," mutters Loki, narrowing his eyes. Is Thor Odin's puppet once again? Or is he here for some reason of his own? To beg forgiveness maybe? Not that Loki could give it.

A streak of lightning turns the realm bright as day.

"What are those shadows in the sky?" Amy says.

"Valkyries," Loki says, the word spitting out of his mouth. His mouth twists. "Not here to beg forgiveness after all."

"Forgiveness?" says Amy.

"We have a few minutes," says Loki twisting to reach into the backseat "Concentrate on the road," he says. "I need to eat something."

Amy is trying to concentrate on the road. Rain and wind are whipping through the sky. It might be her imagination, but both seem to be getting stronger.

She shivers. Her back is still damp from where Loki leaned over her as the grenades went off. Her eyes dart over to him. He's still wet, armor half on, stuffing peanut butter into his mouth with a spoon, a liter bottle of Coca Cola open in his lap. He hasn't spoken to her since grabbing some food. How can he be eating? Her own stomach is heavy with fear, and her mind is swimming with everything that's happened this evening: the elves, the hadrosaurs, and seeing Loki in a lovely robin's egg shade of blue. Trick of the light or not, it had been strange, lovely, and as magical as the fire, the ice, or his astral projections.

She takes a shaky breath. Loki says he's over 1,000 years old. She can't even imagine that.

Whoever's chasing them is likely just as old or older than

him, possibly more powerful...

That's too much to think about. Taking a deep breath, she glances in the rearview mirror. Beatrice is thankfully still asleep. Fenrir is awake, her nose darting from side to side.

Amy looks at the clock on the dash. Fifteen minutes ago Loki said, "It's Thor." It feels like an eternity, and like only a heartbeat. Tightening her grip on the wheel she speeds up.

Lightning rips across the road just 50 yards in front of the car. A humanoid shadow is haloed in its light. Amy screams, hits the brakes, and tries to dodge it.

"Keep going!" Loki yells. His hand shoots to the wheel and holds it straight. Whoever it was hits the car and sinks below the hood. The car bumps sickeningly.

"Hit the gas!" Loki says.

But Amy's foot is on the brake. "No," she says. "We hit someone! We have to stop." Even if it is a criminal.

"He's fine!" Loki says, "Go!"

"No, I can't," Amy says.

Something bangs against the back window of the car. Amy turns and screams again. There is a huge mouth filled with sharp teeth attached to the flat plane of the back window. Fingers with suction cups are at its side.

She hears the sound of a thunk as Loki drops his bottle of cola.

"Drive!" shouts Loki twisting and crawling into the back.

Amy floors it. She looks in the rearview mirror. Loki obscures most of the view, but Amy can see the thing is still there. It doesn't seem to have eyes or nose...just that huge maw.

"Car, open the back window!" Loki says.

"What?" screams Amy.

"Just let Car do it!"

Amy hits the button at her left and the window begins to drop. Over the sound of the wind comes a horrible noise like lips smacking, and then there is a gurgling noise and an inhuman scream.

"Roll up the window!"

Amy doesn't have to be told twice. She raises the window, and Loki pulls back into the front seat, his sword in his hand, something dark and black at the point.

Another bolt of lightning rips across the road.

"Next time I'll just keep going," Amy says. "I'll just keep going."

Looking at the ceiling, Loki says, "There isn't going to be a next time. Thor and the Valkyries are almost upon us."

Amy bites her lips. "What do I do?"

"I'm going to try and make us invisible," Loki says, his voice very calm. "You'll still be able to hear everything...but you'll only be able to see things outside of Car, you won't even be able to see anything inside, not even yourself. I'll need you to keep driving though. Can you do that?"

Amy nods. "Yes...I think so." Not because she thinks she can, just because she doesn't like the idea of what may happen if she can't.

The words are hardly out of her mouth when everything in front and behind her starts to fade from view.

Her foot hits the brakes. She hears the sound of tires on pavement, the thump of rain on the roof, the engine. But she can't see the car, Beatrice, Loki, even herself...She takes a ragged breath.

Loki's voice comes from her right. "It's disorienting."

"Yes!" Amy shouts, maybe just to hear her own voice.

Loki's voice sounds tight. "You must keep driving."

"I can't see the dash, the steering wheel or the pedals!" Amy says.

"You don't even look at those," Loki says, his voice sharp.

That's true. Amy licks her lips, feels the sensation of her tongue, cool and wet against her skin. "I can't see myself...it's almost like I'm not here."

There is a moment of heavy silence. "How can I help?" Loki says, sounding like his voice is coming through gritted teeth.

"Would you touch me?" Amy asks before she's even thought about it, and she almost wants to bang her head on the invisible steering wheel for making the suggestion.

In a voice that is surprisingly clinical Loki says, "You're going to feel my hand on your thigh; it's the best place for me to touch you without obstructing your ability to drive."

Before she even has a chance to react, she feels his hand on her leg, large and warm, and as long as she doesn't look down, seemingly solid. And it does help; she's too grateful to worry about the implications of it. She puts her foot down on the gas and holds the steering wheel at 3 and 9 o'clock.

"Very good," Loki says, giving her leg a pat. It shouldn't be as encouraging as it is.

Amy nods and bites her lip. She's just getting to the point where she's feeling a little more comfortable when bright lights like lasers shoot down on the road and forest in front of them sending off sparks in every direction, lighting up weird hominid shadows as they do.

The shadows leap from the trees on the dark side of the forest. Amy screams again, puts her foot on the brake, and almost runs them off the road, but Loki's hand is suddenly on the wheel, holding it firm. "They're magical flares," he says. "They won't hurt us. Try to dodge them if you can, but keep us on the road!"

Shaking, Amy puts her foot back on the gas.

"They don't want us dead," Loki says as though the words are a revelation to himself. "They're just trying to flush us out."

Amy blinks. "The sparks will hit the car, and they'll see them bounce..."

"Exactly," says Loki, his hand on her leg again.

"I think I can do this." says Amy, speeding up. As long as she doesn't have to worry about the blasts killing them, she feels much better. Also, they're scaring the crazy shadow things away. And that's good.

Amy zigzags through the flares that are falling down on the road.

At one point she thinks they're going to roll over, but a few minutes later, the road ahead of them is clear. She looks in the rearview mirror, all the flares are bursting on the road behind them.

Loki pats her lap. "Well done."

Her heart is in her ears, and she's panting, but she laughs aloud. "We did it!"

The words are barely out of her mouth when she hears a loud clang. Sparks cascade over her head and down the sides of the car like a waterfall. "Uh-oh," she says.

"Drive!" says Loki.

Amy floors the pedal, but up ahead and behind them shapes are falling from the sky. Another flare is fired directly towards them from in front; it explodes on the windshield, and suddenly the car and everything inside is visible again

— but Amy can't see the road at all. She puts her foot on the brakes, gently this time so they don't skid.

She looks to her side. Loki is next to her. His face has a sheen to it, his mouth is open, and she notices he's breathing heavily. He's not looking at her. His eyes are focused on the road ahead of them.

Amy follows his gaze. About 100 yards ahead of them are women carrying spears, standing around an enormous man in front of a chariot without a horse. In the enormous man's hands there is a hammer that is glowing with the pale blue white of lightning.

Loki takes a deep breath, and his voice comes out low, malevolent, but tinged with something desperate. "It is the mighty Thor."

Uh-oh.

CHAPTER 11

"What do I do?" says the girl.

Loki stares at Thor in front of his golden chariot. Valkyries stand beside Thor and are blocking the road behind Car. More are alighting along the sides of the road.

"Drive forward," he says. "Slowly. When I tap the roof, stop." Knocking at the top window, he says, "Car, open up."

"You know..." the girl begins to say.

"What?" he snaps, not bothering to look at her.

"It can wait," she says, gripping Car's door as the window above slides open.

Loki stands up. Heavy but sparse drops of rain fall on him. He can see trees waving madly in the distance, but around him the air is nearly still. They are in the eye of the storm.

Around Car, Valkyries raise their spears, but they do not fire. In front of him, Thor stands up straighter. His eyes meet Loki's, then go over Car, before coming back to meet Loki's gaze again.

Neither Loki nor Thor say anything. When Amy has brought Car within a few paces of Thor, Loki taps the roof. She obediently stops the vehicle.

"Well met," says Thor in the Asgard tongue.

Loki does not respond.

Thor licks his lips and looks distinctly uncomfortable. "I bring grave tidings — "

"If you mean the fire that consumed Hoenir's hut, and all within, including Sigyn and my sons, I already know," Loki snaps.

Appearing genuinely hurt, Thor takes a step forward. "Loki, I did try — "

"To save them," Loki says sharply. His body sags and he looks away. "Yes, I know that, too." It occurs to him how devious it was for Odin to send Thor on this particular outing. Thor is possibly the only Asgardian Loki will hear out at this point. And Thor does have something to say; if he didn't, Loki would be dead by now.

It's uncomfortable standing half in Car, half out. Loki's legs are at odd angles, so he slips onto the roof and sits there, legs dangling into the inside of Car below. The roof buckles a little at his weight, Amy gasps, and Fenrir yips, but Loki ignores them. "Spit it out, Thor. What do you want?"

Thor straightens. He takes a deep breath and appears almost to go a little green, as though he has just been asked to eat something extremely distasteful. "I have been sent...to beg you to return."

Loki stares at him for several long heartbeats. Then he bursts out laughing. The sound seems brittle and hard even to him. Waving at the Valkyries, Loki says, "You came to beg me...at spear point?"

Thor doesn't back down. Raising an eyebrow, he smiles slightly. "It would seem I needed their help to find you."

Loki sighs. Once he might have warmed to that; now he feels only emptiness. "Flattery will get you nowhere, Thor."

The slight smile on Thor's face vanishes. "Nonetheless, everything I say is true. Loki, my father needs you to come home. "

Loki's lip curls into a sneer. "And he would have the gall to ask me after killing Hoenir, Mimir, Sigyn and my boys!"

Scowling, Thor takes a step forward. "It wasn't like that! The fire — "

"Wouldn't have happened if he hadn't tried to execute my sons!"

"Let me finish!" Thor's voice rips so loudly through the darkness of the stormy dawn that Car reverberates. Lifting his hammer, Thor shouts, "My father tried to stop the flames — but even Gungnir couldn't halt them. Something is growing in the nine realms, something that is twisting magic and time and will pull the World Tree asunder." Thor swings his hammer for emphasis and a stray bit of lightning sprays off into the trees. There is a loud crack, and a small scream from Amy. The Valkyries shift on their feet.

Stepping back with one foot, Thor's face contorts into something like disbelief or revulsion. "My father believes only you can stop it." Loki crosses his arms. Of course Thor would feel ashamed if there was some threat to the realms he couldn't resolve with a few pounds of his hammer.

Not that Loki believes this little story. "Would saving the realms involve me remaining in a cave doused in snake venom for a few centuries?"

"It isn't like that!" Thor says. "You will be absolved of all wrongdoing in this matter. This is the truth!"

Absolved? As though he was the one who needs absolution. His sons, Sigyn, Mimir and Hoenir are dead. Loki grits his teeth and feels his eyes get hot. Thinking about them all gone — his body feels hollow, as though he is an empty shell.

He takes a deep breath and pulls himself back into the moment. Absolution is a farce. As soon as Loki returns to Asgard, there will be some dire punishment, and this time there will be no Sigyn to tend to him. Loki rolls his eyes at Thor's naivete. When will Thor realize Odin is as capable at lying as Loki, perhaps more so? Anything to "protect" the realms, or rather, his own power.

"Lovely," says Loki, tapping his fingers on Car's roof. "But I'm afraid I have to refuse." Shrugging, he points down at Car and says, "I have some mortals I have sworn to return to their own realm. You know I always keep my oaths."

Thor scowls. "Father said that you could slip between the realms..." He walks around the car towards the driver's side — as he does so, the Valkyries raise their spears a bit higher. Loki scowls at them and then turns his attention to Thor. Odin's son is now peeking in the driver's side window. Thor smiles and waggles a finger at Amy as one might waggle a finger at a pretty bird in a cage. In the back seat Fenrir growls warningly.

Looking up, Thor raises his eyebrows and says brightly, "She is a pretty thing, Loki. And just your type." Raising one hand to his chest, Thor makes groping motions with his fingers in what is probably a universal symbol for large breasts. "I suppose the old woman in the back is her kin. Convince them to come back to Asgard with you. Keep the girl as your plaything for a decade. When she withers she can remain your servant, a much better life than she'd have in her own realm."

Somewhere a Valkyrie's spear must fire accidentally because Loki sees a flare of orange flame in the periphery of his vision. His sons are dead. As are his ex-wife and two best friends. Thor dares talk of playthings? Loki is too furious to speak.

"What did he just say?" says Amy in English, her voice sounding indignant.

Loki looks down at her. She is staring hard out the window at Thor who is waggling his finger at her again and smiling like an idiot. It is probably innate contrariness that makes Loki translate. "Oh, he's just suggested I bring you home to Asgard and keep you as a plaything and servant. Perhaps you'd like to answer?"

Eyes going wide, Amy's brows draw together and she springs up through the window in the roof between Loki's knees. Facing Thor she says, "You can tell the God of Blunder he can take that idea and shove it up his great big Viking butt!"

Loki blinks. Well, that was absolutely priceless. The corners of his lips pull up.

Thor's face goes completely red, his lips curve into something between a frown and a grimace, and his brows draw into one line. The hand holding his hammer starts to tremble.

"Actually," Loki says, keeping his gaze fixed on Thor, "Thor understands English well enough."

"Oh," says Amy, sounding not at all brave. Putting a hand gently on her head, Loki pushes her back into the car.

Thor is breathing deeply, but Loki nor Car nor the girl are dead. Odin must want Loki very badly.

In English, Thor says very slowly, "You can tell your whore that my orders are to bring you back to Asgard alive. Father will not care about her puny little mortal life."

Head darting out of the car again, in a voice that is plaintive rather than angry, Amy says, "I am not a whore!"

Putting his hand on her head not so gently this time, Loki pushes her back inside. With a smirk he says, "She has my oath of protection. You'll have to kill me first."

With a bellow, Thor swings his hammer in empty air like a toddler having a tantrum. Something cracks in the distance, like lightning hitting tree branches. Loki smiles. He hears the Valkyries at the dark side of the forest give angry cries.

In Car, Amy starts pulling at his leg. "Loki!" she whispers.

"Not now!" he snaps down at her.

In the distance he hears more cracking in rapid succession. Thor looks away. Someone shouts, "Dark Elves!"

"Loki!" says Amy.

He scowls at her. But she gives a ferocious tug at his leg. Letting himself be tugged into Car, he finds his face just inches from hers. Her eyes are wide with fear — and so help him he's about to make her more afraid with the words at the tip of his tongue. But before he can even breathe she says, "Do elves have automatic weapons? Because that sounds like automatic weapons."

Loki's eyes go wide. He looks towards the dark forest. Something hits the side of Car and there is the sharp clang of metal on metal. In the dark forest there are loud angry popping noises getting closer. Valkyries from the left side of the road are streaming past Car to the dark side. Car makes a sharp beep.

Turning back to Amy, he sees her hands are already at the wheel.

"That does sound like automatic weapons fire," he says.

He hasn't heard it since World War II.

Amy hits the gas. Loki puts a hand on her leg and says, "I'm making us invisible again!"

From the backseat Beatrice says quietly, "Oh, the elves have fireworks." Loki looks back at her; her eyes are still closed. Everything around them begins to shimmer as his spell takes effect. He hears Thor yelling orders.

Loki looks at the shimmering Amy, now steering them around Thor's chariot. "How do you know what automatic weapons sound like?" he asks.

"I live in Chicago," she says, as though that is explanation.

Her shimmering form hunching over the wheel, Amy says, "Elves have guns?"

"No," says Loki. More gunshots go off, and the car shoots forward. "Not that I know of."

"Oh, what lovely fireworks," says Beatrice.

An explosion goes off in the distance behind them and something whizzes past. Amy jumps beneath his hand. Loki follows the whizzing shape with his eyes and turns his head. "That was just another flare."

He turns around. "Thor's broken off from the rest and is pursuing us!"

Car shoots forward.

It's like a video game Amy tells herself. The flares aren't going to hurt them. No one dies if they get hit.

"Veer left," Loki says. Amy veers left and a bolt of blue shoots by the car. She's not sure how long she's been driving since the Valkyries were overtaken by dark elves. It seems like forever, but it's probably only a few minutes.

"We're almost at the gate," Loki says. "Slow down."

"How will you open it?" Amy says, putting a foot gently on the brake. "Will you have to get out of the car?"

"Of course I'll have to get out of the car," Loki snaps. "Stop here!"

Amy stops so quickly she bumps the steering wheel.

Loki's hand leaves her knee, and she is suspended in absolute nothingness.

"Car, open up the top hatch!" Loki says.

Amy doesn't try to argue with him. She just searches blindly for the button in the door's armrest. Another flare goes by. She hears what sounds like feet on the hood of the car, and then the only sound is the wind. She can feel rain coming in through the open sunroof and she shivers.

There is the sound of quick steps on the hood again, and then Loki's voice is very close to her ear. "Drive forward!"

Amy does. She sees the rainbow of the gateway again, and her body and the car come into view bathed in early morning light. Dark bricks surround her on either side and she smells garbage and urine and thinks that an alley has never smelled so sweet. She looks up. Loki is half on the hood, half on the roof. His head is above her, looking in the direction they came, a sword in his hand. Glancing in the rear view mirror she sees Beatrice sleeping, the seat behind her Grandmother just coming into view.

Amy smiles and breathes out a long breath of relief. The car is almost through when it suddenly jerks up and backwards, the back wheels seeming to leave the ground. Lines of light surround it on either side. Loki swears. Amy looks back in the window and sees a huge hulking Thor-like shadow seeming to emerge out of nothing behind her. It looks like he's pulling the car backwards by the bumper.

Loki scrambles across the roof towards the back of the car. Amy doesn't think. Shouting "Loki, hold on!" she throws the car into four wheel drive, then reverse, and hits the gas. There is a loud thud. Amy can't see the back of the car; it must still be in Alfheim. But she feels it when the back tires hit the ground and bounce. Heart suddenly very loud, Amy puts the car into first gear and pulls forward but meets resistance.

She looks back. Light flashes in a wide vertical circle behind the car. There is a loud clang, and Loki jumps down off the car and stands in the middle of the circle shouting something in a weird slavic-sounding language. His sword is gone, but in one hand he holds what looks like a tiny book. She thinks she sees Thor again, but then the circle collapses on itself and there's just Loki swaying on his feet.

Turning, with wavering steps he comes around the car. Amy hears the scrape of metal on pavement, and then Loki climbs into the passenger side, sword in his hand.

Beatrice is rubbing her eyes. Fenrir is standing on top of her, looking out the backseat. There is no Thor, but the last six inches of the rear of the car is just gone.

Closing the door and hanging his head, Loki says softly, "Will Car be alright?"

Amy looks back at the missing rear end, and over at Loki. "You know...it's just a machine."

Loki turns his head to look at her. "How can you say that?"

Feeling like a heel, she turns to the steering wheel. Her hands are shaking so much she doesn't really want to go anywhere for a few minutes.

"Dude!" comes a loud voice from outside the car.

Raising her eyes, she sees three guys with spiky hair in hipster clothing standing directly in front of them in the alley. Their mouths are open. The middle one's got a bottle of something in his hands. It falls to the ground and lands with a crash.

Somewhere a police siren wails.

Swallowing, Amy revs the engine a bit. The hipsters move to the side. She pulls out into the alley and heads home. Thankfully, they don't run into any police. She's sure driving with a hole in the back of your car is some sort of moving violation.

Loki says nothing the entire way. He just slouches over in the seat, his breathing ragged and uneven as though he's extremely tired or might weep.

It's still mostly dark out when she backs into the garage, and she doesn't see any neighbors about. Beatrice says, "Oh, my, are we home already?"

Before Amy's even parked, Loki jumps out of his seat and walks out of the garage.

"I'll be right back, Grandma!" Amy says, following him.

She catches him just a few feet outside of the garage. "Loki," she says putting a hand on his left arm that doesn't have any armor on it. He stops but doesn't look at her.

Jaw tight he says, "I think you should know, I have tangled the branch of the world tree we came through. Neither Odin or Heimdall will be able to follow it and find you — " He stops, closes his eyes, takes a deep breath and disappears. For an instant Amy feels him beneath her hand, warm and solid, but then that's gone, too.

Fenrir barks in the garage. Amy just stands staring in the empty alley, feeling hollow and empty.

CHAPTER 12

It's nearly 9:00 PM, three days after Loki disappeared. Amy is just coming home from a shift as vet tech at a clinic up on the North Side. She only gets about eight hours a week from the clinic, and she has managed to get another four as a hostess at a restaurant, but jobs are surprisingly hard to come by this summer.

As Amy climbs the stairs with Fenrir scampering at her feet, she sees Beatrice's door ajar, the light on. She peeks in. Beatrice is sitting on her bed. The dress from Alfheim is hanging on her closet door. It still glows.

Beatrice must hear her because she turns to Amy, a little girl smile on her face. "Would it be wrong to put on our dresses occasionally and throw tea parties?"

Amy blinks, feeling her eyes get wet. Beatrice's memories of Alfheim are only good. Despite Amy's decidedly more mixed experience, she understands what Beatrice means. "I'd be happy to join you for tea," Amy says.

Beatrice sighs and relaxes. "I'm not just going senile. It was real, it really happened!"

Amy stares at the dress.

Beatrice sighs. "Still no sign of Loki. He left his sword." She turns to Amy. "That must be a sign he will come back?"

Amy bites her lip. She is worried it might be a sign of something worse, something self-destructive. "I hope so," she says. Loki in some ways reminds her of the worst frat-boy she's ever met, except with magic. But there is a part of her that believes he's good, and noble even. She remembers the way he stood up to Thor when that big overgrown oaf suggested keeping her as a pet. And Loki did save her from Malson. And then the way he danced with Beatrice... She swallows. Hopefully he's out there, and okay.

Amy looks at Beatrice's beautiful dress and then down at her slightly stained blue scrubs. Suddenly realizing how much she smells like ill cats and dogs, she says, "I'm going to go take a shower."

Beatrice nods.

When Amy comes out of the shower, Beatrice's light is off. With Fenrir by her side, Amy curls up in her own bed and tries to read a book. She's exhausted, but she's still having trouble sleeping. After an hour or so, she turns off her light. She lies in the dark gazing at the ceiling for far too long, but she must eventually drift off because she lifts her head at one point and Fenrir says in a deep masculine voice, "Amy, get up."

Amy stares at her little dog. Fenrir is lying down at her feet, her ears cocked, seemingly staring at a point at the end of her nose.

Amy blinks. It must be a dream — if Fenrir spoke it would be with a girl's voice. At least I'm sleeping, she thinks. With that sleep-induced logic at the forefront of her mind, she lies back down and closes her eyes.

"Ahem!"

Amy opens her eyes. Where her little Fenrir was lying at the end of her bed, there is now a giant wolf sitting on its haunches.

Amy screams, scrambles backwards, and hits the back-board of her bed so hard her head bounces. She tries to jump out of her bed, catches her feet on the sheets, and promptly falls flat on the floor.

"Oh, I'm sorry," says the wolf in a voice that is still masculine, but also familiar...and slightly slurred.

Amy turns her head. "Loki?" she asks cautiously.

The wolf raises a paw to its mouth and snickers. Putting the paw down, it says in a loud voice, "I am the spirit of Fenrir!" Letting loose a howl, it lies down on the bed, rolls over on its back, and closes its eyes. From tail to nose it completely fills the bed. Amy's mouth opens, and the real Fenrir runs over and starts barking at the wolf.

From the door comes a knock. "Amy?"

"It's alright, Grandma. I think it's just...Fenrir."

The wolf blinks its eyes open. "Actually, you were right the first time. Sort of. I think I'm more Loki's subconscious."

"Loki's subconscious?" says Amy.

"Loki's subconscious?" says Beatrice through the door.

Rolling on its stomach, the wolf says, "Yes, that tiny, tiny, little part of him that doesn't want to drown in his own vomit in your backyard."

Amy springs up and opens her bedroom door. "Grandma,"

she says. "I think Loki is in the backyard."

Beatrice looks past Amy and says, "Who were you talking to?"

"The wolf."

"Wolf?" says Beatrice.

Amy looks back. The bed is empty.

"Never mind," she says, turning and running down the hall. She hears Beatrice following more slowly behind her.

A few moments later Amy throws open the kitchen door. Sure enough there is Loki sprawled out on the lawn on his back, an arm thrown over his eyes, his attire flickering from armor to street clothes and back again. She sees something wet glistening on his chin and winces. Magical frat boy indeed.

Behind her she hears Beatrice tsk-tsk. Her grandmother walks right by Amy and out onto the lawn. As she goes over to Loki, a light in the neighbor's house goes on. A window opens and said neighbor, Harry, a sixty five-ish year old man who's lived there forever, says, "Beatrice, I saw that bum pissing in your bushes! Want me to call the cops?"

Amy sags. Whatever hope she had for nobility in Loki is flushed down the drain. Or peed into the hedge.

"No, no, no! That's alright, Harry!" Beatrice shouts. "We know him."

"What's that he's wearing?" Harry shouts. Several other lights down the block go on.

Beatrice taps Loki with a foot, then looks up at Harry again. "Clothes, Harry! Clothes!"

Loki begins to cough.

"Amy!" Beatrice says. "Help me roll him over!"

Startled out of her reverie, Amy runs out and helps Beatrice roll Loki onto his side. He smells like a wino, and up close she can see he hasn't shaven, probably since Alfheim.

"Ugh," says Amy.

Beatrice turns her head and winces.

Fenrir, Amy's Fenrir, moves closer and licks his face. Which is probably a testament to just how disgusting whatever is on his chin is.

"Eww..." says Amy.

Beatrice puts a hand over her nose and her mouth and kicks Loki in the ribs with surprising force.

Loki's eyes flutter but don't open.

"Get in the house, Loki!" Beatrice says.

"Grandma," Amy says, "I don't think that's going to work."

Beatrice kicks him again. To Amy's surprise, Loki rolls over onto his stomach and pulls himself up onto his feet, but he tips dangerously.

"You get under that arm," says Beatrice resolutely. "I'll get under this one."

Together they manage to get Loki across the lawn and up the stoop. They've just stepped into the kitchen and Amy's head is bent over when Beatrice screams and drops the arm she's holding.

Loki falls to the side and crashes on the floor. Amy looks up and there is wolf Fenrir sitting in front of the kitchen sink.

Grabbing her grandmother, Amy narrows her eyes. "Couldn't you have just made yourself look like yourself!"

"That would be needlessly straightforward," says the wolf.

"Wha - wha - wha -" says Beatrice.

"It's alright, Grandma," Amy says, patting her back. "It's just Loki's subconscious."

Tilting its head, the wolf says, "Shouldn't you move him

to the couch?"

Amy looks down at Loki lying on his side on the floor in a semi-fetal position.

"Should we, Grandma?"

Eyeing the wolf carefully, Beatrice says shakily, "No, it'll be easier to clean up if he throws up here."

The wolf puts back its ears, bobs its head, thumps its tail and opens its eyes wide.

"No," says Beatrice, the self-assuredness back in her voice.

Straightening, the wolf sighs. "It was worth a try."

The real Loki mutters in his sleep.

Wincing, Amy says, "What happened?"

"He went on a three day bender," says Beatrice, her voice very dry, a scowl settling on her features.

"Why?" says Amy, walking over to get a dish towel. The spittle or whatever it is on his chin is grossing her out.

"They killed his sons...and Hoenir, Mimir and Sigyn," the wolf says.

Amy looks up from where she is about to wipe Loki's face.

She looks over at Beatrice. The hard lines in her grandmother's brow have softened.

The wolf settles down on the floor with a whimper. "Gone now like Aggie and Helen."

"Helen?" says Amy.

The wolf stares at Loki, his voice far off. "You know her as Hel."

"And Aggie..." says Beatrice. "Angrboða?"

Turning its eyes to Beatrice, the wolf snarls. "Her name was Anganboða, bringer of joy! Do not call her by the name Baldur gave!"

Beatrice puts her hand to her mouth and steps back.

Snarling, the wolf says. "Baldur destroyed her! Called her a troll and a witch. Even Odin spoke ill against her." The wolf's voice takes on a sing-song quality. "Because no one would ever gainsay the words of Baldur the Brave."

And then dropping its head down, the wolf that is maybe a figment of Loki's imagination puts its paws over his nose. "She saw Baldur for what he was. What she saw in Loki..." The wolf whimpers.

The great hall of Odin's palace is filled with golden firelight and the buzz of conversation. Loki stands just to the right of the thrones of Odin, Frigga and crown prince Baldur.

Loki's lips were released from the dwarf wire just a month ago, and he isn't quite healed. Small circles of white scar tissue dot his upper lip and chin. As proficient as he is with magic, the wire itself was magical; the scars are slow to heal and difficult to cover with an illusion.

Odin has commanded he be here. Asgard is receiving King Frosthyrr from Jotunheim, land of the Frost Giants. Loki has never been to Jotunheim — not since Odin rescued him as an infant during a campaign, anyway. He doesn't know Jotunn customs, and the scars on his lips don't speak well of his treatment in Asgard. He has no idea what his presence is supposed to accomplish.

Now as they wait for their guests to enter, Loki scans the hall. He catches Thor's eyes. Thor smiles with too many teeth and raises his hammer. Loki looks away.

He sees Sigyn in a distant corner and looks away again. Hoenir is standing near her in the shadows. Mimir is with him. For the occasion Mimir has been mounted on the end of a long staff. Loki contains a wince. Mimir loves being on the staff point. It gives him a better view. It also is a quite gruesome sight to the uninitiated. Loki wonders how Hoenir convinced Odin to allow it.

Catching his gaze, Mimir smiles brightly at Loki and lifts his eyebrows. It's a Mimir rendition of a wave. Loki nods in his direction.

Horns announce the Jotunn's arrival, and the hall goes quiet. Great double doors opposite the thrones open up and the Jotunn delegation marches in. King Frosthyrr is just one of many kings of Jotunheim squabbling for control of that realm. The civil wars on Jotunheim have given Frost Giants a reputation for primitive savagery, but you would not know it from looking at King Frost-hyrr or the lords and ladies accompanying him. Their armor and clothing are fine, their bearing regal. But whereas Odin's palace is bathed in warm colors — oranges, reds and golds — the Frost Giants wear whites, silvers and blues. The giantesses wear jewelry of cool crystal. Like Loki, to a one they are pale, their skin almost translucent.

At the head of the procession marches King Frosthyrr with his daughter, Princess Járnsaxa. Odin has instructed Baldur to pay special attention to the princess. Loki notices with some disap-pointment that she is actually quite lovely. Her pale cheeks are rosy, her eyes blue and sparkling beneath dark blonde locks. She is smiling perhaps more than a princess should, but overall...Loki sighs. Why does Baldur always get the pleasant tasks?

He looks over at the crown prince. To his surprise, Baldur's eyes are riveted at the far end of the procession. Loki blinks, and then he sees what has caught Baldur's attention. A giantess stands there, her attire somewhat more modest than her companions. She has the darkest hair Loki has ever seen, falling behind her

212 C. GOCKEL

shoulders like a black curtain. Her features are delicate and fine except for wide generous lips. Tall, and voluptuous without being fat, her bearing is as regal as a queen's.

She is the most beautiful woman Loki has ever seen; and next to her, Princess Járnsaxa is only plain.

He shifts on his feet and finds her eyes on his. Her gaze quickly drops and wanders over the royal family beside him, and then it comes back to Loki. She smiles slightly as though they are sharing some secret joke, and then the man standing next to her whispers something in her ear and she frowns and looks away.

Loki stands transfixed for a moment, Odin's words to King Frosthyrr are an unintelligible murmur at the edge of his consciousness. He looks to the crown prince. Baldur's eyes are still riveted on the giantess.

If she has the attention of the golden prince, she is a lost cause. Loki looks away, but over the next few hours his eyes keep going back to her.

Much later in the evening, after the feasting is mostly done and the festivities are turning to dancing, Loki eyes are still wandering to the giantess. He's learned her name is Anganboða. She is unmarried; the man she was speaking to earlier is her brother. Now she stands between said brother and Baldur. Loki scowls.

Thor's loud voice bellows over his shoulder. "What's wrong, Scar Lip? Won't anyone dance with you?"

Loki glares at Thor. "I simply have not asked anyone."

Thor's eyes sparkle and he smiles wickedly. "And you think anyone would give you that honor?"

Loki feels his blood go hot. Without thinking he says, "I bet you six months of your princely stipend that the very first individual I ask will be unable to refuse me."

Thor's smile drops. "If I win I get your stipend for same."

"Done," says Loki, smirking despite the fact he has no idea how he's going to pull this off. His eyes pass over the room. The only woman who might dance with him is Sigyn, but he recoils at that idea. And then he blinks, and recalling his wager, he turns and walks, nay nearly skips, over to Hoenir and Mimir. Bowing low before the staff that Mimir is mounted on, Loki says, "Mimir, would you do me the honor of dancing with me?"

Before Mimir can even respond, Loki pulls the staff from Hoenir's hands and starts moving towards the floor. Behind him Loki can hear Hoenir snort. At the top of the staff Mimir says loudly, "Well, it's not like I can refuse, is it?"

Across the room Loki sees Thor's face go red. Loki smiles with all his teeth and steps with Mimir into the line of dancers, twirling the staff as he does so. From the crowd he hears laughter and cries of "fool," but imagining what he'll do with six months of a princeling's allowance more than makes up for it.

"I say, Loki," says Mimir. "This actually isn't half bad. I can see so much this way. Spin me again!"

Now that Loki's technically fulfilled the requirements of his wager he could quit, but seeing Thor's furious glare across the hall is just too priceless to let go. He dances with Mimir, spins him, dips him, catches the staff on his foot, and tips it back up into his hands.

"I say," says Mimir, "dip me again! I didn't realize the frescoes on the ceiling had changed. I miss being able to bend my neck..."

Loki grins, even though the hall is filling with raucous laughter at his expense. The music gets louder and faster. The torches start to flicker madly, the fires in their pits send sparks shooting up into the air, and then the laughter takes on a nervous edge and someone screams.

"Or maybe we should stop," says Mimir.

The music is slowing anyway. Loki tilts Mimir back for a final, proper dip and as he bows, Mimir's staff in hand, he hears curses and shouts, but above it all the sound of one set of hands clapping.

Loki looks up and there is Anganboða not two paces away, clapping happily. "Well done!" she says, smiling at him. He does not smile back. She is so beautiful and so close. He wants to go to her, to smile in return, but she has the eye of Baldur and he knows who will win in such a contest. The effort it takes to stifle his natural impulses makes his lips twist into a frown; his body flushes with heat and rage.

Screams rise in the hall. Anganboða turns, and Loki follows her gaze. Sparks of fire are jumping madly from candles and the fire pits. Loki's mouth opens in surprise, and his rage cools a bit just as the sparks subside.

"Oh, dear," says Mimir.

Baldur and Anganboða's brother are suddenly at her side, steering her away.

Loki watches them go, his face a mask of indifference. And then beside him he hears Odin's voice. "I grow weary of playing politics. I need a drink. Come with us, Loki."

Loki turns and there is Hoenir and Odin. A drink sounds like a very good idea.

Away from the party, in Odin's own rooms, one drink turns into a few. Loki manages to lose all the money he won from Thor in a wager over a chess game while he is only slightly drunk.

...and then he proceeds to win it all back — and a rather nice guest house thrown in for good measure, while he is incredibly, mind-bendingly drunk during a second chess match.

His head is lying on the board and he hears Mimir nagging

with Odin somewhere far, far, far, off in the distance. "It's your fault! You should never have played him while he was so drunk. You had to know with those odds he'd win! Now look, you're all drunk...Hoenir, don't animate the chess pieces! You know they'll squabble and cause all sorts of trouble — and you haven't given them mouths! You've doomed them to die!"

Loki hears Odin guffaw and Hoenir snort. Loki manages to raise his head. The chess pieces are sliding at each other and not paying attention to the rules of the board at all. He drops his head again.

"Come on, Hoenir," says Mimir. "Let's take Loki home... you're less drunk than he is...Well then, heal yourself...I don't care if you don't want to be sober!"

Loki feels a hand slap his back, and then suddenly his head stops spinning and the world comes into focus. The chess pieces are knocking one another off the board, Odin has his hand on Hoenir's shoulder, and they're both laughing hysterically. Mimir's staff is propped against the wall. For his part, Mimir looks extremely put out.

Loki sits up and meets Odin's unblinking eye. Odin points his finger at him and laughs, "Ha! You get to be the responsible one for once! Take Hoenir home or I'll lift my eye patch and give you a fright!"

At that Hoenir snickers with such force he falls off his stool. The stool promptly hops backwards and begins to scamper around like a small dog.

"Loki, let's go before Hoenir animates something dangerous," Mimir mutters.

Suddenly noticing the wide array of weapons decorating the walls of Odin's private chamber, Loki gets off his chair and slides one of Hoenir's arms under his shoulder. With the other hand he *grabs Mimir's staff. They leave Odin talking with the chess pieces, idly patting Hoenir's stool.*

"Well, that was just like old times," Mimir says as they make their way down a long hallway past Odin's guard. Loki can't be bothered to respond. Hoenir is heavy. Also, Loki is watching for signs that he will throw up.

Loki decides to cut through the guest wing of the palace. There is a servants' corridor and exit that will let them out closer to Hoenir's hut than the front or back entrance. He is passing through some long unremarkable corridor when he hears a female voice echoing down the hall. "For so long you have said my honor was my most important possession, and now you want me to give it away to some so-called-golden prince so that you may rise in power!"

It takes a moment for Loki to realize it is Anganboða's voice. And another moment more to comprehend what she is saying. So-called-golden prince? She is not smitten? He must have heard wrong. He finds himself stopping, his hands tightening on Mimir's staff. There is a sound like a slap and then a door slams. Loki watches as Anganboða's brother strides off down the hall in the opposite direction, passing by another servant as he does.

That servant meets Loki's eyes. In his hands, Mimir whispers, "There really is nothing you can do at this point that won't make the lady's situation worse."

Loki frowns but continues slowly on his way.

By the time he reaches the small door that exits to the garden, he doesn't think his mood can get worse. There is a lantern by the door that he gives to Mimir to hold in his teeth, and then they step out into the night and Loki realizes it's raining. Soon Loki is wet and chilled and Hoenir is getting heavier and heavier, and less and less cooperative. It would be better if Loki could swing him over his shoulder, but he also has to tote Mimir along.

Loki thinks of Odin warm and drunk and happy in his rooms and scowls. He hates being the responsible one.

Head bent over, he continues on. The rain picks up, and they're just turning into a walkway lined with long hedges when Mimir mumbles through the lantern handle in his mouth. "'ook!"

Loki looks up; a hooded figure is pressed against the hedge. Whoever it is doesn't seem to be aware of their approach until they are nearly upon them, and then the figure turns. The hood spills off and Loki and Mimir are facing a very red-eyed Anganboða.

"What are you doing here?" he says, the words harsher than he intends.

"Is it any of your business?" she says.

Loki stares at her and he knows. "You're running away," he says. At least temporarily. From Baldur. Maybe from her family.

She doesn't deny it.

He twists his hands on Mimir's staff. Choosing to run away in the rain, probably without a plan, or without really knowing where she was going...She's obviously a bit mad.

The right thing for Loki to do, if he values his position at court, is to convince her to go back to the palace, grit her teeth, and allow Baldur's "affections."

He holds out Mimir's staff to her and says, "You can come with us." Apparently Loki can only be responsible to a point.

She takes the staff, looks up at Mimir and says, "Would you like me to take the lantern?"

"Yesh!" says the head, dropping it from his mouth into her hands.

It was quite nice of her to think of Mimir that way. For some reason it irritates him. Swinging the nearly unconscious Hoenir over his shoulder, he begins to walk away. A few paces later he turns back. Anganboða hasn't moved.

"You need not worry about your honor. You have my oath it is safe with me," Loki says, the words spilling out before he even thinks about them.

She tilts her head and then says, "I trust you." And she does. Loki has a rather keen sense for disambiguation. She's definitely mad.

Heaving a breath, she says, "But it doesn't seem to matter what you do, it's what people say you do..."

"Ahem," says Mimir. "Consider me your chaperone."

Looking up at the head, Anganboða's lips part. Those very wide, generous lips. Loki can't help but stare.

Why did he just make an oath to protect her honor? Scowling, Loki says, "Come on, Hoenir's heavy," and starts walking again. This time she hurries to catch up.

"Did you have any plans?" Loki gasps out as they trudge along. "Since you have chosen to run rather than accept the suit of Baldur the Beautiful, Wise and Brave."

"Is he those things?" Anganboða says.

Loki turns to her. Rain has plastered her raven locks to her face, and he realizes what he took for a cloak is actually just a blanket, probably stolen from her rooms in the palace. She is very desperate.

Turning her eyes to the muddy ground she says, "I look at him...and I see a golden prince, but when I turn away, from the corner of my eye I see something quite different. Something I don't like, something dark. When I hear his words they sound sweet, but when I replay them in my mind they are cruel." She laughs and there is something frantic in it. "Yet everyone says he is beautiful, wise and brave."

Loki turns to her, mouth open. No one else has ever doubted

Baldur. A knot in his stomach uncoils with a force so strong it hurts.

"I must be mad," she says softly. "And yet...he bartered for my honor with my brother...am I worth so little that a man can do that and still be good?"

"No, my lady," Loki says.

She turns to him and smiles softly, and he finds himself silently vowing that if Baldur ever lays a finger on her, ever hurts her, he will make him die a slow and painful death.

They turn round a hedge and step through the large trees that shield Hoenir's hut from the rest of Asgard. "What a meager abode for Odin's brother," Anganboða says out of nowhere.

Loki blinks and shoves Hoenir against the door. "Hoenir is not Odin's brother. Whatever made you think that?"

Hoenir grunts, the door gives way, and Mimir is overcome with a minor coughing fit.

Following him in the door, Anganboða says, "But the three of you...you're brothers, surely..."

"We aren't related," says Loki.

Mimir's minor coughing fit turns to a major coughing fit. Loki looks at him sharply, wondering what's amiss. Mimir says nothing, just turns very red.

"Brothers," the wolf mutters nonsensically. "She was mad...but I still loved her. And Sigyn..." It whimpers again.

Amy looks down at Loki. Beside her, Beatrice kneels down, too. Surely losing your children, best friends and wife warranted a little sympathy? She touches the cloth gingerly to Loki's chin, the reek suddenly not bothering her as much.

Underneath his unshaven face she begins to see that nobility again.

"So sad," says Beatrice with a sigh.

Loki's eyes flutter open. "Where am I?" he asks, rolling onto his back.

Leaning over him, gently brushing his cheeks, Amy says, "You're safe. You're back with Beatrice and me."

Loki's eyes go over to Beatrice and then rove down Amy's body. He mutters something. Even though it is in a strange foreign language, it sounds heavy with gratitude.

His eyes close again and Amy says to the wolf. "What did he just say?"

Blinking, the wolf says, "Oh, he said 'By the World Tree you have nice tits.'" And then it pops out of existence.

Amy leans away, just a little bit horrified.

Beatrice shakes her head ruefully. "Well, he's not the god of niceness." Standing up she says, "I'm going to bed."

CHAPTER 13

The next morning when Amy comes into the kitchen Beatrice is already there, and so is Loki. Beatrice is buzzing around the stove; Loki is sitting at the table, hunched over a cup of coffee and a half eaten plate of eggs. His hair is wet like he's just come out of the shower, but he still hasn't shaved. He isn't in his armor. He's wearing one of her grandfather's old tee shirts and a pair of Grandpa's utility pants that fit Loki like capris.

He doesn't raise his eyes when she comes in, just stares at a point on the table next to the sugar jar.

"Hi," Amy says.

Loki doesn't move or speak. But Beatrice says, "Good morning, Dear." And then her grandmother takes a cup of tea and goes and sits down next to Loki at the table.

Amy pours herself a cup of coffee and joins them.

Loki doesn't do anything, just sits hunched over, as though

inhabiting his own dark world. It's frightening, and sad.

Swallowing, Amy says, "You told us what happened."

Loki's eyes shoot up to hers. For a moment Amy thinks they are completely black, but she blinks, and they're that eerie light gray color again.

"You told us last night," Amy says. Or his subconscious did. It doesn't seem worthwhile to go into the whole wolf Fenrir thing. "I'm sorry about your family, and your friends."

Loki looks away.

Beatrice shakily puts down her teacup. "I hope you won't do anything ...rash..."

Amy blinks. A three-day bender seems pretty rash to her.

Loki's eyes slide to Beatrice and then he smirks. "Are you are referring to Ragnarok, Beatrice?"

"It had crossed my mind." Beatrice's eyes are steady, but her hands are shaking on her teacup.

Amy's heart stops. If she remembers Loki's Wikipedia entry correctly, he's the one who leads the dead in the battle against the Norse gods at Ragnarok, the end of the world.

Loki snorts, and then he begins to laugh quietly. Playing idly with his fork he says, "Oh, if only I could hop aboard the ship Naglfar and lead the armies of Hel against Asgard, I would, definitely. But there are no armies in the realm of Hel. Just my daughter's corpse, and the corpses of her maids." His smile drops and he looks away. "There is no Hel for the meek, no Valhalla for warriors slain in battle. Those are just dreams you humans use to console yourselves during your fleeting lives. There is just nothingness."

"You don't know that!" says Beatrice, fingering the cross hanging around her neck.

Loki looks up at her and glares. And then he stands from

the table and walks out the door. Beatrice and Amy watch him walk into the garage. Amy looks around the kitchen. Nothing is on fire. For some reason that makes her sad.

Sitting with her laptop and checkbook on the kitchen table, Amy's looking at her bank accounts trying not to feel depressed. It's the evening after Loki's return. She had a temp job in the afternoon, and now she's obsessively reconciling her checkbook, calculating how much she has earned and how much she'll need to earn to have enough money to pay the school fees her scholarship doesn't cover, and to make a down payment on a new place to live in the fall.

Hearing a knock at the door, Amy looks up. Through the window she sees Loki wearing the same clothes he had on earlier.

Grateful for the distraction and relieved that he looks sober and shaven, Amy walks over and opens the door. Face almost expressionless, Loki says, "Miss Lewis, it seems I will be a guest of your world for awhile. I was wondering if..." He looks away. "If you might help me get acclimated to your world's current magic...technologies."

Amy's stares at him. That seems so healthy and proactive. "Wow. Good for you," she says, too shocked to move from the doorway.

Shrugging, he says in a flat voice, "If I'm going to see Odin kneel before me while I hold his testicles in my hands as all of Asgard burns, I have to start somewhere."

Amy's mouth drops.

Straightening, Loki says, "I will make it worth your while

somehow, I give you my — "

Amy waves a hand. "No, no, no. It's okay...of course I'll help you if I can; you don't owe me anything." She'll just take that Odin's testicle thing and Asgard burning thing as a slight bit of hyperbole brought on by grief.

Loki tilts his head and his expression softens just a bit.

Her brow furrows. "Is there any place you'd like to start?"

Loki's eyes go over to her laptop on the kitchen table. "Computers and the internets. The last time I was here I had some access to ENIAC — but things have come so far since then."

Amy blinks at him. ENIAC? Shaking her head she steps aside and motions for him to come in. "Have a seat. I'll get us something to drink."

"Thank you," says Loki, walking over and sitting in front of her computer. As she turns to the refrigerator, he's staring at the blank screen of power save mode.

Taking out a pitcher of freshly made peach tea, she pours two glasses and turns around. Loki has one finger hovering above the keyboard and he's staring at her bank account information.

"Whoa," says Amy, going to the table and closing that tab.

Loki looks at her, brows slightly raised.

Wincing, Amy says, "You probably shouldn't have seen that."

Loki holds up two hands. "I just touched it and — "

"No, no, no...It's okay." She grabs her checkbook and then brings the two glasses of tea over to the table. Handing him one, she takes a sip of her own. It's not as cold as she expected. "Drats, I'll have to get some ice," she says.

Holding out a hand to her, Loki says, "Sit down and allow me."

She hands him the glasses. He gives her a twisted half smile and frost climbs up the outside of both. "Here," he says, handing one back.

Amy finds herself smiling...more than she should. Is she being flirty? She shouldn't be flirty. He just lost his family and his best friends and that would be inappropriate. She schools her face to neutral. Is it her imagination or is her pulse a little quick? Just knowing about his family...he doesn't seem so much like an obnoxious flirt anymore. He has children, he's —

Loki clinks his glass with hers which snaps her back to the moment. She takes a sip. "It's perfect," she says, staring over her glass at him.

Loki raises an eyebrow. "Where should we start?"

Realizing she's staring, she spins back to her computer. "Well, I guess, first...this is a mouse." She toggles the wireless mouse she has next to her iMac. Remembering his confusion over Car, she says, "It's just what it's called...it's not actually alive."

Loki holds out a hand and she hands it to him. Eying the mouse he murmurs, "Hoenir would have fun with this." Expression hardening, he says, "How does it work?"

Amy has some experience teaching techie neophytes. She expects hours of back and forth, and obvious questions that make her want to tear her hair out. That doesn't happen.

Loki grasps the point and click concept immediately. They move quickly from mice to the internet, and he begins asking questions that are too technical. He accidentally calls up the browser's options and gets a menu she has never seen. He clicks on something, and when the page of gobbledygook comes up, he recognizes it immediately as the code for the page.

That's when she looks down and sees it. "Um..." she says. "Loki, your fingertips are blue..." It's that lovely, robin's egg shade she had seen before, and it almost seems to be alight from within.

He looks down and his brow furrows. He takes a breath and the color fades away, like a wave draining from sand. Turning to her, his expression sharp, he says, "It is just an illusion."

Amy can't help it; she puts a hand on his shoulder. "It's okay."

Turning back to the computer he says dryly, "I blame you for putting the damned idea in my head."

Removing her hand and taking a deep uncomfortable breath, Amy says, "Okay, maybe we should go next to Google. It's an internet site that can tell you just about everything...."

Once Loki has access to Google, it quickly becomes apparent that Amy isn't so much helping as holding Loki back. She gets up and lets him explore 'How the Internet Works' and 'Static Versus Dynamic Web Pages' by himself.

Beatrice comes in, they all eat dinner together, and then Loki is at the computer again. When Amy goes to bed, Loki is still there, the screen flashing from one page to another. His eyes look very dark, and she swears his skin has a blue cast but decides not to say anything.

The next day when Beatrice goes to fetch Loki for breakfast, Amy clicks on the browser's history — just out of curiosity. She's not sure what she expected to find, but she doesn't expect to find a whole bunch of entries on something called Schrödinger's cat, the Heisenberg uncertainty principle, quantum computing, random number generators and something on financial derivatives. She backs slowly away.

At breakfast when she asks him what he was browsing the night before, he just smirks and says, "Magic."

With the help of Google, Loki fixes the ceiling fan in her grandmother's room — turns out the problem was actually in the fuse box. During his first week with them, among other acts of computer wizardry, Loki cleans up the hard drive on Beatrice's PC — something Amy would have thought impossible since her grandmother seems to open every attachment and click on every link she's ever gotten in an email. And he also manages to get a nasty virus off of nosy-neighbor Harry's computer — Harry's on Beatrice's email list. Sometime that first week he also hooks up the television, the DVD player and the stereo so that all share one remote, something Amy never managed to do. After that Amy finds herself regularly watching TV with Loki late into the night. He lies on the couch, feet propped up on one end. She sits on the EZ-boy chair — she starts sleeping better there than anywhere else.

Overall, Beatrice and Amy are both really impressed by the way Loki immerses himself in modern technology and modern life. But there are some incidents.

Amy comes home just after lunchtime during Loki's second week with them. She had a job as a hostess at a local restaurant that morning. Beatrice meets her in the backyard, water pot in hand. "He's in the kitchen," Beatrice says. "I think you need to talk to him. We just don't do that!"

Puzzled, Amy heads into the kitchen. Loki is wearing her grandmother's apron...which is a little odd considering it is pink and far too small...but that isn't what really grabs her attention.

"Why is there a dead pig on our kitchen table?" She's been around enough dead animals in vet school to recognize it without most of its skin and to not be disgusted — even if she is mostly vegetarian.

Loki looks up from where he is leaning over said pig with a very big cleaver. His brows furrow. "It has come to my attention that I am, in Beatrice's words, 'Eating you out of house and home.' I am trying to do my 'fair share'."

"By butchering a pig..."

"It is a free-range pig, much higher quality than you would get in the the grocery store. Also, it is freshly slaughtered. It will be delicious...even you will want to eat this bacon." He smacks the pig's hindquarters and smiles.

Tilting his chin and rubbing the back of his cheek with a bloody hand, he says, "Though tonight I think we should eat the head. I make a delicious sweetbread." He looks at her, holding up the cleaver in a way that is kind of psycho-esque. "What?"

"You cook?" she says. That is probably the least important question in her mind, but somehow it pops up first.

He rolls his eyes. "Odin was always sending me out to babysit Thor when he went adventuring. Thor was a prince; a bastard, but a prince... I got to cook."

Amy looks at the dead animal stretched out and filling the whole kitchen table. "Where did you get the pig?"

He blinks at her and then leans down and starts sliding the knife under the pig's skin. "From a butcher on Fulton. I read about it on the internet and went this morning."

"You don't drive...did you take this thing on the bus?" She had taught him how to use the bus and left a pass out for him. The one time Amy tried to teach Loki how to drive, he turned the Subaru into a load bearing part of the garage wall. Amy doesn't know how he can build her a personal website on 'server space' she didn't know she had and hook it up to 'RSS feeds' on veterinary medicine but can't manage to put a car in reverse. It probably relates somehow to him setting the toaster on fire, though.

He looks up at her. "You know they wouldn't let me?" He shakes his head as though amazed. "I carried it back. I got a lot of stares. You'd think people never had seen a hog before."

Amy can hear the neighborhood gossip mill grinding in her head. Trying not to think about it she says, "How did you pay for it?"

He blinks again.

Oh, no. "Did you steal this pig?"

"I have no money. Of course I stole the pig," he says.

"We don't do that!" says Amy.

He stares at her. Then frowning and crossing his arms, cleaver still in hand, he says, "Do you want me to return it?"

Amy looks at the partially butchered animal and rubs her eyes. "No, just tell me where you stole it from and give me your oath that you won't do it again." She tells herself she'll send the butcher compensation. Somehow. Anonymously.

"Fine...you have my oath, while I reside at your house, I will not steal another pig — "

"Anything," says Amy.

He glowers at her.

She glowers right back even though she feels a pang of

fear. "It could attract attention and the police."

Narrowing his eyes, he uncrosses his arms and rolls his eyes. "Fine, you have my oath I will not steal while I reside under your roof."

Amy decides that is the best she is going to do. Later that night, despite her better judgment, she tries some pig cheek — it just smells so good. It is delicious.

It is near the end of the second week when the second incident occurs. Amy is just coming home late from her hostessing job. There is a light in the living room. She follows it and finds Loki kneeling in front of the TV cabinet fiddling with the remote.

Without thinking, she puts her hostessing apron with the $66.73 she got in tips from takeaway orders on the coffee table next to her laptop. It was a long day, she made hardly any money, and she has no idea how she's going to pay all her expenses at this rate. Settling into the EZ boy, she just sighs.

Without looking at her, Loki flops down on the couch. "I've hooked the television up to your computer. We can watch YouTube, Netflix, Hulu..."

"Whatever," Amy says.

Without looking at her, Loki points the remote at the TV and some strange menu with cute icons comes up. He selects some talk on YouTube about Higgs Boson particles. Physics really isn't Amy's thing, but it is interesting — until it isn't. Amy finds herself drifting off into sleep, Loki talking in the background...Something about, "Humans can't see magic, but you've found all these ways to look at it indirectly. I really can see why Hoenir is so fond of you..."

She jerks awake when the program ends. The strange menu comes up and Loki flips to Netflix and Star Trek TOS reruns.

Spock's making eyes at some incredibly elegant woman, and Amy's just drifting off to sleep again when Loki says, "She's scrawny."

"Mmmm..." says Amy.

And then out of the blue Loki says, "You know, Amy, you really are just my type, but I don't even feel like having sex right now."

Amy bolts upright. Loki isn't even looking at her. He's just lying on the couch, head turned to the television screen. Her heart rate goes from racing back to normal. For a moment she'd felt like her sanctuary was going to collapse on her.

Staring at the flickering light without even seeing it, Amy feels exhausted again. "Sex is overrated," she says. Sex is a tease. Your body convinces you you want it, and then during it you hardly feel like you're even there, your mind wanders, the sensations become muted. Once it's over you're left feeling incomplete, and empty, wondering why you'd bothered in the first place. And then your partner describes it as awesome. She huffs at a recent memory and stares at her fingernails on the arm of the chair.

"Ordinarily I'd take that as a challenge," Loki says, not moving.

Amy's cheeks flush. "Glad I can be here during your time of personal growth."

"This isn't growth," says Loki, his voice flat.

He isn't looking at her; he hasn't even moved. And then she remembers him laughing about getting his lips sewn shut, and flirting with her in Alfheim. Where did the Loki that could laugh about his own torture go? She's been enjoying his company these last few weeks; he's been mellower. There have been no horrible pick-up lines; she feels so safe she falls asleep with him in her living room. But the reason he's been so mellow, the reason she feels so comfortable — it's because he's depressed, isn't it?

She swallows. And why shouldn't he be? He's lost everything.

The images on the screen stop. "I'm bored with this show," says Loki. He flips back to the cute icon-y menu.

Suddenly anxious to draw him out, Amy says, "Did you hook my computer up to the DVD player somehow?" Talking about technology is about the only thing that seems to perk his interest lately.

Loki actually laughs. "Oh, your DVD player isn't involved in the slightest. I'm utilizing a device called an Apple TV. It's a little box that connects your TV to your computer and the internet. The hard part was getting a username and then a password to initialize it." He shakes his head and sighs. "Actually, it wasn't that hard. You know, if you humans used more pass phrases instead of passwords the internet would be so much more secure. And think of it — 'the pink hadrosaur jumps over 13 purple griffins in the icebox,' you'd never forget it, and it would be nearly impossible to hack."

He actually sounds happy, and that's good, but he talks so fast it takes Amy a moment to decipher all of it. And then she flushes. "Did you steal an Apple TV?"

He waves a hand at her and puffs. "No, I borrowed an Apple TV. I have every intention of returning it."

"You can't do that!"

Loki looks at a point on the wall. "No, I really can. I make myself invisible, walk into the Apple Store and — "

"That's stealing!"

He glares at her. "I do not break my oaths!"

What follows is an argument that she thinks she technically wins, but he refuses to acknowledge her victory. In the end she extracts an oath that he will return the Apple TV the next day and that he won't borrow again without a merchant's express consent...as long as he resides on their property.

That night she goes to sleep in her own bed, leaving him taking the Apple TV box thingy out of the TV cabinet.

Later, she comes down the stairs to let Fenrir out. Loki is stretched out asleep on the couch. A box she supposes is the Apple TV is on the coffee table beside him.

His face is drawn, his fingers are blue and twitching, and he's mumbling something in another language, sounding strained. Her change apron is still on the coffee table, too. She decides not to move it. It's so close to his face, it will jingle and Loki obviously needs his sleep, pained as it may be.

She has his oath not to steal in her house; and she's seen that the man takes his oaths very seriously.

It isn't until she's settled back in bed and closing her eyes that she realizes the true significance of her argument with Loki earlier in the evening.

Her eyes bolt open.

...forget borrowing things without asking. What's really scary is that he's been here two weeks and he's already hacking into computers.

Stumbling out of the rain into Hoenir's hut, Anganboða, Mimir, Loki and the nearly unconscious Hoenir find themselves in a sitting room. Panting, Loki drops Hoenir on the small sofa. Hoenir mumbles something in his sleep, and Loki crumples to the floor.

"That's going to hurt in the morning," says Mimir with a tsk, tsk.

"His head or my back?" Loki grumbles.

"Both," says Mimir. His eyes slide over to Anganboða. "Would you please lean me against that wall?" He waggles his eyebrows in the direction of a wall just to the side of an unlit fireplace.

As Anganboða complies, Loki stares at the logs in the fireplace, concentrates just a moment and the logs leap into flame.

Anganboða gives a small gasp and she backs away from Mimir and the roaring fire. Loki just stares at her silently, his mind an uncomfortable jumble.

"Now, Miss," says Mimir, "Loki did ask a very good question out there. Do you have a plan?"

Anganboða lets the blanket covering her shoulders fall away. Beneath it is a thick satchel. "I was thinking, I have heard some wealthy families will hire a young lady to educate their daughters and young children." Opening the satchel, she pulls out a large and well worn tome. "I have no experience, but I am well read."

Curiosity getting the better of him, Loki says, "That doesn't look like a book for children."

Anganboða sighs. "It isn't, but it is one of my favorites. I couldn't leave it." She hands it to Loki. He opens the dust jacket and smiles. "Ah, it is Hellbendi's, Magic: Mathematical, Scientific and Philosophical Inquiries Beyond Practical Applications." Shaking his head he says almost to himself, "This is a very, very, good book."

Although the Aesir can sense magic and bend it to their will, few have tried to understand it like Hellbendi, a sorcerer from ancient times. Loki has found that understanding the science of magic has greatly improved his practical abilities.

"You've read it?" says Anganboða. She sounds impressed, not bored or mildly disgusted.

He should reply with confidence; however, all that happens is that his jaw drops open.

Fortunately, Mimir comes to Loki's aid. In his most courtly tones he says, "Loki has read that and more. When he isn't causing mischief for his or Odin's amusement, he is often ransacking Hoenir's library."

"Library?" says Anganboða, her face visibly brightening. She looks at Loki expectantly.

Pulling himself together, he says, "Yes, Hoenir's rivals Odin's." Going to retrieve Mimir, he steps towards a wall lined with several doors. "Come, we'll show you," he says.

"Are you sure you know which door? Even I can't keep them straight," Mimir whispers.

Loki isn't sure, but he doesn't answer. Instead, he smiles as confidently as he can at Anganboða, who smiles back wildly. Lifting his eyebrows at her, he opens the first door just slightly. The sound of claws on metal and a furious screeching fills his ears. Loki peeks in the opening. It is a room he has never seen before, lined with giant cages, inside of which are velociraptors as tall as him. Their heads swivel as one towards the doorway. For a moment they just stare, and then they jump against the bars of their cages, shaking and screeching with all their might.

Loki closes the door quickly.

"What were those?" says Anganboða, eyes wide.

"Errrr...." says Mimir.

"*Nothing but harmless hadrosaurs, gentle herbivorous drag-ons,*" says Loki.

"*They didn't look gentle,*" says Anganboða.

"*Let's try the next door,*" says Loki, quickly moving on. Fortunately, that door does lead to the library.

Perhaps an hour later, they are still there. Mimir is leaning against a wall, sound asleep. Loki and Anganboða are sitting at a table, two stacks of books in front of Anganboða. One stack for her to read, the other a stack of children's books Loki is insisting that she borrow from Hoenir.

Leaning on his elbows, Loki says, "*You are so well read, and yet you do not use magic yourself. I don't understand.*"

Anganboða looks down. "*I would love to use magic. But I can't. I see magic but am unable to bend it to my will.*"

She frowns a little. Upset that his line of questioning has made her unhappy, Loki reaches forward and pulls an illusion of a flower from her nose.

Anganboða laughs, and Loki smirks and lifts an eyebrow. He waves his hand and the imaginary flower turns into butterflies — he's more a fan of spiders, but they seldom go over well. The butterflies flap their wings, fly up towards the ceiling and disappear.

Still smiling, Anganboða looks to the books. "*Do you really think Hoenir won't mind if I borrow these?*"

Loki waves a hand. "*Of course he won't mind.*" He leans back in his chair and puts a hand to his chin. "*What's more of a worry is how Baldur reacts to your not coming to see him this evening. Falling out of favor of the crown prince is a sure way to find yourself unemployable.*"

Unless of course, you are Loki. Odin insists Loki remain in Asgard, no matter how Baldur complains.

Tapping his chin, Loki says, "You were supposed to meet him somewhere in the palace, were you not?"

Anganboða's face falls and she nods.

"Don't worry," says Loki. "We will tell the court I transformed myself into Baldur and nearly led you astray, but the fine Mimir saw what I was up to, put an end to my antics, and protected your honor. Eternally grateful, you helped him find his way back to Hoenir's hut." Loki straightens and smiles mischievously. "Your honor is preserved, and Baldur can't possibly be mad at you because everyone knows what a horrible prankster I am." He narrows his eyes. But somehow he has to find a way to keep Baldur away from her in the future.

"I don't like that plan," Anganboða says.

Loki raises an eyebrow. "Why ever not?"

"What of your honor, and how it will be damaged by such a lie?" Anganboða says.

Loki smirks. "Everyone knows I have no honor."

Anganboða's eyes narrow. "Yes, if it wasn't for the eagle eyes of Mimir over there, I'd be ruined by now."

Mimir chooses that moment to release a giant snore.

Loki flushes. His jaw tenses. Pretending that Mimir is protecting her is one of the little mental games he plays to keep his oath to her. "It is not for lack of desire, my Lady." His words sound too cutting, and too cruel, even to him.

Anganboða's gaze moves away. She looks at the books in front of her. "After I am employed, will I see you again?"

Her voice is soft...almost hopeful. Or perhaps he is imagining it. "That can be arranged," he says cautiously.

She smiles, and he feels his lips threaten to pull up.

"But first," he says, "we must make sure you can be employed. You must lie to the court."

Shaking her head, she puts a hand on his. "I won't tell them that story. It is unfair to you."

It's ridiculous how arousing her soft fingers are against his knuckles. He sighs and brings her hand to his lips. "My Lady," he says. "At court you must lie. It is how you survive."

"Loki, Loki, Loki!"

Loki's eyes open to darkness. It takes him a moment to realize he is on Midgard curled up on Beatrice's couch. He puts his hand to his temples, closes his eyes and sees Anganboða's face.

"Aggie...." He sighs. Was there ever a time he was so hopelessly romantic? "I could not protect you..." Or even the much more formidable Sigyn.

"Loki, Loki, Loki!"

Loki feels a chill pass through him. Red mist creeps along the edges of his vision. "What do you want?" he whispers.

"I need your help," the mist says, as usual in Russian.

Loki scowls. "And why would I do that?" The mist swirls around him and the hairs on the back of his neck rise.

"I know what I am," the child's voice says.

Loki says nothing, just narrows his eyes.

"Cera," the child's voice whispers.

Loki raises an eyebrow at the word. Cera means power.

"And I can be your Cera," the red mist says. It is so dense around Loki that he has to blink his eyes to see. His whole body hums and his skin starts to turn blue. Scowling, he fights back the illusion concocted by his obviously slipping sanity and grief.

He blinks again. The thing, Cera, is right. Loki's pulse starts to race. He's been delving into mortal magics these past few weeks looking for some way to exact revenge. Humans are so close to being able to give him what he needs — yet still decades, maybe centuries away. But Cera...if whatever Cera is, is as powerful as Loki thinks, vengeance may be very close.

"What do you want?" Loki whispers.

"Be my Josef!" Cera wails. "Save me from the God people!"

Loki throws his legs over the edge of the couch. "Where are you?"

He feels an anxiety in the pit of his stomach and knows it isn't his own. The thing is projecting emotions now. He scowls.

"I don't know where I am," Cera wails. "But I know where I've been..."

It is way too early in the morning after Loki and Amy's Apple TV discussion, but Amy is dashing down the stairs. The vet clinic called. They are short handed for the day; they asked her if she can be there in half an hour for a ten hour shift. She tears into the kitchen in her scrubs and finds Loki staring out the window, a frown on his face. She runs to retrieve her change apron from the next room. When she gets back in the kitchen, apron in hand, she says, "What's wrong?" She doesn't really have time for the answer, but she remembers him murmuring in his sleep the night before, his fingers twitching, and it makes her physically ache for him.

"I need money," he says, shooting her a look like a

challenge. "And I am forbidden to steal while I am under your roof, so — "

"You could ask to borrow some," says Amy.

Loki's frown vanishes. "Ask?"

"Of course," says Amy. She heaves a breath. "Look, you lost your family, your friends...your world. Of course you'll need some help getting back on your feet." She takes two tens out of the change apron, slips them in the pocket of her scrubs and drops the apron on the table. The change rattles in the pockets. Loki follows it with his eyes.

"Take as much as you need; everything if you need it," Amy says.

"I don't think I could...." says Loki. His eyes have gone wide, and he has the expression of a surprised puppy on his face.

His earnestness surprises Amy and makes butterflies flutter in her stomach. "Look, you know where it all is. Take it. Everything. It's okay. Really."

Loki comes forward and drops to one knee in front of her. "Amy Lewis, I am in your debt. You have my oath that I will pay you back with interest."

"Ummm..." she says. "Well, if you think that is necessary," she says, looking at her change purse. What is it, forty six bucks and some change maybe?

Kissing her hand, he says, "I do think it is necessary."

Amy swallows as warmth rushes through her limbs at his touch. "Okay..." Loki looks up at her, his face shining with something close to happiness. "I wondered why I heard you in the forest, I wondered how your voice came to be in my head, and how you intersected with my higher purpose. Now I know. My gratitude is eternal, and you have my oath, I will pay it back with interest!"

He kisses her hand again, and Amy's mouth drops open. "Ummmm...." is all that comes out. She feels her face go red, and then Loki looks up at her like he might actually kiss her — really kiss her. That is appealing and scary. "I have to go," she squeaks and runs out the kitchen door.

She nearly crashes into Beatrice on the back walk. Clutching a watering can to her chest, Beatrice says, "Did you talk to Loki this morning?"

Amy blinks. "Yes."

Beatrice's eyes narrow. "I heard him talking in Russian." Beatrice learned Russian as a child in the Ukraine — under less than ideal circumstances.

Amy's bites her lip. She has to run, but she doesn't like to rush away from her grandmother. Not when she's talking about her life before.

Shaking her head, Beatrice says, "Something about Cera and Tunguska."

"What?" says Amy.

"Cera is power, dear," says Beatrice. She purses her lips. "I think Tunguska is a place." And then Beatrice starts walking towards the front yard. "Well, I better go. My impatiens are thirsty."

Amy watches her go, her stomach tying in a knot. But then she shakes her head and makes a beeline for the bus stop, waving to the little Mexican man on a bicycle ice cream cart that always seems to be around their house as she goes.

Later that evening when she comes home, her change apron is lying on the table. She peeks in. Loki has left her with $20. A note is on top, written in an oddly near perfect hand.

Miss Lewis,

I must leave for a while and do not know when I shall return; but rest assured, I never forget my oaths. We never discussed terms of my loan, I hope 33% per annum will be sufficient.

Again my gratitude is eternal,

Loki

Amy's heart falls at the "leave for a while" bit. She rubs her hand over the note and sighs.

After a few minutes she picks up the change apron and shakes her head. All that gratitude for what could have only been about $26 bucks?

About a week and a half later, Amy is walking up the sidewalk to her grandmother's house. It's dusk, and the windows are all dark. The day was hot and muggy, and the evening isn't much better, but she sees Beatrice out watering her flowers in the relatively cool air. Her grandmother nods without smiling, and goes around the back of the house, watering can in hand. Her grandmother's expression, the darkness of the house, she doesn't have to ask; Loki is still gone. She bites her lip, and the magic is gone with him. Bowing her head, she trudges up the steps.

Going in the door, she picks up the mail that's been thrust through the mail slot. She rifles through the envelopes, purposefully not looking at the couch where Loki slept.

Her eyebrows rise. There is a letter from her school.

Opening it, she finds that the check she sent in to pay for her miscellaneous school fees has bounced. Shaking her head, she goes to her laptop to check her bank account. She's never bounced a check in her life; there must be a mistake.

A few minutes later, Amy's sitting at the kitchen table, staring at the computer screen, face in her hands. There is only $1 left in her checking. She feels cold, even though the room is warm. Realization hits hard and fast. Loki stole from her, after giving her his precious oath. And he hasn't come back, and she won't be able to go back to school.

She swallows and scoots back from the table feeling sick.

How will she get the money? Should she borrow it from Beatrice? Is it too late to apply for financial aid?

She looks up and her gaze goes to the kitchen window. She's vaguely aware of Beatrice standing up and lowering the the watering can in her hands. Amy closes her eyes, remembering Loki's words, "I will pay you back with interest." Maybe it's all been a mistake? He'll come back, it will all be okay... But it won't be, because she needs the money now.

Outside, Beatrice must see Amy, and her face must look stricken, because Beatrice comes running. And then Beatrice just sort of isn't there.

Amy bolts from her seat, the sickening feeling in her stomach instantly getting worse. She runs through the door and finds Beatrice on the ground at the bottom of the stoop, her leg at an odd angle. Her head is tilted back and her eyes are closed. Blood is on the sidewalk.

"Grandma!" Amy screams. Sinking to her knees, she pulls out her phone, and dials 911. As the phone rings, she takes her grandmothers hand in her own. She looks down at the delicate veins visible through her grandmother's aged skin. Beatrice does not stir. Amy swallows, her eyes hot. Now everything is gone.

A few hours later she is at the hospital, sitting in the waiting room in a daze. On the periphery of her vision she sees several men approaching.

"Miss Lewis?" Amy turns her head, and her brow furrows. There is the older man with the too-square jaw in the too conservative gray suit who she saw in her neighborhood eating ice cream. He's still in a gray suit. Next to him are two other men. The first looks Mexican, and vaguely familiar. She blinks. It's the ice cream vendor, but now he's in a suit, too.

The last man is young. He's wearing a suit too, but he looks a little more rumpled. Looking down at a little device of some kind, he says, "She's clean."

Holding up a badge, the older guy says, "Miss Lewis, I'm agent Merryl and these are agents Hernandez and Ericson. We're from the FBI. We need to bring you in for questioning."

"Am I in trouble?" Amy stammers.

The old guy just tilts his head.

Continued in "Monsters – Part II of I Bring the Fire"

AUTHOR'S NOTE:

Thank you for taking a chance on this self-published novel and seeing it to the end.

Because I self-publish, I depend on my readers to help me get the word out. If you enjoyed this story, please let people know on Facebook, Twitter, in your blogs, and when you talk books with your friends and family.

Want to know about upcoming releases & get sneak peeks and exclusive content?
Follow me on Tumblr: ibringthefireodin.tumblr.com/
Facebook: www.facebook.com/CGockelWrites
Or email me: cgockel.publishing@gmail.com
Thank you again!

Made in the USA
Lexington, KY
08 December 2014